P9-BYS-230

LAST NIGHT

I SANG TO

THE MONSTER

~~LAST NIGHT~~

I SANG TO

~~THE MONSTER~~

A NOVEL

BENJAMIN ALIRE SÁENZ

CINCO PUNTOS PRESS
www.cincopuntos.com

PROPERTY OF
PLACENTIA LIBRARY DISTRICT
411 EAST CHAPMAN AVENUE
PLACENTIA, CA 92870

Last Night I Sang to the Monster. Copyright © 2009 by Benjamin Alire Sáenz. All rights reserved. No part of this book may be used or reproduced in any manner whatsoever without written consent from the publisher, except for brief quotations for reviews. For further information, write Cinco Puntos Press, 701 Texas Avenue, El Paso, TX 79901; or call 1-915-838-1625.

SUMMERTIME (from "Porgy and Bess"). Music and lyrics by George Gershwin, Dubose and Dorothy Heyward and Ira Gershwin © 1935 (Renewed) George Gershwin Music, Ira Gershwin Music and Dubose and Dorothy Heyward Memorial Fund. All Rights Administered by WB Music Corp. Gershwin ®, George Gershwin ® and Ira Gershwin ™ are trademarks of Gershwin Enterprises. Porgy and Bess ® is a Registered Trademark of Porgy and Bess Enterprises. All Rights Reserved.

This book is a work of fiction. All names, characters, places, and incidents are either the product of the author's imagination or are used fictitiously. No reference to any real person is intended or should be inferred.

FIRST EDITION
10 9 8 7 6 5 4 3 2 1

Library of Congress Cataloging-in-Publication Data

Sáenz, Benjamin Alire.
 Last night I sang to the monster / by Benjamin Alire Saenz. — 1st ed.
  p. cm.
Summary: Eighteen-year-old Zach does not remember how he came to be in a treatment center for alcoholics, but through therapy and caring friends, his amnesia fades and he learns to face his past while working toward a better future.
 ISBN 978-1-933693-58-3 (alk. paper)
 [1. Self-esteem—Fiction. 2. Psychotherapy—Fiction. 3. Alcoholism—Fiction. 4. Emotional problems—Fiction. 5. Family problems—Fiction.] I. Title.

PZ7.S1273Las 2009
[Fic]—dc22

2009015833

Thanks to our great readers: Jonathan Hunt, Becky Powers, John Fortunado and Ailbhe Cormack Aboud

Cover and book design by Antonio Castro H.
Home at last! Isn't El Paso always better than New York City?

Many thanks to David González whose image graces this cover.

3 6018 05445413 7

Brian, do you still want

to know if I believe in miracles?

In a monstrous time, the heart breaks and breaks
And lives in the breaking.

—Stanley Kunitz

LITTLE PIECES OF PAPER

I want to gather up all the words in the world and write them down on little pieces of paper—then throw them in the air. They would look like tiny sparrows flying toward the sun. Without all those words, the sky would be clear and perfect and blue. The deafening world would be beautiful in all that silence.

WHAT GOD WRITES ON YOUR HEART

-1-

Some people have dogs. Not me. I have a therapist. His name is Adam.

I'd rather have a dog.

After our first session, Adam asked me a lot of questions. I don't think he liked my answers. I kept saying, "I'm not sure. I don't remember."

I think he got tired of my answers. "You're not sure about a lot of things, are you, Zach?"

"Guess not," I said. I *did not* want to be talking to him.

He just looked at me and nodded. I knew he was thinking. Adam, he likes to think—and he's a friendly guy but I was *not* into friendly. "I have homework for you," he said. Homework. Okay. "I want you to tell me something significant about yourself."

I just looked at him. "Something significant? Like what?"

"I think you know what I mean, Zach."

"Sure."

He smiled at the way I said *sure.* "You can do it in writing or you can draw something."

"Yeah, okay," I said.

"It's all right if you're angry with me," he said.

"I'm not angry with you."

"You sound a little angry."

"I'm tired."

"Who are you angry at?"

"Nobody."

"Can I be honest with you, Zach?"

"Sure, go ahead, be honest."

"I don't think that's true. I think you're really angry."

I wanted to say something. Something that began with *F* and ended with *you.* But I didn't. "I'll do the homework," I said.

When I got back to my room, this is what I wrote down:

> I don't like remembering.
> Remembering makes me feel things.
> I don't like feeling things.

As I'm staring down at the piece of paper, I'm thinking I could spend the rest of my life becoming an expert on forgetting.

It's entered into my head that I exist in this in-between space. Maybe that's just the way it is with some people. And there's nothing anybody can do to change it.

I have it in my head that when we're born, God writes things down on our hearts. See, on some people's hearts he writes *happy* and on some people's hearts he writes *sad* and on some people's hearts he writes *crazy* and on some people's hearts he writes *genius* and on some people's hearts he writes *angry* and on some people's hearts he writes *winner* and on some people's hearts he writes *loser.*

I keep seeing a newspaper being tossed around in the wind. And then a strong gust comes along and the newspaper is thrown against a barbed wire fence and it gets ripped to shreds in an instant. That's how I feel. I think God is the wind. It's all like a game to him. *Him.* God. And it's all pretty much random. He takes out his pen and starts writing on our blank hearts. When it came to my turn, he wrote *sad.* I don't like God very much. Apparently, he doesn't like me very much either.

Adam asked me, "What do you remember—about coming here?"

"Nothing," I said. "I don't remember anything."

"Nothing?"

"I was somewhere else. And then I was here."

"Somewhere else?"

"Yeah."

"Where was that?"

"Home."

"Where's home?"

"El Paso. El Paso, Texas."

"And that's where you were before you came here?"

"Yeah. That's where I used to live."

"Used to live?"

"I don't live anywhere anymore."

"What else do you remember, Zach?"

"Nothing."

"You're sure?"

I really just wanted Adam to stop interviewing me. I just kept staring at him so that he was sure I was serious. And then I said, "I want you to stop asking me what I remember."

"Well, listen, Zach, amnesia is not uncommon in cases of trauma." Trauma. Yeah. Okay. They like that word around here—they're in love with that word. So maybe I *can't* remember or maybe I *don't want to* remember. If God wrote *amnesia* on my heart, who am I to un-write what he wrote?

Look, if I could get my hands on a bottle of bourbon, I'd feel a little better. Maybe I'll tell Adam that bourbon might help jog my memory. Maybe bourbon is a miracle cure for amnesia. Like he'd go for that. I can just hear Adam's response: "So blackouts are a cure for amnesia? Tell me how that works, buddy."

The thing is that I only remember my past life in little pieces. There's a piece here and there's another piece over there. There are pieces of paper scattered everywhere on the floor of my brain. And there's writing on those pieces of paper and if I could just gather them and put them all in order, I might be able to read the writing and get at a story that made sense.

I have these dreams. And in some of those dreams, I keep hitting myself.

Adam wants to know why I hit myself in my dreams.

"I probably did something wrong."

"No," he said. "You didn't do anything wrong."

Like he knows. I hate that he thinks he knows.

"Okay, Zach, if you did something wrong, tell me what it is. Make me a list—of all the things you did that were wrong."

Shit. That could be a long list.

Adam's trying to tell me that my thinking is all screwed-up. He says that it's my addict who does all the thinking for me. My addict. Who the hell is that guy? Did I miss something? Okay, you don't have to be a trained therapist to know that I am one screwed-up guy. But do I have to blame that on my addict self? I don't even know if my addict self exists.

The way I see it, Adam is trying to get me to create more pieces of paper. Why would I want to do that? I wish I could get rid of all those pieces of paper, and I wish I could get rid of my dreams. And I wish to God I wasn't living in this place full of people who are even more screwed-up than I am.

Okay, maybe they're not all as screwed-up as I am, but, okay, okay, like Adam said, "It's not a contest, Zach." You know, all the people that the world screwed over, they're all here. It makes me sad and it makes me sick. I mean, okay, let's say we're all going to get better. Let's just pretend we will. Fine. Where are we going to go after we get all better? What are we going to do with all of our newfound healthy behaviors? Back out into the world that screwed us up and screwed us over. This does not sound promising.

I wish I didn't have a heart that God wrote *Sad* on.

Some people think it's all very cool to have a therapist. Me, I'm not into this.

Will somebody please just give me a dog?

-2-

I have this dream. I'm out in the desert with two of my friends, Antonio and Gloria. All three of us are in the middle of the desert and there's an ocean right there in front of us. An ocean with real water. It's so fantastic and beautiful, and part of me just wants to jump into the water. But I don't because I don't know how to swim. But then I think that it would be okay to jump into the water anyway. I would drown. But it would be such a beautiful way to die.

God, it's all so perfect and beautiful, the desert and the sky and the ocean.

Gloria's long black hair is blowing in the breeze as she sits there and smokes pot and she has this look on her face that's better than anything I've ever seen. She is as perfect as the sky or the clear blue water in the ocean or the desert sand we're sitting on. She's laughing. She's so happy. She's so happy that it breaks my heart. And Antonio, he's as perfect as Gloria, with his green eyes that seem to swallow up everything around him. He is shooting up—which is his favorite thing to do. And he's as happy as Gloria. He's so, so happy.

And me, I'm sitting there with my bottle of Jack Daniels. I don't know if I'm happy or not. But maybe I *am* happy because I'm watching Antonio and Gloria.

And then we're talking to each other and Gloria says, "Zach, where are you from?"

And I say, "I don't know."

And Antonio asks me, "Where do you live?"

And I say, "I don't live anywhere."

And they look at each other and then they start having a conversation in Spanish. And I wish I could understand because it seems like they're saying such beautiful things to each other. And it seems like they're becoming one person, like they belong to each other—and I don't belong to anyone. That makes me feel sad. I'm crying. I can see Gloria and Antonio. They're happy and they're talking and they're beautiful. They're beautiful like the sky and the desert and the ocean. And me? I'm not beautiful. And I can't talk. And I can't understand anything.

I'm seeing the whole scene. Happy Antonio and happy Gloria. And sad me.

I drink and drink and drink. Until it doesn't hurt anymore.

I hate dreams almost as much as I hate remembering.

3

I had this plan. The plan first entered my head when I was in the first grade. I was going to make nothing but A's. I was going to get a scholarship and go to Stanford or Harvard or Princeton or Georgetown or one of those famous schools where all the students were very smart. And very happy. And very alive.

Something went wrong with my plan. Shit.

If Mr. Garcia could only see me now. Mr. Garcia, he was a very cool guy. He was young and smart and he was real. Mostly, I think people are fake. Well, what do you expect? The fake world we live in conspires to make us all fakes. I get it.

But somehow Mr. Garcia escaped the monster named *fake*. He had this really cool goatee and he wore tennis shoes and jeans and a sports coat and he always wore white shirts that were a little wrinkled and, well, I really liked the guy. He had the friendliest face I'd ever seen. And he had really black eyes and hair so black it was almost blue. His voice was soft and clear and he made people want to listen. "You have to respect words." He said weird and interesting things like that. He memorized poems and recited those poems to us out loud. It was like his *whole body* was a book—not just his head, but his heart and his arms and his legs—his whole body. I got this idea into my head that I wanted to be like him when I grew up. Not that I think it's such a good idea to want to be like other people. It never works out.

Once, he wrote on a paper I turned in: *Zach, this is really fine work. You blow me away, sometimes. I'd like to talk to you after school. If you get a chance, do you think you can come by?* So I made my feet wander over to his classroom after school. When I walked in, he was pacing around the room with a book in his hand. I could tell he was memorizing a poem. He smiled. It was like the guy was glad to see me. Wow, he was really wigging me out. He pointed to his desk. "Sit here," he said.

I pointed to the chair behind his desk. "There?"

He nodded. "Yeah. That's a good place, don't you think so, Zach?"

So I sat there like I was the teacher or something.

"How does that feel?"

"Okay," I said. "It feels okay. Weird."

"Maybe you'd like to sit there someday. You know, teach kids about poetry and literature. Memorize poems, read books, teach them. How would that feel?" He smiled. You know, the thing about Mr. Garcia was that he smiled a lot and sometimes it would wig me out because I just wasn't used to people who smiled a lot. Especially adults. And even though Mr. Garcia hadn't been an adult for a long time, he was still an adult.

It was just strange to see someone like him. The world sucked. Didn't he know that? Maybe he was a freak of nature. Look, the guy had no right to be that naïve. And then out of nowhere he looked at me and said, "Zach, did anyone ever tell you that you're a brilliant kid?" Brilliant? The dude was absolutely stunning me out. What exactly did he expect me to say in response to that?

"You don't like compliments, do you?"

"They're okay," I said.

He looked at me and nodded. "Okay," he said. "Okay." He sort of grinned. And then he said. "The papers you write, they're amazing."

"They're okay."

"They're better than okay. I think I used the word amazing." He walked up to the board and spelled it out. Always the teacher, that dude.

I stared at the word. I knew that word did not apply to me. But I just wasn't going to get into an argument with him so I just said, "Okay."

"Yeah," he said. "Okay." And then he sort of shook his head and smiled. "You know something? I like you, Zach. Is that okay, too, if I like you?"

Well, big deal, the guy liked everyone. How could you go through life liking so many people? There just weren't that many people in the world worth liking. "Yeah," I said. "I guess that's okay."

"Good," he said. "You like music?"

"Yeah, music is good. It's okay."

"You want to hear something?"

"Sure," I said.

He walked to his closet and pulled a trumpet out of its case. He blew into it, you know, like he was clearing it all out. He ran his fingers along the valves and played a scale. And then he said, "Okay, Zach, ready?" And then he started playing. I mean the guy could play. He played this really soft and beautiful song. I never knew a trumpet could whisper. I kept looking at his fingers. I wanted him to keep playing forever. It was better than any of the poems he'd read to us in class. It was like the whole loud world had gone really, really quiet, and there was nothing but this one song, this one sweet and gentle and brilliant song that was as soft as a breeze blowing through the leaves of a tree. The world just disappeared. I wanted to live in that stillness forever. I wanted to clap. And then, I just didn't know what to do or what to say. I was high. I mean it. High and torn up to shreds.

"How was that?" He was smiling again.

He looked like an angel. He did. And thinking that really wigged me out. I didn't know what to think about myself with that thought in my head. "Well," I said, "it was better than okay."

"Better than okay? Wow," he said. "That's the best thing anybody's said to me all day."

I mean, the guy was trying to connect with me. Only it was freaking me out. And then I just knew I had to get out of there. The guy was normal and I wasn't, I don't know, I was just, well, I was feeling these things that I just didn't like. And then for a moment I just froze. I watched him put his trumpet away. "Anytime you want to listen to a song—"

"Okay," I said. *But I had to get the hell out of there. I had to.* We sort of shook hands, you know, like we were friends. We nodded at each other.

As I was walking out the door, I heard his voice. "Zach, I know you're sad sometimes. And if you ever want to talk, well, you know where to find me."

My heart was beating and my palms were all sweaty and I felt like there was a hummingbird inside my heart and a pump inside my stomach. I found the nearest bathroom and threw up. I was completely torn up. I kept seeing Mr. Garcia's black eyes, his hands, his face, his eyes, his hair. What was he doing in my head?

I cried all the way home. I just, hell, I don't know, I just cried.

4

When I walked into the house, I went in search of one of my dad's bottles. Not that they were that hard to find. He hid bottles all over the house. I knew where they all were. That was one of my hobbies, finding where my dad hid his bottles. It was my version of looking for Easter eggs. In my house, Easter lasted forever.

I took a pint of bourbon, put it in my coat pocket and left the house. I walked around drinking and smoking and I kept crying and crying. I was, I don't know *I don't know I don't know* wigged out, sad, drunk, torn to shreds, shit. I hated Mr. Garcia. Why did he tell me things like *you're a brilliant kid?* Why did he write *amazing* on the board? That word was not a true word. It was not a word that lived inside me. And if he thought my papers were *amazing,* why didn't he keep that thought to himself? And why did he say, *"Is it okay if I like you?"* Who the fuck wanted to like a kid like me? I hated that he noticed that I was sad. And I hated that he played that beautiful song. Why would I want to hear a trumpet whispering beautiful lies into my ears? And why the fuck was the guy wasting his time on a kid like me?

So I walked around and drank and smoked. And cried and yelled at Mr. Garcia. *I hate you. I hate you.* I thought the liquor was supposed to help. And it sort of *did* help. It made everything feel farther away. The farther away things felt, the better.

Mr. Garcia—he's one of the pieces of paper on my floor. So was the bourbon I liked to drink.

Pieces of paper.

Yeah, see, maybe this place that's supposed to heal me will just hand me a good broom. So I can sweep up the floor that's in my brain. Maybe I'll tell Adam that I don't need to remember. I just need a really good broom.

REMEMBERING

Somebody put a calendar on the bulletin board in my room. I guess they wanted to make sure I knew what day it was. I think I heard a voice say, "You can mark the days." That's a funny thing to do with days. Mark them. Put an X on them. Cross them out.

I arrived here on New Year's Day, 2008. There was a big storm on the night of January 2nd. All that noise woke me up. I lay there and listened to the wind and I swear it was trying to tear down the cabin.

The wind was like the world. It was this thief that came along and tried to take whatever I had that was left.

I have this storm inside me. It's trying to kill me. I wonder sometimes if that's such a bad thing.

I know about storms.

I'm tired.

I just want to sleep forever.

Maybe I should tell the storm to go ahead and kill me.

PERFECT

-1-

I always felt guilty about my plan. The plan about getting perfect grades and going to college. I can be seriously mean and selfish. My mom and dad, they loved me. It's not like they would hug me or touch me or things like that. Not that I like to be touched. This family thing, it's complicated. Everyone's got stuff. My mom and dad were trying to deal. My brother was trying to deal. I was trying to deal. Running out on them— maybe that's not dealing. Maybe that's just running.

My mom and dad were doing the best they could. I could see that. Things were not easy for them. I knew my mom was seriously depressed and my dad's only hobby was drinking. And the thing of it was that I had school and they didn't. What did they have?

High school was like going to work. I got paid with A's. I was really into the studying and the A thing. This one time I thought I was going to explode over a B- I got on a pop quiz in history class. I mean there were firecrackers going off in my stomach and in my head. I was wigging. I went home and started swigging down bourbon. It always felt good, to take a drink, the way that the liquor burned in my throat and sort of exploded in my stomach. Liquor really tore me up. In a good way.

I went a little mental that night. Well, maybe I went a lot mental. Seriously. I took my baseball bat and went walking around and broke a few windshields. Okay, that doesn't sound cool, but that's what I did. I went totally mental. I admit it.

I ran into some problems and had to run a lot because lots of those cars had alarms. But I really got off on beating the shit out of some of those fancy BMWs. Maybe I was just pissed off because I didn't have a car. My brother, Santiago, he dropped out of high school and he didn't have a job but he got a car. I never understood whatever passed between my parents and my brother. Just never got it. Families don't make sense. You can't explain them because families, well, they aren't intellectual. And they aren't emotional either—at least not mine. We didn't do the emotion thing very well in my family.

See, I think there are roads that lead us to each other. But in my family, there were no roads—just underground tunnels. I think we all got lost in those underground tunnels. No, not lost. We just lived there.

So yeah, my brother—the raging ingrate—he gets the car. I make straight A's and do all kinds of stuff around the house and I *don't* get squat.

-2-

Sometimes, I get these ideas in my head and I just can't stop them from entering and it's like the ideas tell me what to do. When I did stuff like break windshields and crap like that, it wasn't even as if there were any thoughts in my head. There were just these feelings running through me, bad feelings. Really, really bad feelings. I just wanted to get rid of the feelings. I'm not sure God knew what he was doing when he put feelings inside of us. What is the purpose for human emotions? Will somebody please tell me?

So there were two things I really worked hard at: not feeling and getting good grades. The getting good grades was easy. The not-feeling part was hard. But I'm working on that. The way I see it is that if I didn't feel anything, then I wouldn't wig out anymore. No feelings = no wigging out. The solution was simple. So why is everything so hard?

My friends were really into drugs and booze. But it's not as if I wasn't into the mood-altering substance thing. I tried to be careful. I didn't want to screw up my plan. And the drinking was cool. It helped, you know? And the other thing was that I was really into cigarettes. Love to smoke. And I'm good at it too.

Substance abuse. That was a joke me and my friends liked to make. We wanted to write a song about *substance abuse*. These are some of the lyrics I wrote when we were all stoned out of our heads:

What is this thing you call substance abuse?
All I wanna do is forget and get loose.
Drinking and smoking over and over
What's so great about a life that's sober?

There's nothing cool about being young
When the monsters of night have stolen the sun.

I'm tired of searching for words in the sky.
All I wanna do is drink and die.
Nothing is real. It's all a big lie.
All I wanna do is drink and die.

There's nothing cool about being young
When the monsters of night have stolen the sun.

You know, that song, it's another one of those pieces of paper on the floor of my brain. Anyway, my friends, I really liked them. Antonio and Gloria and Tommy and Mitzie and Albert. God wrote *crazy* on their hearts when they were born. But it was good when I was with them. It was like we all belonged to each other.

And they were all really smart. I know people think that druggies are really nothing but a bunch of losers. But the truth is that the smartest kids, they're the ones doing the drugs. We're thinkers and we don't like rules and we have imagination. All right, so we're also all fucked up. But hey, you think sober people aren't all fucked up? The world is being run by sober people—and it doesn't look like it's working out all that well. Just take me and tear me up.

My friends, they always made me laugh. Not that I remember a lot of the things we did together. We got smashed. But I didn't feel alone—that's what counts. The rest of the time, I just felt like crying. You know, the word *sad* that's written on my heart, *that* word. *Sad.* Yeah. Crying. Okay. But my friends made me laugh.

We played games. That was cool. We liked Scrabble. I think we were all sort of in love with words—but we liked to keep those words in our heads most of the time. We had this game. Every week, we'd pick a different word. They were like our own personal passwords—and we couldn't tell anybody what our passwords were. At the end of each week, we'd pick a new word, and then we'd get high and yell out the old words, the words we were tossing out. I remember one time, these were the words we yelled out:

Eschatology
Ephemeral
Capricious
Coyote
Luchar
Soledad

Some of the words were in Spanish and some of them were in English. Gloria and Antonio were really into speaking Spanish and even though I had a Mexican last name, it was a language that had been lost in my family. Yeah, well, a lot of things got lost in my family.

But with my friends, I didn't feel lost. I liked our words, liked the sound of them as they floated out of their voices. As we got stoned out of our minds, we'd make up sentences using our words. The sentences sounded like entire stories to me. All week long I would write sentences in my head using our words.

It was like having little pieces of my friends in my head.

-3-

At home, well, things were not great. My mom was depressed. I don't mean that in the regular sense. Sometimes people say things like, "Man, I'm really depressed." But my mom, she was depressed in the clinical sense.

Not that you needed a psych doc to recognize her condition. I don't know how it all started for her. Long before I was born, that's for sure. I grew up taking her to different psych docs. She liked to change doctors. That really tore me up.

I started driving when I was thirteen. Not that I knew what I was doing—but I got the hang of it. The thing of it was that my mom could never drive when she was having what my father called "episodes." Driving without a license? That's nothing.

My mom, she was always on some kind of medication, and things would be okay for a while. She'd cook and clean the house and stuff like that—but then for some reason, she would stop taking her medications. I never really understood that. I'm not her.

I could always tell when she got off her meds because she'd hug me and tell me that she was well now. "It's all going to be lovely, Zach." Lovely. I hate that word.

I don't remember a lot of things about growing up. I spent a lot of time playing in the backyard. I think I remember being in love with a tree. That's weird, I know, but there are worse things than being in love with a tree. Trees are very cool. And they're alive. More alive than some people.

We used to have a dog. Her name was Lilly. She slept with me. When I was about five, I found her sleeping under the tree, the tree I was in love with. But she wouldn't wake up. I was yelling and crying and just, you know, going mental.

My dad came out. He saw Lilly. He smelled like the bourbon he'd been drinking. "Dogs die," he said. And then he walked back into the house—to get himself another drink.

I remember lying down next to Lilly. After a while I just got up and dug a grave. It took me a long time. But I couldn't just leave Lilly lying there. It wasn't right.

I kept asking if I could have another dog but my mom said they were too much trouble. Like she knew. My mom, she didn't know a thing about taking care of dogs. I mean she didn't even know anything about taking care of boys. Boys, as in Zach. Not that it mattered. I managed. Look, I'm being mean to my mom. I hate that, when I'm mean. She had to deal with a lot of stuff. I know that. What Adam calls the internal-life stuff. I know it's hell. Believe me, I know. Shit. I wish I didn't. But there it is.

My mom, mostly she stayed inside a dark room that was all hers. She had agoraphobia. That's what my dad said. Just like her sister. I guess it ran in her family.

Agoraphobia. That was another way of saying that she was allergic to the sky.

When she was feeling okay, she'd leave her room and talk to me. I remember this one time she said: "Zach, you're just like me. You know that, don't you?" I looked at my mom and tried to smile. Look, smiling is hard for me. "You are," she said. "You even have my smile." Shit.

And then she kissed me. "I miss you." She said it like I had gone somewhere. I wanted to say, "I miss you too." I mean, she *had* gone somewhere. And then she said, "I miss everyone."

I didn't know what to say.

"Your father doesn't touch me anymore."

Wig me out. It was none of my business whether my parents touched each other or not.

And then she looked at me and said, "Do you understand what I'm saying?" She squeezed my arm. "Zach, you can touch me if you want."

My heart was beating really fast and I felt as if my heart was freezing up, like it was in the middle of a storm and there were things running through my mind, things that were stomping on me, telling me things I didn't want to know—bad things—and I wanted to take a bat to my own brain. I didn't, I mean, I just didn't know what to do so I just smiled at her and nodded. God, there I was with a stupid smile and I hated myself and I thought that maybe there was a knife inside of me, trying to cut me up. I don't know how I did it, but I did it—I got up and got my book bag. "I have a study session with Antonio and Gloria." I was trembling and I don't know how I made myself move or talk or do anything.

"Do you have to go?" She sounded like a little girl. It was like she was begging me to stay. I was breathing so damn fast that I couldn't breathe. I know that doesn't make any sense.

I needed something. *I really needed something.* I found my feet moving towards Tommy's house. I don't know what I would have done if he hadn't been there.

"Dude," he said, "You look really weirded out, man. I mean, you could really use something."

"Yeah," I whispered.

That was the first time I did coke.

My body, it was electric. For the first time in my life I felt as if I had a real heart and a real body and I knew that there was this fire in me that could have lit up the entire universe. No book had ever made me feel that way. No human being had ever made me feel like that.

God, it was incredible to feel so perfect. Look, God didn't write the word *perfect* on my heart. But cocaine did what God didn't. Wow. *Perfect.*

I was on fire. I mean it. *On fire!* The truth is that I wanted to die. It would have been beautiful to die feeling so alive. I knew I'd never be that perfect again.

REMEMBERING

I'm riding a tricycle. I'm four. What I'm remembering must be a dream because I have lots of brothers and sisters. I'm wearing a white shirt and black pants and nice dress shoes that hurt my feet. I'm playing with all my brothers and sisters on my dad's perfect lawn.

I just want to be alone. I walk away from everyone and I find this very cool tricycle. I start riding it and I'm singing to myself. I'm happy. I look back and see that all my brothers and sisters and my mom and my dad are all piling into the car. My mom is carrying a present. It's really pretty with a white silk ribbon. And then the car drives away.

I wave at them. Bye. Bye. I keep riding my tricycle. I keep singing. I'm happy. I don't like it when there's a lot of noise.

But then, the car comes back and my mother says. "Where were you?"

And I say, "I was here."

"You scared us. We didn't know where you were. You're a bad boy scaring me like that."

She sounds really, really mad. "I'm sorry," I say. I feel a knot in my stomach.

And my mom says, "You're a bad boy."

I want to know why I'm a bad boy. Sometimes, that's what I say: *Zach, you're a bad boy.* That's really weird, I know. I tear myself up sometimes.

WHY I DON'T BELIEVE IN CHANGE

-1-

It's not as if my dad was the only father in the world who drank.

He worked hard and he never missed work. Not ever. Every day, up at 5:30 in the morning, making his own coffee, making his own lunch, going to work.

And, hell, at the end of the day, the guy was all beat to shit. Sometimes, he came in after work and he could barely talk he was so tired. He'd take a shower and pour himself a drink. He didn't hook up with other women and stuff like that. He stuck it out, took care of us. So the guy drank. Hey, there are worse things. And look, my mom, she could be great, but there were days she just sat there, tears rolling down her face. She wasn't very interactive.

Santiago came home and made noise, threatening to kill us all, then laughed, stoned, that guy. Crazy. But he always took off. And left us to our quiet house.

The really sad part was that I was afraid of my mom. That's not normal. You think I don't know that? Sometimes, I would sit next to her and ask her if she needed anything and she would look at me like I was some kind of demon and she would just slap me. The first time she did that I went to my room and cried. I was a lot younger then. But after a while I sort of expected it. One time, she really went crazy and wouldn't stop slapping me. And then she cried and cried and I felt really bad for her. I knew that she didn't mean it. But the whole situation didn't make me want to come too close. And then there was that conversation about touching that I just couldn't get out of my mind.

But there were good days too, days when she would get up early and make breakfast and clean and cook the most amazing meals for dinner. But the last time we had a dinner together, it didn't work out too well. She'd spent all afternoon making homemade ravioli. "I wanted to be Italian. Instead, I was just a boring girl from Ohio." My mom was a lot of things. But she wasn't boring. Boring would have been really great.

So that night, we were enjoying her ravioli and everything was going really good. My dad was making jokes, trying to make my mom laugh, and my mom, she was smiling. God, she could smile. And Dad wasn't too drunk and, you know, I was starting to feel a little relaxed. I'm not a relaxed kind of guy. I'm all tied up in knots. You know, around here they call that anxiety. And, well, I'm on some meds for that. Look, I think God wrote *anxious* on my heart.

But that night, I was starting to feel chilled. It all fell apart when my brother Santiago came home, stoned out of his mind. He was seriously crazed. He looked at all of us and yelled, "Typical. No one fucking invited me." I mean, the guy lived there. *He was always invited.*

My brother really tore me up. He looked right at my mom and said, "It's about fucking time you cooked." He spit on her plate and then started in on my dad, throwing cuss words around like confetti. His words were flying all over the room. He grabbed my dad's plate and threw it across the room and it shattered against the wall.

And then my mom, she immediately went back to her internal life, to that place where she lived. I just sat there, hoping my brother wouldn't go after me. But of course he did. "Suckass." He made this sucking thing with his lips. "You got any money, suckass?"

He knew I always had a few bucks on me. It was like I was the guy's ATM machine. I reached into my wallet and pulled out two twenties.

"That all you got?"

"Yeah." I tried to pretend I wasn't scared.

He grabbed the money. "Let me see your wallet." He threw the wallet on the floor and looked at me like I was nothing. "This isn't over," he said. "Don't fucking believe this is over." He pushed me against the wall and

I could smell his breath. It smelled like he'd eaten a dead dog. God, my heart was beating so fast that I thought it was going to fly out of my chest. He looked at me with that look of his, that look that said I was nothing, that look that said I wasn't even worth hating.

He left me standing there. I felt stupid and naked even though I was wearing clothes.

I heard the door slam and I jumped. Man, I was a knot of nerves.

My mom got up from where she was sitting and left the room. I got up from my chair and cleaned up the mess. My dad just sat there and poured himself another glass of wine. I served him another plate of my mom's ravioli and we sat there and finished eating.

He didn't say a word. I didn't either. It was like Santiago stole our mouths and all the words that were in them.

-2-

I always wanted to have Santiago's name. We were both named after our grandfathers. Santiago was named after my dad's father. And I was named after my mom's father. My dad never liked the idea of me being named Zachariah. Zachariah? What kind of name was that for a guy whose last name was Gonzalez and who lived in El Paso, Texas? And my mother didn't even like her father. My dad's father was born in Mexico City. My mom's father was born in Cuyahoga Falls, Ohio. My dad's father was an artist and a musician. My mom's father was an accountant. So I was named after an accountant from Ohio, a guy who my mother hated—and my brother was named after an artist-musician from Mexico City. Shit. I always got the short end. Shit. My brother's full name is Santiago Mauricio Gonzalez, and me, my full name is Zachariah Johnson Gonzalez.

I'm skinny like my mom and Santiago is big like my dad. And I must have looked like my mom's dad because my skin is so white—not like Santiago's. Santiago looked like his name. I guess I looked like mine. Maybe we got the names we deserved.

I know the deal. You don't get to pick what you look like.

You don't get to pick your name.

And you don't get to pick your parents.

You can't pick your brother, either. Mine didn't exactly love me. The guy didn't love anybody. He didn't know how. That wasn't his fault. He just didn't get that love thing. He was mad all the time. He used to hit me. He broke one of my ribs once. Everyone pretended that it didn't happen. Including me.

Another time, he came home drunk and beat the holy shit out of me. Yeah, look, I didn't cry. I didn't yell. See, when my brother hit me, I sort of went away. I don't know how to explain that. I guess I got that from my mom. I don't know exactly where I went, but, look, I just went away. That's all I can say about it.

One time, my dad had taken my mom to the movies. That was a big deal because they *never* went out. When they came home, my brother was gone and I was all black and blue. I don't want to go into the details of what I looked like. It tore me up to look at myself in the mirror. I told my dad that some guys at school had jumped me as I came out of the library. I didn't get the feeling that he was all that worried. That made it easier because Santiago said he'd fucking kill me if I ever told anyone. I didn't go to school for a few days. That was okay. Well, it wasn't so okay really. No, no, it was not okay. I had to study extra hard to catch up.

I really loved Santiago. I always loved him. It was like he was the sky and the air. It felt that way when I was a little boy. I knew that even though he was way into mood-altering substances and he had this really bad temper that there was something really beautiful inside him. Just because no one else could see it didn't mean it wasn't there.

I remember this one time, he was about thirteen and I was about ten. I don't remember why exactly, but I heard him crying. So my feet just took me to his room. I sat next to him on his bed and I said, "Santiago, don't cry, it's okay."

He put his head on my shoulder and he cried like a baby. His tears soaked my t-shirt and I felt as if my skin was soaking in everything that had ever hurt him. And I was so happy. That sounds screwed-up, I know. But I was happy. Because I was with my brother. *I was really with him.* That was the first time in my life that I knew that he loved me, that he really loved me. And I wanted to tell him that I loved him back. I just didn't know how to say it.

When he stopped crying, we caught a bus and went to a movie. I was happy and a part of me wanted to hold my brother's hand. I know that's really weird and when I think about it I wig myself out. I'm always thinking really crazy things.

Sometimes, after Santiago would hit me, he'd cry and tell me he was sorry. And he would buy me things, you know, like a CD of Rage Against the Machine or Juanes. He knew I really liked Juanes. It made me happy that he'd buy me CDs I liked.

Once, my brother came home really messed up. I don't know what he was on. He started beating the crap out of Dad and then he started in on me. I missed school again for a couple of days. Missing school made me really anxious. School, it was like an addiction. I had to go. *I had to.* And when I couldn't get there, I would just get all anxious.

When I went back to school, Mr. Garcia noticed the bruises. He started asking questions. You know, Mr. Garcia, he was too sincere for his own good. And really, his questions made me even more anxious.

"It looks like it hurts."

"Not much," I said.

"Who did that? Who did that to you, Zach?" He sounded a little mad.

"Some guy at a party," I said. "I like to party."

"Really? A party, huh?"

"Yup."

"Maybe you should stop going to those parties, Zach."

"Maybe I should."

I don't think Mr. Garcia was buying my story. He asked me to come by after school.

When the last bell rang, I really didn't want to go see Mr. Garcia, but my feet took me there anyway. When I got to his room, his door was open and he had an open book of poems in his hand.

"Sit," he said. He put down the book of poems on his desk and I saw the title: *Words Like Fate and Pain.* I watched him as he took out his trumpet and played something real soft and smooth. Maybe he was trying to make me cry. Why was he trying to make me cry? When he finished playing, he looked at me. "Everything okay at home?"

"Yeah," I said.

"Mom's okay?"

"Yeah."

"Dad's okay?"

"Yeah, everything's okay."

"What if I told you that I knew your mom suffers from depression?"

I don't know how he knew that. And I hated that he'd let me know that he knew. "It's not so bad," I said.

"What if I told you that I know your dad drinks?"

"It isn't that bad."

"Maybe it is bad. Who hit you, Zach?"

I got up from where I was sitting. "What if I told you that it's none of your fucking business?" That's what I said. "You're just a teacher. Your job is here—in this fucking classroom." I knew I was yelling.

Mr. Garcia, he sort of gave me one of his smiles. God, his smile really tore me up. "No cussing in my classroom," he said.

"Okay," I said.

"Okay," he said. "Look, Zach, I didn't mean to upset you."

"I'm not upset."

"Okay," he said. He wrote down his cell number and gave it to me. "Look, if you ever need anything, you just call."

I nodded. I took it. Another piece of paper.

-3-

Mr. Garcia had it wrong. I mean, it wasn't as bad as all that. We had a decent house. And my dad liked having a nice lawn. I had it in my head that the nice lawn was my father's way of telling the world that a real family lived there. A man, even a man who drinks too much, has to have some pride. *Pride. Maybe God wrote that word on my dad's heart.*

But the thing was that he spent more time with the grass than he did with me. That messed me up when I thought about it. That's the thing about remembering. If remembering messed me up, then why do it?

When I turned seventeen, my dad remembered that it was my birthday. I don't know how that happened because he'd really been hitting the bottle especially hard. I mean, even for him, things seemed really bad. But he remembered. He remembered. Me. Zach.

My mom was having an episode so I didn't expect her to remember. And Santiago, I mean the guy didn't even remember his own birthday. But my dad, hell, he remembered. He really remembered. Wow.

He asked me what I wanted to do. I didn't know. I just made something up. I told him I wanted to go hiking. I don't know why I said that.

And, you know, that's what we did. We went hiking out in the desert. And it was beautiful and brilliant and amazing. And my dad only drank water and I didn't smoke and, my dad, he knew the names of all the different kinds of cacti and bushes. I didn't know he knew stuff like that. And he even smiled that day and it had been a long time since I'd seen him like that. And that really tore me up.

I asked him how he knew about all the plants and their names.

"My dad," he said. "My dad taught me."

I wanted to ask him if he'd teach me too. But I didn't.

After the hike, we went out for pizza and we talked about things, not important things, but just things. I told him about Mr. Garcia, how he played the trumpet and Dad wanted to know if I had ever wanted to play an instrument, and I told him, "No. I'm not musical. But I like to draw."

"Really?" he said. "I didn't know that."

"Yeah," I said. "I like to draw and I like to paint."

There was an almost-smile on his face. Maybe he was thinking of his father who had been an artist. "I've never seen anything you've done."

"I keep it all at school. In the art room."

"I'd like to see your work." God, my dad looked so brilliant. Like there was a light inside him. He put his hand on my shoulder. "I mean it," he whispered. He looked into my eyes. And it was really weird because I thought he was really looking at me. And I wasn't used to that. I wanted to cry—but I didn't.

"Are you any good?"

I knew he was making a joke.

"I'm okay."

"I bet you're better than okay."

Not that he knew. "I'm not awful."

"You're a good kid," he said.

I wanted to tell him that I liked to drink and that I'd done coke and that I wasn't a good kid at all. It killed me that he thought I was good. But I just sort of nodded. Even though I knew I wasn't a good kid, I'm glad my dad said that—even though he was lying to himself.

The really screwy thing was this: I got it into my head that maybe things could be different. Maybe things couldn't be different for mom or for Santiago. But things could be different for me and my dad. Maybe they could be. That's what I got into my head that night before I went to sleep.

Maybe our lives would get better.

Maybe Dad wouldn't drink as much.

Maybe I wouldn't drink as much.

Maybe we didn't have to be so sad all the time.

Maybe we didn't have to walk around looking at the ground. Maybe we could look up sometimes and see the sky. I mean, why not? I was happy that night before I went to sleep.

But nothing changed.

My dad's drinking got worse after that.

My drinking got worse too.

I never showed my dad any of my art. Maybe he'd never really wanted to see it.

My mom started living internally—all the time. Her life had become one long episode.

One night she climbed in my bed. She called me Ernesto. Ernesto, that was my father's name. She reached down and put her hand between my thighs. I didn't know what to do. I was stunned out of my mind.

My heart was beating really fast and all these things were racing through my head. I jumped out of bed and threw on some clothes and I grabbed one of my dad's bottles and ran out of the house. I didn't come home for two days.

When I came back no one said a word. It was as if I'd never been gone. Nothing got better.

Adam is a big believer in change. I don't know where that guy came from. Same place as Mr. Garcia—that's my thinking. Monday through Friday he shows up. He says that in life you have to show up every day. He's an expert at showing up. I wonder what kind of parents he had, him and his eyes that are as blue as the sea, eyes that see me but don't see me. No one sees me. He tells me I should look in the mirror and say: "I am capable of change." Like I'm really going to do that. God did not write *change* on my heart.

I think sometimes I hate Adam.

I think sometimes I want to get a bat and pretend he's a windshield.

My father wasn't right about me. I'm not a good kid. Yeah, look, I'm just a piece of paper with the word *sad* and a bunch of cuss words written on it.

A lousy piece of paper. That's me.

A piece of paper that's waiting to be torn up.

REMEMBERING

I was talking to Adam in his office. I don't know why we call it talking since really it's an official appointment with my therapist. You know,
therapist to patient. It's not as if we're friends. He was saying something to
me. I guess I wasn't paying attention. My mind wanders sometimes. And
then I heard Adam ask me, "What do you see when you see that picture?"

"What picture?"

"The picture you're staring at."

I guess I *had* been staring at the picture. I didn't know what to say.
"They're your sons," I said.

"Yes."

"So, well, I guess I see your sons."

Adam, he doesn't roll his eyes. He's a real professional. But he does
sometimes give people a snarky smile. That's what he gave me. "But what
does it make you think of?"

"I have a brother."

"How old is he?"

"He's three years older than me."

"What's his name?"

"His name's Santiago."

"Do you have a picture like that, of the both of you—when you
were little?"

"Yeah. My mom had one in her room."

"What's going on in the photograph?"

"My brother is hugging me."

"How old are you in the photograph?"

"Two."

"Are you smiling?"

"Look, Adam, I don't want to talk about the photograph. It's just an old picture. It doesn't mean anything."

"Okay. Listen, is it all right if I ask you a question, Zach?"

"Yeah, sure, go ahead."

"Did you love your brother?"

"I don't remember."

"You don't remember?"

"No, Adam, I don't."

He knew I was lying. I guess I didn't care. Look, *I don't want to remember* should count as *I don't remember.* That's what I was thinking.

IN THE COUNTRY OF DREAMS

I have this idea stuck in my head that you have
to be born *beautiful* in order to dream beautiful
things. God didn't write *beautiful* on my heart.
I'm stuck with all my bad dreams. Bad dreams
for bad boys. I guess that's the way it is for me.
Look, there's nothing I can do about it.

DREAMS AND THINGS I HATE

-1-

I keep having this dream. It's like being in hell. It's like I'm being punished and I have to watch the same scary movie over and over. And even though I know the movie by heart, it still scares me because there's always a monster lurking in the dark.

That monster wants me dead.

I wonder if I'm the only one who has a monster.

It's just a dream. It's just a dream.

I think I know why there are so many addicts in the world.

Running, that's what I'm doing in the dream. I'm running through the streets and I'm barefoot. My feet are bleeding but I can't stop and I'm trembling and scared, the storm inside me, strong as a tornado, twisting and twisting. All the pieces of paper I have on the floor of my brain are flying around like birds gone crazy and I'm torn up as hell and I'm running and running and it seems as though I'll be running forever. It's night and it's cold and everything is dead and quiet and hollow and I can hear the echoes of my own breathing in the dark and empty streets. I can't see where I'm going because the darkness stretches forever and the sweat is stinging my eyes. But that doesn't stop my feet from running. It's like my feet can tell my brain what to do. My feet, they're always taking me places I don't want to go—especially in my dreams. I'm scared. I hate that I'm so scared. It feels as if my heart if going to be torn out of my body. I don't even know what I'm scared of.

The monster. I'm scared of the monster.

And all of a sudden I'm home. The lawn is soft as cotton and cool on my bloody feet and I think of my father who is the god of the lawn and I want to cry. I want the lawn to hold me but that's a crazy thought because a lawn doesn't have arms and hands and a heart and what good is it to have arms and a heart anyway because, hell, they've never done me any good.

When I go inside the house, it's as empty as the streets. I start to realize that I'm dying of thirst so I try to get a glass of water from the faucet but nothing comes out. No water. I'm going to die, I'm going to die. I know that if I don't drink *I really am going to die,* so finally I remember that the only thing left to drink in the house is my father's bourbon. So I go looking in hiding places for his bottles and I find a pint and I drink it down. The whole bottle. And I feel a fire inside but that fire only makes me thirstier.

So now I'm even thirstier than before and I keep trying to get the faucets in the house to work but they just won't give up any water and, god, I'm thirsty, thirsty, thirsty, and I know I have to drink something so I keep looking for bottles of bourbon and finding them all over the place and I keep drinking them down and as I drink there are explosions in my throat and in my stomach and I'm half on fire and I'm thinking I'm going to die because I keep getting thirstier and thirstier until I just can't stand it and my feet are really bleeding.

I want to die. I begin to think that maybe the monster will come and I'll let him take me.

And then my brother appears and he looks really mad and he's coming at me. He's screaming at me and calling me all kinds of names. I want to yell for help but nothing comes out and I know it wouldn't do any good anyway because everyone in the whole world has gone away. I know they've gone away because of something I've done. My heart is beating so fast that I know it's going to burst and I can't stand the panic in my brain.

It would be so peaceful just to die.

That's when I wake up.

This is not the only dream I have. There are more. How can there be so many dreams living inside me? How do they all fit? Since I've been here, it seems like I dream all the time. I almost don't want to go to sleep—except that I'm so tired by the end of the day that I can't keep my eyes open.

So I sleep. And I dream.

Sleep and dream.

Sleep and dream. Over and over. This is what my days are made of.
So this is where I live now, in the country of dreams.

Some nights, I wake up in the middle of the night. And I'm scared.
Sometimes it's as though I've been crying. The dreams make me tired and
I hate myself. There's blood in my dreams—in all of them. And there's
always something that wants to hurt me. I know it's the monster. I never see
the monster but I know he's there.

I think the monster comes to me at night.

One of my roommates, Rafael, he's an expert on monsters. Not that
he talks about them. I can just tell. People who have monsters recognize
each other. They know each other without even saying a word.

One night, Rafael was sitting on my bed and shaking me. "It's okay,"
he was whispering. "It's only a dream, Zach. It's only a dream." I must have
been screaming or something. I could feel the beating of my heart. My
heart that had the words *anxious* and *sad* and *scared* and *messed up* written on it.

"It's okay," Rafael said. "It was only a bad dream."

I didn't say anything. I waited until my heart stopped running.
Sometimes, my heart ran faster than my bloody feet. When my heart relaxed and got quiet, I told Rafael I needed a cigarette.

"Just go back to sleep," he said.

"Will you stay? Until I fall asleep again?"

He didn't say anything. But he stayed.

I felt like a little boy. Shit. But I couldn't stop shaking. And I didn't
want Rafael to leave. I fell asleep listening to the sound of his breathing.
In the morning, Rafael asked me about my dream. "I don't remember,"
I said.

"Try."

"Why?"

"Because you won't get better if you don't."

"Are you teaming up with Adam?"

Rafael shook his head and then just grinned. "Okay," he said. "But,
listen, Zach, I care about you. I care what happens to you."

I mean the guy hardly knew me. But the thing was that, you know, I believed the guy. And he wasn't scary or anything like that. And to tell you the truth I liked that he liked me. I guess I thought he would change his mind about me once he got to know me. Not that I planned on letting him get to know me.

"Did you hear me, Zach? I care about you."

"Okay," I said. "It's okay with me that you care about me. But can we please not talk about it? Would that be okay with you?"

"Yeah, that would be okay," he said.

-2-

The thing I like about Rafael is that he's a nice guy. For-real nice. Mr. Garcia-nice. On the first night he was in Cabin 9, I heard him crying. His crying was real soft and quiet and it made me sad. The thing is that Rafael and I, well, we have this dream thing going on and we're both sad as hell. That makes us the same. Even though he's fifty-something and I just turned eighteen, we're both in the same boat. We're in the middle of a flood, floating down a wild, untamable river. The real difference between me and Rafael is not our ages, but that he's working hard to remember and I'm working hard to forget.

Another thing Rafael and I have in common—he hates himself. I hate myself too. But there's another part of Rafael, I think, a part of him that just doesn't want to hate himself anymore. He wants to be done with all that I-hate-myself shit.

Look, this dream thing, I just don't talk about my dreams to anyone. I don't talk about them with Rafael. I don't talk about them with any members of the group. And I don't talk about them with Adam. Yeah, okay, I know my dreams are intrusive. That's what they call them here. The psych doc, he asked me, "Do you have intrusive dreams?"

I looked at him and said, "I'm not sure what you mean by that."

"Are your dreams so real that they intrude into your waking hours?"

"Yes," I said.

"Do you want to tell me about them?"

"Why would I want to do that?"

"It's not good to keep all those things inside you."

"Maybe not," I said.

"It would be good if you talked about them with someone."

"Who would it be good for?"

He was trying to ignore the fact that I was being non-compliant. Non-compliant is a therapy word they toss around this place. Non-compliant is a very nice way of saying I was being a jerk. He was a jerk too so it all evened out. Do *not* get me started on the psych doc. I *did not* like the psych doc. *No, I did not.*

There are some things that I just don't like talking about and that's the way it is. I'll give the psych doc credit. He knew enough to change the subject. But he wrote something down on his pad. I knew the score. Everything he wrote down on that pad was going to make its way to Adam. I knew that Adam would bring up the issue of my "intrusive dreams" sooner or later. Adam, he was pretty good at getting down to my issues when we talked. Or things he thought were my issues. He has theories about me. I'm more or less hoping he'll keep those theories to himself.

Sometimes I think everything and everyone here is intrusive. My dreams don't leave me alone, Adam doesn't leave me alone, the other therapists don't leave me alone. Not even my two roommates, Sharkey and Rafael—they don't even leave me alone.

I've been here for three weeks. I know that I was at another place before coming here. That other place was a hospital. I don't remember anything about it except that I was really sick. Sometimes I have dreams about that other place. Everyone's dressed in white and all the walls are white and the bed sheets are white and I'm wearing white pajamas which is really weird because I don't wear pajamas. Everything's white and blinding and things seem like they're always moving. I just want to shut my eyes. I'm really tired and everything is blurry and I hear voices calling my name.

And then one day, well, I woke up and I was lying in Bed 3. Bed 3, Cabin 9. I remember being interviewed by the psych doc. I remember talking to Adam. He was really nice to me and his voice was kind and I almost wanted to cry. I mean, Adam is not a bad person. But the guy just won't lay off. Always showing up, that guy. And what is it about remembering that really gets him going? What is that?

When I first got here, the staff showed me around the grounds. There were like fifteen cabins scattered around and a main building where we ate and sat around if we wanted to sit around. A lot of people hung out at the main building. I wasn't one of those people. You know some people just didn't know how to be alone. Me, I was all about being alone.

Adam says I isolate.

I have no comment about some of Adam's observations. I did want to ask him if the word "isolate" was intended to be used as a verb. I wondered what Mr. Garcia would think about that.

If I want to hang out in Cabin 9, *what is so fucking bad about that?* It's a perfectly good cabin.

-3-

They let us smoke. Not that the counselors encouraged that kind of addict behavior. But the thing is that most of us have bigger problems. Yeah, smoking is not healthy. Yeah. They offered a "Quit Smoking Class." I was *not* interested in that subject.

There was a rule that we could only smoke in this one designated spot. Everyone called it the smoking pit even though it wasn't a pit. I bought a couple of packs of cigarettes off Sharkey when he arrived. He got here ten days after me. I was fucking dying for a cigarette. Sharkey, he's twenty-seven. He likes to talk a lot. Talk, talk, talk. Makes me fucking crazy.

The first few days I was in Cabin 9 alone. I liked that. I'd go to all the group sessions I was supposed to attend. You know, it was like school only you didn't get grades. I didn't mind listening to all the stuff the therapists had to say and what the screwed-up people had to say. I mean, the thing about screwed-up people is that they're very interesting. Interesting in a very stun-the-hell-out-of-me kind of way. I mean people get upset and angry and emotional and all of that. That's not really a big deal. Okay, so

I don't join in on all the emoting. It's bad enough that my dreams make me cry sometimes. I don't mind listening. And if someone wants to put all his emotional stuff out in front of everyone, well, that doesn't bother me. Well, it does bother me, but as long as there's a therapist around, it doesn't make me too anxious.

The thing about being at this place is that I am supposed to engage in healthy behaviors. Going to meals is a healthy behavior. Not that I was ever hungry. And not that I talked to anyone. I sort of just listened. Look, I'm consistent. This is not a bad thing. I mean, they *do* tell us that we need to be consistent. And the thing about meals is that there's a lot of drama. *I do not like drama.* Someone is crying or someone is saying something snarky or someone is complaining that this place sucks or someone is offering an opinion about one of the therapists or someone is telling their life story or someone is getting into it with someone else about shit that just doesn't matter—and it all makes me fucking crazy. Adam says that I need to engage in behaviors that are good for my sobriety. In my opinion, the meals here are extremely bad for my sobriety. Not the food, the people. And, another thing, I am not exactly nuts about being sober.

After meals, if I wasn't on clean-up duty, I'd just go to my cabin and read. Not such a bad life really, when you think about it. I was supposed to be doing homework, but I didn't feel like doing it. You know, the therapists were always trying to get you to talk about yourself. Like I really wanted to do that. And I'd always get an assignment. What does your addiction look like? Draw a picture of your home life. Write a letter to your mother. My addiction looks sad. My home life was sad. My mother was sad. Next assignment please. Let's keep moving. Shit.

I was pretty much doing okay living in Cabin 9 all by myself. It was okay. I was fine. Fine. Every time I said that word, Adam repeated it. Like, yeah, sure, *fine.*

Then Rafael came along. He'd been in another cabin and I knew him because he was in my group and I liked him okay. Not that I was all that present in group. Look, the guy didn't bother me. But that didn't mean I wanted to have him as a roommate. I don't know whose bright idea it was to have him move in with me, *but I was not happy.* I got this idea into my head that Adam was behind the whole thing and I told Adam I didn't think it was a good idea that Rafael roomed with me.

"Why not?"

"He's old," I said.

"We don't put people together based on age."

"His hair is turning gray."

Adam was giving me this look. "And?"

"He needs a haircut."

"So do you."

"I'm growing my hair long."

"So is he."

"Can't he stay where he was?"

"What?" he said. "Does this interfere with all that isolation?" I wanted to pop the guy. I knew it wasn't going to do any good if I told Adam that Rafael seemed too sad and kinda broken and maybe it wasn't good for me to have a sad and kinda broken older gentleman as a roommate. I wanted to say, "Maybe he'll be bad for my sobriety."

Look, I was stuck with the guy. When he moved in, he shook my hand, and I don't know, I guess I thought the guy wasn't going to be so bad. His smile *was* kind of sad but it was real and I liked that. And the best thing was that he didn't take up a lot of space and he was friendly and respectful and all of that. The guy had manners and so maybe I thought it was a good thing that he was my roommate because I knew other guys would be arriving because people arrived all the time and I figured it was better to have Rafael for a roommate than some ill-mannered, screwed-up jerk.

After Rafael moved in, we talked a little bit, but I could tell right away he didn't want to get inside my head, which was really cool, because I really wigged out when people tried to get inside my head. And Rafael, well, he seemed, well, I hate to say this, kinda normal. A lot more normal than me, anyway. He knew how to talk to people. And I felt bad for having gone to Adam to complain about the guy when really I didn't know shit about him.

The thing that really tore me up about Rafael was that when he smiled he almost looked like a boy. But, you know, well, there was that sadness thing about him. I could see it in his dark eyes. I mean, the guy was seriously sad. He was almost as sad as my mom, but somehow he seemed to be more connected to the world. Not that being connected to the world was all that great a thing. Not the way I saw it. What did being connected to the world get you? It got you sadder. *Look, the world is not sane.* If you stay connected to an insane world, well, you just go crazy. This is not a complicated theory. It's just simple logic.

-4-

And then Sharkey came along.

He was all smiles and talk and bullshit. But I liked him. See Rafael didn't take up a lot of space, but Sharkey, the guy took up space. I mean, he just about took over Cabin 9. And the guy had stuff. Three suitcases. Not small suitcases either. I'm serious. He had different kinds of sneakers and all kinds of pairs of shoes and clothes and clothes and more clothes. How long was the guy planning on staying? And sunglasses. Man, the guy was all about sunglasses. I got a big kick out of watching Steve go through Sharkey's things. Steve, he's on staff. They do that here, they go through your things. You know, make sure you don't have any sharpies to hurt yourself with and most especially they want to make sure you're not sneaking in any drugs. They don't trust you here. Not that any of us are worth trusting.

But man, did I get a kick out of seeing the look on Steve's face—especially when he got to Sharkey's underwear. I mean Sharkey had a stack of designer underwear still in the boxes. Designer underwear, it comes in a box. The dude had money. Maybe he was a dealer. That's what I was thinking.

When Sharkey walked into the cabin, Rafael was reading a book. And me, that's exactly what I was doing. He looked at both of us and said, "Well, you guys are gonna be a barrel of fucking laughs."

Rafael and I looked at each other and smiled. The good thing was that Sharkey made Rafael laugh. I mean, Rafael had a sense of humor. In some ways, he seemed younger than a guy in his fifties. It wasn't so much the way he looked, it was the way he existed in the world. See, I have this theory:

some people exist in the world in an old way and some people exist in the world in a young way. My dad, he existed in an old way. Rafael, he existed in a young way. Adam, he existed in a young way too. See, some guys, they'll always be like boys in some ways. I don't know if this is a good thing or a bad thing. I haven't decided yet.

But see, I liked the young thing about Rafael.

And Rafael, he put up with Sharkey's bullshit. I mean, Sharkey was the kind of guy who always told you what he thought. Like we wanted to know. But see, guys like that, they don't always believe that everything is a two-way street. They tell you what they think. That's cool. But when you look guys like Sharkey straight in the eye and tell them what *you* think, well, that's not always so cool.

When Rafael first arrived, me and him would talk a little. Not much. I didn't like to talk and he was sad and we both liked to read. So it was a good match. The cabin was nice and quiet. But with Sharkey on the loose, the whole cabin changed. His first night, he started asking a lot of questions. "What are you in for?" He looked straight at Rafael. It wasn't hardly a question.

Rafael gave him a crooked smile. "I'm an alcoholic," he said.

"Is that all?"

Rafael shook his head. "There's more to it than that."

"Well, I got nothing but time. I'm stuck here for thirty days."

Rafael laughed. "You can leave any time you want. This isn't a prison. We're not doing time."

"The fuck we're not."

"Have you ever actually done time?"

"Fuck yes. And I'm not going back. That's why I'm here."

"So you have yourself some legal consequences?"

Sharkey laughed. "You could say that. Look, I'm not coppin' to shit. But, see, I figure the judge is gonna smile at someone's who's trying to get his act together by coming to a place like this. See, I'll spend thirty days here, get my therapist to write a nice letter and, you know, the judge will see that I'm ready to join the earth people. Not that I want to be an earth person. But there's no harm in pretending to be one if it'll keep me out of the fucking slammer."

Rafael smiled. I mean, I could tell Rafael was getting a kick out of the guy. "What were you into?"

"This a fucking interview?"

Rafael shot him a smile. "Yes. If Zach and I don't like you, they'll move your ass to another cabin."

"Bullshit."

"Maybe. Maybe not." Then Rafael just broke out laughing. Then Sharkey went at it too. And me too. So we were all there in Cabin 9, laughing our asses off.

Then the room got real quiet.

"Look," Sharkey said. "I guess I was pretty much into everything. Cocaine, heroin, alcohol—you name it, I did it." He seemed pretty proud of himself. He looked at Rafael. I mean the guy had no remorse in his voice. I know remorse when I hear it. Rafael, he had remorse coming out his ears. Sharkey, he had zero remorse. "And you, dude, what was your drink of choice?"

"Wine."

"Wine? Shit, that's lame."

"It did the job."

And then he looked across the room at me. "What about you, Zachy?" The guy already had a nickname for me.

"Bourbon," I said.

"Just bourbon?"

"Well, coke. I liked that too."

"Now we're talking."

He got this look on his face. Euphoric memory. That's what Adam called it. "Some of you guys even get high remembering." That Adam, he had a name for everything. But that was exactly the look Sharkey had on his face. Euphoria. The guy was a disaster. But I liked him. He wasn't normal. If you were normal, he called you an earth person. He didn't care for them. No way. I think that's what I liked about him.

I wanted to ask him what he did to get himself into legal trouble, but I figured I'd find out soon enough. I figured I wouldn't even have to ask. After a few days, I'd know more about the guy than God did. That was my thinking.

Sharkey got quiet for a little while and looked around the room. But soon enough he started in again. "What is this bullshit of going through your stuff? It's such bullshit. And what's with this sex contract that we have to sign that we won't have sexual contact with anyone while we're here. What's that about?"

Rafael was trying like hell to read. He looked up from his book. "It's a no-touch facility."

"What the fuck does that mean?"

Rafael kinda shook his head. "You know what it means, Sharkey. And I think you know why."

That seemed to quiet down Sharkey's complaints. Not that Sharkey was happy about the whole thing. See, I was already getting it into my head that Sharkey just liked to complain. "You know," he said, "there's probably not any girl here I'd want to have sex with anyway."

Rafael looked up from his book and smirked. Rafael, that guy could smirk. "What makes you so sure there's a girl in here that would want to have sex with *you*, buddy?"

That pissed Sharkey off. "What's that supposed to mean?"

See, I knew what Rafael was doing. Sharkey was a really handsome guy. You know, the kind of guy who thought everyone was in love with him because, well, a face like that went a long way—especially with girls. Guys like Sharkey thought they owned the world. Rafael, he didn't go in for that.

Rafael didn't say anything. He just kept reading his book.

"Look," Sharkey said, "any girl would be lucky to have me."

"Maybe," Rafael said, "but if I had a daughter, I wouldn't let you past the front porch."

"Look, dude, you don't know me. Maybe I'm a really nice guy."

"Yeah. You probably *are* a nice guy. Tell me something, how many girls have you been with?"

"Is this still a part of that interview?" Sharkey sort of laughed, but I could tell Rafael was making him nervous.

"I have a guess." Rafael peered over his book.

"I'm game, dude."

"How old are you? Twenty-seven? Twenty-eight?" Rafael, he was good with ages.

"Twenty-seven."

Rafael nodded. "I'd say you've been with, let me see, more than fifty girls—more than fifty but under a hundred."

Sharkey smiled. "So what?"

"See what I mean about not letting you past the front porch?"

Sharkey laughed. He didn't say anything for a while, but I knew he was thinking of something else to say. Finally, he looked at Rafael. "What is it with you and that book?"

Rafael laughed. "We have a personal relationship."

That made Sharkey laugh. But then he said, "Doesn't seem like you need to be in place like this."

"Trust me, I need to be here."

"Not me."

Rafael smiled. "Maybe not. Well, there is that thing about your legal consequences."

"Consequences? What's up with you and that word, dude?"

"What about that word don't you like?"

"What are you, a counselor? You're not supposed to play therapist. It says so right in the rules."

"If you want to get technical, the rules don't actually say that. And anyway, I'm not much interested in playing therapist. I'm a garden-variety drunk. Nothing special about that."

I hated to hear Rafael say that. I don't know why. I just didn't like to hear him talk about himself that way.

"Look, they screwed me over. I didn't do what they said I did."

Rafael nodded like, you know, he wasn't going there. "Look, I didn't mean to upset you."

"I'm not upset." Yeah, not upset. Sharkey was definitely upset.

"Good," Rafael said.

"Look," Sharkey said. "Why don't you go back to your personal relationship with that book?" He looked up at me. "Aren't you a little young to be acting like him?"

I guess Sharkey thought that reading books was an old people's thing. I didn't know what to say so I just sort of shrugged.

"Hell," he said, "I think I'll go to the smoking pit."

That's when I decided Sharkey and I were going to be best friends. "You smoke?" I said.

"Yup."

"Can I buy a smoke from you?"

He smiled. Look, if the guy would sell me some smokes, I'd listen to him complain till the leaves grew back on their trees.

It was funny, when we walked out to the smoking pit, Sharkey got real quiet. We stood out there in the cold and smoked a couple of cigarettes.

"Life sucks," he said.

"Yeah," I said. "Rafael says it sucks better sober."

That made Sharkey laugh. "I can't decide if I like that guy."

"I like him," I said. I didn't know why I said that. Well, it was the truth. I did like Rafael. So, what was wrong with saying you liked someone when you did like them?

"He's a helluva lot nicer than my father." He took a really deep drag off his cigarette. "Don't get me going on my father."

I guess his father really tore him up. God, it was cold. I hated winter.

"You have dreams?" I heard Sharkey's voice in the dark.

"Yeah," I said. "I don't like having them."

"I have them too," he said. "I want to get rid of them."

"Me too," I said.

I wondered if he had a monster. Yes, he had a monster. Sharkey definitely had a monster.

Maybe everyone had one. Maybe I was just making that up. It was strange and funny and sad that we were standing there smoking and think-ing that we could get rid of our bad dreams. Maybe we were both hoping that something would happen and things would be different. Maybe the changed Zach and the changed Sharkey would have different dreams. It wasn't good for me to think these things. I knew that. Thinking things like that only made me sad. It was like that time when I thought that things between me and my dad could be different.

I kept the smoke in my lungs as long as I could, then just let it out slowly.

I hated winter.

I hated dreams.

I hated remembering.

I hated talking to Adam.

And I hated the fact that change was a word that existed in a dream I would never have.

REMEMBERING

There was this guy at school. His name was Sam. He was really tall and kind of a jock. Not that he hung with other jocks. I guess he was like me, kind of a loner. You know, like some coyotes. Coyotes really stun me out. They're very fantastic animals. They're really good parents for one thing. They take care of their pups and they raise them and they play with them and they teach them all the things they need to know in order to make it in the mean world. And even though coyotes like hanging out with each other and sing and howl at night, some of them like to just go off and be alone. They're okay with being alone. I was one of those coyotes who liked to be off by himself. I think Sam was like that too.

He was always trying to talk to me and stuff. I talked to him too. Not that I'm all that good at talking. Talking is fantastically overrated. Too many people do too much of it. It stuns the hell out of me how so many people like to talk. Sharkey, for example. If talking is so good for you, what the hell is Sharkey doing here? The guy tears me up. Talking *does not* heal you. Talking just adds to the noise pollution in the world. If we were really serious about going green, then maybe we'd all just be quiet.

Maybe that's why I felt connected to Sam. He was friendly and all of that and even though he wasn't an extreme introvert (that would be me), he was quiet about the fact that he was an extrovert. I mean, God did not write *anxiety* on Sam's heart. That really stunned me out.

One day Sam goes by my locker at school and asks me if I wanted to go hang out. I said sure. It was a Friday, and normally on Friday I'd go and get stoned out of my mind with my friends. I thought it might be good to change it up, you know? So Sam picks me up in his car and we go riding around and we're listening to music and talking and I'm trying not to want to smoke because I knew the guy didn't smoke. And then he says, why don't we go to a movie, and I say cool and so we go. I don't remember what we watched but I knew that Sam was watching me more than he was watching the movie. And that was really stunning me out. But I pretended not to notice. I mean, what the hell did he see?

So, when he takes me home, he says to me, we're just sitting in his car, and he says to me, "Listen, Zach, have you ever kissed anybody?"

And then I see where we're going with this, but I want to play it cool because, well, I liked Sam, and I didn't want to freak out because I freak out way too much and really it's no big deal that the guy wants to kiss me because, well, it wasn't as if he was scary or anything. But I have to say I started to feel really anxious and I wasn't about to kiss him. I mean, the guy was good looking and smart and he had these serious green eyes and he was all the things most guys really want to be and all of that and I knew a lot of girls that would have really liked to kiss the guy, but I, well, that just was not going to happen.

I just sat there and finally I said, "Why would anyone want to kiss me?" It was a really stupid thing to say. I don't even know why I said that. I mean, the words just came out of my mouth. I really tear myself up sometimes.

"Why wouldn't somebody want to kiss you? I mean, you're really beautiful."

That really wigged me out. Stunned the hell out of me. In a bad way. In a very bad way. I mean, I didn't like that he said that. Why did he say that? I hated that. I really needed a drink and I really needed a cigarette. Look, I didn't know what to do and he was bigger than me and he was a jock and what if he hit me? I didn't like that. I mean, I'd had enough of that hitting crap with my brother.

I just got out of the car and reached in my coat pocket and lit a cigarette. I took a drag and walked inside the house. And then I found myself walking around some street, smoking and drinking. I mean, my feet didn't have to ask my brain when they took me places. I got really drunk and I stumbled home. I don't even remember how I got into bed.

But the next night, Sam was in my dream. He kept looking at me. God, I hate that I'm lying here in Bed 3 of Cabin 9 and remembering a guy named Sam. Sam with serious green eyes. I didn't even know the guy. This doesn't feel good. Nothing feels good. Nothing.

THINGS I DON'T WANT TO KNOW

-1-

There are things I don't know that I really know. That's one of the categories of things around this place—at least in our group. We keep lists and categories for things so we can keep track. It's weird. Of course it's weird. Everyone in here is weird. And it stands to reason that most of the things we do are equally weird. Weird people have weird behavior. And if we weren't weird we wouldn't be here.

There's this lady in our group, she could be my mom. Her name's Elizabeth, but she likes to be called Lizzie. She calls this place "Trauma Camp." I like Lizzie. She has her issues but I like her voice and she says funny things and she's not all checked out like my mom.

See, that's the thing in our group. We all suffer from trauma. Only, I'm not exactly sure what my trauma's supposed to be. Everyone else in our group pretty much knows what their trauma is. Except me. I pretty much keep quiet about that. Well, I pretty much keep quiet about everything. Look, at least I listen. I don't think we all have to participate in the same way. That's my thinking. Sometimes, Sharkey tells me I have to speak up in group. "Look, dude," he says, "we're not here just for giggles and grins." Sharkey, he's not at all consistent. One minute he's all into this place and says he's ready to do the work. And the next minute he's carping and whining and calling this place a shithole. But Sharkey, he speaks up in group, I'll tell you that. Some days, he stuns the hell out of the whole group.

Our group is called Summer. You know, the season. There's a big painting that hangs on the wall of our meeting room. There's a huge tree in the center of the painting. And I mean to tell you that this tree is seriously full of leaves. And there's a group of people sitting under the tree and they're all talking and smiling. And instead of fruit, the tree is growing letters and the letters spell out Summer. Adam says that summer is the fullest season, the season of the sun, the season when the sky is bluest, the season when the whole world is most alive. I guess that's a nice thing. Yeah, okay, nice. Summer. The thing of it is that right now it's the middle of winter. Winter, it's the empty season. It's the season when the sky is the grayest. The world is leafless and dead. Winter tears me up.

There are other groups and the people in the other groups have other things going on. You know, other issues. We all have issues. Like Sharkey says, "We're not here for grins and giggles." The world has stunned the hell out of us, torn us apart, beat us down. Sharkey says we're lucky to be walking around.

Some people have eating disorders and there's a special group for that. Some people have more than one person living inside them and there's a special group for that. That's serious stuff. *That really does stun the hell out of me.* I mean, I only have one of me living inside me and that's bad enough. If I had more than one of me inside me, I'd off myself.

Look, let's say I had two other guys inside me. That would make three of us. That would mean that God would have written *sad* three times on my heart. Just think about that. Man, I would be smoking for three and drinking for three. It would not be good.

Some people are addicted to love or to sex and there's a special group for that too. I mean, that's kind of weird too. Look, I'm not into touch so it's hard for me to think too much about sex. I know I'm not normal. What's normal? And anyway, at this place, normal doesn't count. Not even the therapists are normies. Sharkey says that the only really cool thing about this place is that there are no earth people hanging out.

And there's another group. I'm not sure what that group is all about. I think maybe the people in that group are like the people in our group. A trauma group. Maybe in that trauma group, they're not addicts. That's the other thing about our group, we're all either alcoholics or drug addicts or both. And then it gets a little complicated because each group has other kinds of troubled people. I guess that's how I like to think about us, we're troubled. Sharkey likes to say we're damaged. But he's way into drama. I mean, I think the guy is addicted to having a crisis. Okay, so God wrote *troubled* and *damaged* on our hearts. That really tears me up, that God did that to us.

And the thing is that a lot of people who are troubled hurt themselves. That's a special kind of addiction. Around here, they call these types of people "self-harmers." They cut themselves and stuff like that. I can't take it. I just can't. There's enough blood in my dreams.

I guess I'm thinking that we're all self-harmers. In a way we are. Yeah, well, maybe not. Like I would know. I understand that there's something wrong with me. But I don't have more than one person living inside of me and I don't cut myself and I don't yell and scream or cry all the time like some people around here do, so I figure that I'm about as close to being a normie as it gets. At least around here. Yeah, yeah, yeah, I know what Adam says, this isn't a contest. *You belong here, Zach, trust me.* Like that's supposed to me make me feel good.

See, I just want to get back to my plan. Finish school with all my A's and go to college. I want my plan back. That doesn't sound so complicated. I'm going to talk to Adam about this. Let's just get me back to my plan.

But every time I want to talk to Adam about what I want to talk about, he brings other stuff up and we wind up talking about all kinds of issues that I just do not want to talk about.

-2-

Adam says I almost died from alcohol withdrawal. He says I was in a hospital for ten days before I came here. "Do you know how serious that is, Zach?" He didn't say it like it was some kind of accusation. He said it, well, like maybe I was lucky to be alive. Okay. Lucky.

I don't remember much about the hospital. I knew I was in there. But that's it. The details didn't hang around in my head. This is a good thing. I don't like the ugly details of my life loitering around. Look, if Adam says that's what happened, I guess that's what happened. I don't take Adam for a liar. The guy does not have it in him to go around bullshitting people. He's a straight-up guy. I mean, the guy is Mr. Get-Honest-With-Yourself. So, I guess I'm an alcoholic. But I just turned eighteen. So how can I be an alcoholic? If I was an alcoholic, I think I would know.

This is my thinking. I'm not really an alcoholic. I just overdid it one night and got some kind of alcohol poisoning. Okay, maybe I overdid it for a period of several days. Maybe weeks. But I'm okay now. That's my thinking on the subject. No use in wigging out over things you shouldn't wig out over. No use in getting all stunned out over alcohol. I'm okay. I'm fine. I may be torn up about a lot of things, but this alcohol thing, well, I'm okay on that score. I really am.

Like I said, we have these categories in our group and every day I'm supposed to try to add something to the list. Category 1: Things I know. Category 2: Things I don't know. Category 3: Things I know that I don't know. Category 4: Things I don't know that I know. It's hard to explain. Sometimes I understand the categories. Sometimes, I just get all confused. But this is the thing: There are things about myself I really don't want to know. What would knowing get me? I hate trying to come up with things for the list. Adam is always asking me how I'm doing on my list. I tell him that I'm working really hard on it. Like he believes me.

I think the therapists around this place think that if you know yourself, then somehow you'll be better and healthier and you'll be able to leave this place and live out your days as a happy and loving human being. Happy. Loving. I hate those words. I'm supposed to like them. I'm supposed to want them. I don't. Don't like them, don't want them.

This is the way I see it: if you get to know yourself really well, you might discover that deep down inside you're just a dirty, disgusting, and selfish piece of shit. What if my heart is all rotted out and corrupted? What about that? What am I supposed to do with that information? *Just tell me that.*

Most of the time I get the feeling that I'm just an animal disguised as an eighteen-year-old guy. At least I'm hoping that maybe deep down inside I'm a coyote.

Coyotes are decent.

Not like people.

People are not decent. That's the real secret nobody wants to talk about. I talk to myself a lot.

Adam is always asking me, "Zach, how much time do you spend talking to yourself?" I shrug and don't say anything. After a while, he starts shooting numbers at me and we come up with an honest figure. Honesty is a very big word when you're in therapy. Don't ask me what I think about that word. Just don't.

Look, I don't believe in honesty. I'd rather have a cup of coffee and a cigarette than live in all that honesty.

Anyway, Adam and I came up with this figure: 85%—which means that 85% of the time, I'm engaging with myself instead of engaging with the people around me. Look, I like the 85% thing. I do. I'm giving other human beings 15% of my time. That's plenty. Believe me. No, no, don't believe me. I'm a liar. Before I came here, I was always lying about all sorts of crap. I mean, I don't even believe the crap I tell myself. I don't. Why should anybody else fucking believe me? Okay, okay, I have to stop with the F-*word*. Adam put me on contract.

When you're on contract around here that means you can't do something. I'm on contract concerning the F-*word*. Can't use it. I use it too much. Not according to me but according to Adam. The group agrees with Adam. Well, except for Sharkey. He thinks we should all use the words we like to use.

-3-

One day Sharkey got all mental during group about the F-*word*. He shot Adam a look and said, "Lizzie likes to use the word *stupendous*." That's what he said. Then he looked around the room, then turned back to Adam. "Look, people need to use the words that best describe what they feel."

And Adam said very calm and sedate-like, "Really?" I hate the way that Adam is always so relaxed. It really pisses me off sometimes. So he said all calm and sedate, "Sharkey, don't just talk to me. Talk to the group."

And Sharkey shot back, "It's not the group that put Zach on contract over the F-*word*."

Adam sort of nodded. "Is that what this is about? This is about Zach?"

"No, this is about freedom of expression. I should be able to say *fuck* anytime I want to. And so should Zach."

That's when Adam interrupted him. "You can speak for you, Sharkey, and Zach can speak for Zach."

"Yeah, you like that because Zach never says a fucking thing."

Adam looked at me and asked, "You want to say anything here, Zach?"

"I like the word *fuck*," I said.

Adam smiled. "I get that." He nodded and then he looked at Sharkey. "What are you angry at, Sharkey?"

"I don't believe in censorship. That's all I'm saying. Lizzie can use the word stupendous if she likes even though I fucking hate that word. And she can use that stupid expression *terminally unique* all she wants. I don't give a shit. I don't have to like her words. She doesn't have to like mine. And the group can go to hell if they get all offended at the word fuck."

I could go on and on about what happened next. Lizzie let loose on Sharkey and told him that he was pretty much behaving like a selfish adolescent. And then she added: "There is nothing wrong with the term *terminally unique.* It means that you think you're so special that no one could possibly understand you. It means you should wake up and smell the coffee, Sharkey. You're twenty-seven years old. Zach is more mature— and he's eighteen." Man, when Lizzie gets going, she really gets going.

I decided I wanted to be left out of the discussion. You know, the thing about not talking very much is that people think you're mature. They make things up about you.

Then Lizzie put her head between her hands. "I'm sorry," she said. "I didn't mean to say that."

The thing about Lizzie is that every time she said something she really believed, she apologized for it. I really think Lizzie should be put on contract for apologizing. She should not be allowed to apologize. Why was she so afraid of hurting Sharkey's feelings? I mean, Sharkey didn't give a damn. He didn't. If the guy was gonna shove shit down your throat, well, the two-way street rule applied. That was my thinking.

Rafael, who'd been pretty quiet, looked at Sharkey and repeated Adam's question, "What are you really angry at?"

Sharkey completely ignored him. "You say the word *fuck* plenty, Rafael."

"Guess I do."

Sharkey looked at Adam and pointed at Rafael. "Why don't you put him on a fucking contract?"

I could tell Rafael wanted to go for a few rounds with Sharkey. I studied his face. He was deciding. And then he smiled. Rafael smiled a lot. I think sometimes Adam wanted to put him on contract over that smile of his because sometimes he smiled and said the saddest things. It was like Rafael's smile was a way of clearing his throat and it wasn't a smile at all. "See, the thing about that word, Sharkey, the F-*word*, is that sometimes I make that word do too much work. I mean, I say that word as if it clearly articulates what I'm really feeling. And it doesn't. It's a shortcut."

"A shortcut to fucking what?"

"To my anger. Maybe I cheat myself when I use that word. Maybe I cheat you too. Maybe the people around me deserve a better word."

"Are you saying I'm disrespecting the group? Is that what you're saying, Rafael?"

"I wasn't talking about you, Sharkey. I was talking about me."

"I think you're accusing me of disrespecting the group because I like to say *fuck*."

Rafael was trying to stay calm. Sometimes he *was* really calm. And sometimes he got all worked up. "Nope," he said. "I'm having a tough enough time owning my own shit. You own yours, Sharkey." He sort of sat back on his chair. "And if I want to accuse you of something, I don't need to be circumspect."

That's when Sharkey really lost it. "See!" I mean the guy was almost yelling. "Circumspect! What the fuck kind of word is that?" Sharkey was acting as if Rafael had stolen his car or something.

He went on and on for a while. We all knew Sharkey. That's what he did. When he was done, Adam got up from his chair and went up to the board. *The board.* That meant that Adam was about to do some serious analyzing. He wrote all our names down across the top of the board and then he went around the group and asked each one of us what they thought was really going on in the discussion.

The whole thing made me really anxious.

See, Adam had a way of putting the brakes on things. He re-focused us. That was Rafael's theory. Rafael watched Adam. It's like he was studying him. It was like he was learning from him. I noticed that. So Adam says, "What's coming up for all of you? What's this about?"

Then Maggie says, "It's hard for me to trust this group when everybody's angry." She crossed her arms. Maggie, she was pretty. She always wore dangling earrings. She was nervous about things. Especially about anger. I mean, she would *not* have liked my brother.

Adam asked her if she was angry too. "Yes," she said.

"Who are you angry at?"

"You," she said.

"Okay," he said. "Why are you angry with me?"

"Because you let Sharkey run this group."

"Does Sharkey run this group?" He let the question hang in the air.

Sheila pulled her hair back really tight. She did that. She looked right at Adam and said, "You run this group."

"No," he said, "I don't run this group."

And then Rafael said, "Well, I'd say you're pretty much in charge."

"In charge of what?"

"You fucking get paid," Sharkey said. "Don't they pay you to be in charge?"

Adam wrote the question on the board. WHO IS IN CHARGE? Then he wrote:

ADAM IS IN CHARGE
SHARKEY IS IN CHARGE
SHEILA IS IN CHARGE
RAFAEL IS IN CHARGE

LIZZIE IS IN CHARGE
ZACH IS IN CHARGE
MARK IS IN CHARGE
KELLY IS IN CHARGE
MAGGIE IS IN CHARGE

We all stared at the board. Rafael got this big smile on his face. "Well," he said, "I'm just thinking that if Sharkey's in charge of the group, it's because we let him." And then he laughed. He looked right at Maggie. "Can I tell you something, Maggie?" That was the thing in Group. If we wanted to say something to someone, we were supposed to ask them if it was okay. Not that we always followed the rules. Maggie nodded.

"If you feel Sharkey's taking over the group, maybe you should say something to him."

"Well," she said, "don't you feel Sharkey's taken over the group?"

Rafael smiled. "I guess I don't. He hasn't got that much power."

Everyone laughed. Even Sharkey. "You got that right," he said.

Then Adam looked at me and asked, "What comes up for you, Zach, when you look at the board?"

I hated to say stuff in Group. Like Adam didn't know that. "Look," I said, "all I know is that the only thing I'm in charge of is Zach."

Adam smiled. "And how are you doing with that?"

"I'm doing a pretty shitty job if you ask me."

He nodded. "That's honest. That's really honest, Zach."

He looked at Rafael. "What about you, Rafael?"

"In charge?" He laughed. It was a really sad laugh. "It's all gotten away. Everything. It's all gotten away."

"What's gotten away?" Adam got this really serious look on his face.

"My life," he said. "It's gotten away."

Everyone got real quiet.

Then Adam said, "Homework." I knew that was coming. "Everyone make a list of the ways you've lost charge of yourself, lost control of yourself, lost control of your life."

"I thought we were supposed to turn our control over to our higher power." Mark had this cynical look on his face. He was like that sometimes. And the thing was that Mark just did not get into the whole concept of a higher power.

"Is that what you're working on, Mark, turning your life over to your higher power?"

Adam knew damn well this was *not* the case.

"Look, I'm still not into this higher power thing. I just don't get it."

"Sure you do," Adam said. "You turned your life over to cocaine and vodka."

"That's bullshit."

"Is it?"

I mean the guy had been living in some cheesy hotel. He'd left everything, left his house, his wife, his job. He'd told us so himself. "You got me," he said.

"No, Mark, it's not like that." That Adam, he was one sincere guy. "I'm making up that you've handed over all your power to the crap in your life that screws you over. I'm making up that everyone in this room has done that."

He looked at the board. And this is what he wrote:

ADAM IS IN CHARGE

SHARKEY IS IN CHARGE alcohol and marijuana and cocaine and heroin and anger are IN CHARGE

SHEILA IS IN CHARGE alcohol and marijuana are
IN CHARGE

RAFAEL IS IN CHARGE wine and sadness and depression are
IN CHARGE

LIZZIE IS IN CHARGE cocaine and self-loathing and negative self-talk are IN CHARGE

ZACH IS IN CHARGE liquor and isolation and not remembering are IN CHARGE

MARK IS IN CHARGE Heroin and cynicism are IN CHARGE

KELLY IS IN CHARGE marijuana and depression and anxiety are
IN CHARGE

MAGGIE IS IN CHARGE alcohol is IN CHARGE

When he finished, we all looked at the list. Adam studied the board for a moment. "Anybody want me to change anything?"

Maggie spoke right up. "You forgot to add anger next to alcohol on mine."

Adam nodded. "Okay," he said. He added anger next to Maggie's name.

Then Sharkey said, "You forgot to write something next to Adam."

Adam grinned at him. "Don't worry about Adam. Worry about Sharkey."

That sort of made Sharkey quiet down. But, God, it was a sad list, I'll tell you that. And it wasn't like Adam was really making all this stuff up. I wanted to walk up to that list and erase it.

I looked at Rafael who just kept shaking his head.

I don't want to know these things. I don't. I know that Adam—look—he's okay. He reminds me of Mr. Garcia. But he's tearing me up.

I hate this.

The list makes me really sad.

I'm thinking about bourbon.

I'm thinking about how bourbon was my higher power. I'm feeling very anxious.

-4-

At the end of the day, I was still on contract concerning the F-*word*. Sharkey went on contract concerning that word too. In fact we all went on contract. While he was at the board, Adam got this brilliant idea. Yeah, brilliant. We all had to list our favorite expressions and he put us all on contract. We couldn't use those expressions in group for a week.

"Look," he said, "it's not a bad idea for us to take a good look at the way we talk, at the way we express ourselves. Let's call it *change* with a small 'c.' It's only for a week. Let's try it."

So I was okay not using the F-*word* in group. It wasn't going to kill me. I could think it. I didn't have to say it. I could use another word. And it wasn't as if I said that much in group. But I did like to say things like *That really stuns me out* and *that tears me up* or *I'm really wigging out right now.* So I was on contract about using those expressions for a week. Big deal. I'd use them in my head.

No one can put you on contract for the things you keep in your head.

But I'm telling you, Sharkey was one pissed-off dude. After group I heard him tell Adam that he wanted to change therapists. Adam wasn't all that shaken up about it from what I could tell. He kinda smiled at Sharkey and said, "Sorry, buddy, but we're kind of stuck with each other for now."

"I'm serious," Sharkey said.

"Okay," Adam said, "we'll talk about it."

Sharkey, he was just letting off steam. He gets himself all worked up. See, I get Sharkey. He gets all worked up and gets all verbal. I'm like that but different. I get all worked up and get all anxious. Maybe I get verbal too. Only I get verbal in my head. You know, that internal life Adam talks about.

The next day, Adam came back to the whole idea of words and how we use them. He says it wasn't a bad idea for all of us to engage our imaginations and come up with new words that expressed our internal lives—"our rich internal lives." I wonder where he lifted that from. Mentally, I was going to put Adam on contract for that expression.

That Adam, he was certainly an optimist. Look, I'd seen what having internal lives did to my mom and dad. Like I wanted that. He gave us all homework. We had to come up with a list of words that expressed what we felt. No cuss words were allowed on the list. He really pissed me off sometimes. I mean it. Sorry, I can't say he pissed me off. I have to say, he really makes me angry. That's a really boring way to say what I feel. *I am not fucking boring.* Okay, okay, sorry, sorry. No more of that F-*word* stuff. I'm on contract.

And there's another thing I'm on contract for. It has to do with that 85% thing. See, I have to bring that number down. Adam says I isolate. He is addicted to telling me that I spend too much time in my head. It's an unhealthy behavior. Look, I don't see how not bothering other people with your screwed-up vision of the world constitutes unhealthy behavior. Okay, so I hang out in my cabin a lot. What's wrong with lying on your bed and thinking? Like that's a crime. Look, I can do that for hours. See, this is the way I see it: I got this gerbil in my head. And he's always running around up there, stirring things up. I named him Al. So Al, he and I, well, we have this thing going. He stirs things up and I hang out with all the things he stirs up.

Adam thinks I need to shut Al down. Letting Al run wild in my head is not good for me. And he wants me to talk more in group. He calls it sharing. "Can you share more in group?" Look, if I wanted to share more, I would. That's the deal. You know, it isn't as if Adam pushes me. Well, he does push me but in a very subtle kind of way. Well, maybe not all that subtle. He's always trying to figure out some kind of game plan. That's how I see him. He's cool. He is. Mostly I like him. But not all the time.

Sometimes, when I'm in Adam's office, I study that picture he has of his kids. I guess I wonder what it would be like to have Adam as a father. I don't think that I should think those things. Thinking about what kind of father Adam would be is an unhealthy behavior. That's the way I see it. Adam. He even showed up in a dream I had. He was trying to talk to me but I couldn't hear him. I kept trying to get him to talk louder. I could see his lips moving and his hands moving and he was trying to explain some-thing to me. And then I realized that there wasn't anything wrong with Adam. It was me. I'd gone deaf. I hated that dream.

And what was Adam doing in my dreams? I mean, wasn't it bad enough that he was always trying to get inside my head? And who wants to see what's inside of my head anyway? There's all these words blowing around my head right now: *Zach winter remembering dreams summer forgetting blood Adam change change change.*

REMEMBERING

In winter we yearn for summer. That's what Rafael whispered last night as he watched the snow fall. He went with me to the smoking pit. He was talking more to himself than to me. He held his hand out and tried to catch the snow.

I knew he was remembering. He looked sad and alone and I knew he was far away.

"What were you like when you were my age?"

"Like you," he said.

"Like me?"

"I think so. Yes."

I offered him a cigarette.

He shook his head. "I quit ten years ago—and I'm not going back."

"Was it hard to quit?"

"I'm an addict. Everything is hard to quit." He laughed. He looked out at the falling snow. "When I was your age, I used to loiter around the liquor store and talk someone into buying me a pint of bourbon. I'd walk around and smoke and drink. I really liked doing that—especially in the winter when it was cold."

"Why did you drink?"

"Same reason as you. I was in pain. I just didn't know it."

I wanted to ask him why he was in pain—but I didn't.

"Life hasn't been easy on you, has it, Zach?"

"It's been okay."

"That's a lie."

"Yeah, guess so. Not that life's been all that easy on you either."

"That's no excuse for becoming a drunk."

The way he said it—like he was done with drinking. But he was also really angry with himself. "Maybe it is," I said.

"No, Zach, it isn't."

"Does it have to be this hard?"

"You're a sweet kid, you know that?"

I wanted to cry.

"Sorry," he whispered. "I know you don't like compliments."

That made me laugh. I don't know why, but Rafael was laughing too. Maybe just to keep me company. "Does it hurt—to remember?"

"Hurts like hell, Zach."

"Will it ever stop?"

"I have to believe that it *will* stop."

I wished to hell I could have believed him.

SUMMER, WINTER, DREAMS

-1-

I wasn't hungry. I went to breakfast anyway. I was late so the place
was pretty empty. There was a guy sitting by himself at one of the tables.
I decided to sit with him. I mean, it would've been uncool not to sit with
him. I went into my head and tried to retrieve his name: Eddie. I was good
at remembering names. The guy was about Rafael's age and he'd only been
here a couple of days.

I put my plate across from him and sort of smiled. "Hi, Eddie."

"Hi," he said. "Forgot your name." He sort of frowned.

"Zach."

"Yeah," he said. He did not seem interested. I should have left the
guy alone. Shit. Too late.

"So what group are you in?" It was the best I could do to start a conversation.

"I'm in the *I'm-Leaving* group."

"You just got here."

"This place isn't my brand of gin."

I guess I just didn't know what to say. I decided right then and there
that I was going to make a list of people who came and stayed here less than
a week. I mean, I guess I just didn't get that. It sort of made me mad. But
maybe it made me mad because they were doing what I wanted to do. Maybe they were doing the brave thing. They were going back home. I mean,
what was keeping me here? I know I'm still a high school student, but I'm
eighteen—and that makes me an adult. What was keeping me here? Why not

just go home? Maybe I was just hiding out here.

The guy looked at me for a while. "What the fuck are you doing in here anyway?"

I didn't know what to say so I didn't say anything.

"Do you believe in Jesus, kid?"

I thought that was a really weird question. "Yeah, I guess so."

"What's he ever done for you? What's he ever done for any of us?"

"I haven't thought about it that much," I said.

"I got some advice for you. This place will just take your money and throw you back out there again. It's a fucking waste."

"So you're just gonna go back out there and drink?" I didn't know I was going to say that. Sometimes, I really wig myself out.

"What the fuck's it to you?"

I looked down at my plate. I thought maybe he was going to hit me and I started trembling on the inside—just like I did when my brother was about to hit me. The anxiety was owning me again. God, I hated this feeling, hated it, and I just couldn't move, couldn't talk. I don't know how I did it, but somehow I made my legs move. I made my arms move. I made it to the bathroom just in time to throw up. I hugged the toilet bowl until all the words in my head stopped spinning. I got up and washed my face and breathed until I felt myself getting quiet again. I made my way to the smoking pit and lit a cigarette. Sharkey was watching me. "You okay? You look a little pale, dude."

"Something I ate," I said.

"Sure," he said. I hated the way he said *sure*. Sometimes I just wanted to beat the crap out of Sharkey. Why couldn't he just leave a guy alone with his anxiety?

-2-

By the time I got to group, I felt better. Better does not equal good. I kept thinking about Eddie's question, about what Jesus had ever done for me. I took a deep breath and tried to exhale the question. Not that I really thought things worked that way. You can't just breathe out anxiety. You can't just breathe out confusion.

There was a therapy they used around here. It was called Breathwork. Sharkey and Rafael, they did that stuff. Breathwork. Look, you just can't breathe in and out and expect everything to be fine. Sometimes, instead of taking a deep breath, I counted. So I looked around the room and that's what I did. Counted. For some reason, counting calmed me down. Seven people in group now that Mark was gone. Thirty days at this place and now gone back to his family. He left a sober man. Yeah, sober. But, I don't know, I was sort of worried about him. Mark, he still looked a little angry, you know. And it was like he still had too much of the street in him. Like Sharkey. Maybe I thought he could never be tamed and that a house with a wife and kids could never make him happy because there was something too wild inside of him. There was too much fire in his eyes. You know, like he could light into you or anyone he ran into for any reason. That wild thing inside him.

Yeah, what do I know?

Look, I think too much. That's the way I am. Worry, worry, worry. Worry and anxiety go together. It's better now with the meds. But I don't like taking them. They're non-addictive. That's cool. But, you know, it bugs the crap out of me that I have to take something to keep me calmer.

When Mark left, we did our usual goodbye thing in group. Adam has these medals. They look like they're made of copper—or at least that's what it seems like they're made of. On one side the medal says: *To thine own self be true.* And on the other side, there's an angel who looks like he's praying. I'm not into angels. Not that I know anything about angels.

I've done a lot of thinking about that medal we pass around when someone leaves the group. I'm not sure about this *To-thine-own-self-be-true* stuff. Speaking for myself, I'm not sure what that means. Am I being true to myself if I want to forget? Am I being true to myself if I want to remember? The part of me that wants to live in forgetting is pretty real. So am I supposed to be true to that *thine self*? That medal wigs me out.

So we do the ritual of passing the medal around. We hold it and we press something good into it. You know, like a good wish. Rafael pressed a lifetime of sobriety into it. That was cool. I mean, it wasn't like a life-time of sobriety was going to be easy—not in a world that pushed alcohol as a full-time hobby. But still, maybe when Mark wanted to take a drink he'd remember what Rafael had pressed into his coin. And, well, maybe he wouldn't drink. I got the feeling Mark drank like my dad. Not good. Not a healthy behavior.

Sharkey pressed music into the medal. That was cool too. I mean Mark was way too serious and Sharkey said, "Dude, you got to get that music into your head, into your feet. Music, dude, get it?" That made Mark smile. Sharkey, he could make people smile. He went around the world stunning people out.

Sheila cried. You had to know her. She cried about everything. I mean, *it just was not necessary to cry about everything.* Okay, maybe she really liked Mark. That was cool. You were allowed to like anyone you wanted to like. Okay.

When the medal got to me, I pressed peace into it. You know, peace is a good thing. Peace was good enough. Look, I felt bad about the peace thing. Stupid. Peace. Sure. I tear myself up.

This is the thing, people are not supposed to come here and stay forever. They deal with their stuff and they leave. Or sometimes, they don't deal with their stuff and leave. Sometimes they come, look around, and then leave. I mean Eddie was not the only guy to walk in and then walk back out. I was at dinner the other day and I was talking to this other new person. Well, I wasn't really talking, but I said, "Hi."

And she said, "Hi."

And I said, "I'm Zach." I was trying to be friendly and she looked really freaked out. She looked like hell. "I'm in Summer," I said.

"Summer?"

"That's my group."

"Oh," she said.

"What's your group?"

"Doesn't matter," she said. "I'm leaving."

Another member of the *I'm-Leaving* group. "Oh," I said,

"that's too bad."

"Why is that too bad?" She sounded mad.

"Well," I said, "maybe it isn't too bad."

"You like it here?"

"It's okay," I said.

"What's so okay about it?" she said.

"The food is good."

I could tell she thought I was really screwy. "If I want good food, I'll go out to a restaurant and order a nice glass of wine to go with it."

To tell you the truth, that sounded pretty good.

"My husband said if I didn't stick it out here that he was leaving me." She took a sip from her coffee and boy was she shaking. "He can go to hell."

I knew the score. She didn't want to get sober. I didn't blame her for that. Look, I was still thinking how good it would be to get my hands on some bourbon. There were worse things than being a drunk. At least that was my thinking. I said that to Adam once. "Really?" he said. "Make a list, of things that are worse than being a drunk." Shit. More homework. Do you see why it's best not to say too much?

This woman, whose name was Margaret, eyes me up and down and said, "There doesn't seem to be anything wrong with you."

"You can't always tell by looking," I said.

She studied me for a little while. "If I were you," she said, "I'd pack my bags and get the hell out of here before something really bad happens to you."

I had the feeling that something really bad had already happened to me. And it didn't happen here. But I didn't say anything.

"Look," she said, "places like this can make you crazy. Really crazy. Get out while you can."

I wanted to tell her that depression and alcoholism and eating disorders were not communicable diseases. I mean, I didn't know much, but I did know that. You know, it really doesn't do any good to talk to someone who's already made up their mind. But I knew if Adam got her in his office he'd say, "This is just where you belong." I pictured Adam saying that to her. I pictured her wigging out. I got to smiling.

"Why are you smiling?" she asked.

"We do that around here," I said. "We smile for no reason." I could tell I was beginning to freak her out.

"I need a cigarette," she said.

"Listen," I said, "be careful of the people in the smoking pit. Some of them have more than one person living inside them."

She did not like that one bit. She just sort of stomped away. Look, I don't know what gets into me sometimes. It was not a nice thing to wig a lady out who was obviously already wigged out. Not a nice thing. Still, I was sort of laughing to myself.

Later that day, I saw that lady get in a cab and leave. I saw her from the smoking pit.

"We lost another one," Sharkey said. "If I had any brains I'd be getting in that cab with her."

I wondered if Sharkey meant it. Maybe part of him wanted to just get the hell of out here. But the part that was staying, I was interested in that part of him.

This was my new theory: not everybody was interested in doing the work. Rafael said that change hurt like hell. I think Rafael would know. That guy is in some kind of pain. Sometimes it almost hurts me to look at him.

So even though not everyone stayed, me and Sharkey and Rafael, we stayed.

-3-

"Tomorrow," Sharkey said, "the word is that we're getting someone new in group. Another messed-up member of the human race." Sharkey, he kept his eyes and ears open. It wasn't hard to believe he'd spent a lot of time out on the streets. I mean the guy knew everything about our little society. It was like he made himself an insider into every part of this place. He always knew who was coming and who was going. It was like getting to know everything about a place was in his nature. I wondered about that. What was in my nature? Isolating. I was hyper on the inside and dead on the outside. Sharkey was hyper inside, outside, hyper all over.

I'm telling you, Sharkey was nervous as hell. Always pacing up and down. I loved watching him. He'd pace like he needed to go the bathroom or like a tiger that was trying to figure out a way to get out of his cage. He could be funny as hell. And he could be really scary. He tore me up, that guy.

I stared at Sharkey as he lit up another cigarette and looked at his watch. He always had to know what time it was. What was up with that?

Lizzie shook her head. "Any bets on how long she'll stay?"

"How do you know it's a she?"

"Because she's going to be my new roommate."

Sharkey nodded. "I'll give her a week."

"I say she'll stick it out." Lizzie put out her cigarette.

"Since when are you so optimistic?"

"Optimistic? Me? Look, Sharkey, let me tell you something. Just because someone sticks it out for thirty days or forty-four days or sixty days or ninety days, that doesn't mean anything will change. Sticking it out isn't the same thing as doing the work."

"Then what's the point?" I said.

"He speaks," Lizzie said. "Wow. He knows how to pronounce words."

"Knock it off, Lizzie," I said. "Just knock it off."

She laughed. I liked her. We were just joking around.

"I'm serious," I said. "What's the point?"

"Maybe that's what we're here to figure out."

I wanted to ask her if she was better. I mean, if she was getting well. I wondered if something changed inside of you. I mean, there was this talk about change all the time and I wondered how anyone would know if they changed. Did it feel different? What would that feel like? It's not as if I could grow wings. It's not as if I could ever fly. It's not as if I could ever be anything beautiful.

Annie. That was the new member of the group. She came in, looked a little scared, looked down at the floor, than grabbed a chair. We always sat in a circle. The chairs weren't too bad. Not too bad, not really. Adam introduced her. She was supposed to say something about herself. Later, she could tell us her story. Everyone had told their story except for me and Sharkey and Rafael. Look, I didn't mind Storytime—as long as it wasn't me telling the story.

"I'm Annie," she said. "I'm thirty-four. I'm an addict and an alcoholic and I've been sober for twenty days. I'm from Tulsa, Oklahoma."

"Twenty days." Adam said. "Good job."

Yeah, sure, okay.

We all nodded. "Welcome." That's what we all said. It was weird. We were all more or less sincere when we said it. What else were we supposed to say—*run for your fucking life*?

That's when we did our Check-in thing. We went around and said stuff, how we were feeling, what we wanted to work on that day, healthy behaviors, unhealthy behaviors, secrets, stuff like that. Oh, and we always had to say something good about ourselves. We called them affirmations. We were supposed to say three good things.

Rafael was first. "I'm Rafael. I'm an alcoholic."

"Hi Rafael." That's what we said. That's how it went.

And then Rafael just paused and said, "No secrets. I'm sad. Guess that's not much of a secret." And then he paused again and said, "I've been having bad dreams." He looked at me and grinned, "There's a lot of that going around." He looked around the room. "No unhealthy behaviors— well, I thought about drinking. It passed." He took a deep breath. Rafael, he was like me, he hated affirmations. "I am capable of change." He always said that. Sometimes he said it, you know, ironically. Sometimes he sounded sincere. Today, he sounded more or less sincere.

"Yes, you are." That's what we all said at the affirmations. See, I just didn't like this part of the whole group thing. Made me anxious.

"I like being sober."

"Yes, you do." Yeah, we were like this little congregation at church saying *Amen.*

"I like trees," he whispered.

"Yes, you do," we whispered back. *Amen.*

"Trees?" Sharkey interrupted. We were not supposed to interrupt during Check-in. "That's your affirmation? You like trees?" I mean Sharkey was all outraged over the whole thing.

That just made Rafael laugh. "Yes, Sharkey, I like trees."

I could tell Sharkey wanted to tell Rafael that it was all bullshit. But Sharkey just decided to drop it.

"Trees are good," Adam said. "Anyone here not like trees?"

Sharkey just couldn't take it. "What am I? Fucking Tarzan? I like cities—that's what I like."

Adam smiled. "You can express your love for cities when it comes around to your turn." Adam and Sharkey gave each other snarky smiles. I liked watching that. It made me smile.

We moved on—all around the room. Lizzie was happy—sometimes she was happy. "I'm physically, spiritually and emotionally connected." People in group said that a lot. Connected to what?

And me, God, I hated when it was my turn. "I'm Zach. And I think I'm an alcoholic."

"You think?" Adam said.

I shot him a look. "I AM AN ALCOHOLIC." Then I shot him an are-you-happy-now kind of look.

He grinned back at me.

I looked at the card in front of me. The card had affirmations in case we couldn't come up with our own. "I deserve good people in my life." I know I sounded like a wiseass when I said it. Look, let's get real. I had no clue as to what I *did* and *did not* deserve.

"Yes, you do." I didn't doubt the group's sincerity. But who wrote this card?

I stared at the card. It was really pissing me off. "Can we move on here?"

"Why is it so hard to say three good things about yourself?"

"I was born beautiful. There. How's that?"

"Yes, you were." Adam really smiled at that one. So did Rafael. Sharkey thought it was funny as hell. And it was funny as hell.

"My life has a purpose." I read that one off the card.

"Yes, it has."

I ended my Check-in with, "Physically, I'm good. Emotionally, I'm screwed. And spiritually, I'm, well, screwed. That's the sorry dirt of it." Next. God, I really *did not* like Check-in. It made me feel like I was in a really bad television show. The sad thing was that if this was a television show, there are people in the world who would actually watch it. The world is really, really screwed-up.

After Check-in, Rafael took out a picture he'd drawn. You know, we all get time to talk about our artwork and stuff. Or the lists we're always working on. We're supposed to ask for feedback or for whatever else we need. Like I knew what I needed.

I really liked Rafael's painting. The guy wasn't a hack. His art said something. It was real. The sky was really deep blue, not like it was day but like it was night. But there weren't any stars in the painting. And there was this monster that sort of took over the whole sky and he looked like he was about to pounce on this little boy who was reading a book. God, his painting really tore me up and he'd written something on the bottom of the painting and it was like the words were part of the painting and it was as though the boy was sitting on the words.

Adam put the painting in the middle and we all looked at it. And we were all really quiet, you know studying it, and Adam said, "Will you read that for us?"

And Rafael read: *I can hear the warning, the whisper: there's a monster in the room. The whisper becomes a scream. The world is full of madmen. I have evidence. I can prove it. I look around. The room is as empty as my heart. It used to be full, my heart, but that's another story. No one is here. Maybe not even me. I can prove there are madmen—but I can't prove the monster exists. Who was it that whispered the warning? Listen close, the sky is falling. Maybe the monster is outside just waiting for me to step out the door. Maybe he's already swallowed up the sky. What does he want with me anyway? Is he trying to scare me? Is that it? I was born scared— I don't need a monster for that. Maybe the monster lives in the books I'm reading. One of books is about the genocide in Rwanda and the other book is about a little boy who gets raped. Who needs monsters?*

That's what he read. And it really tore me up. Somehow I felt as if Rafael was reading that just for me. His voice—and the way he read it—I don't know, it's just that all of a sudden I felt as if I was going away and I wondered about that because I didn't like it when I did that, sort of went away because that's what my mother did, so I made myself stay in the room. And I kept looking at Rafael's picture and I was only half listening to what everybody was saying and thinking and feeling about Rafael's painting and then I heard Adam ask me what I saw in Rafael's painting and I just looked at Rafael and asked, "Is that boy you or is that boy me?"

And I didn't know why but I was crying. And I hated that. I was just crying. I was hitting and hitting myself, hitting and hitting myself in the chest with my fists. And then I felt someone taking my fists and holding them until I unclenched them—and then I felt a hand holding my open hand. And I heard Adam's voice saying, "I see you, Zach. I see you."

But I didn't know what that meant.

Maybe it was all a dream. A bad dream. But Rafael's voice had been so beautiful so maybe it wasn't all bad. And Adam's voice sounded so kind when he said *Zach, I see you.* And I kept thinking to myself: *Some people have dogs. What do I have? I have dreams I don't want to remember. I have two roommates named Rafael and Sharkey. And I have a monster and a therapist named Adam. What happened to me that I couldn't just have a dog like normal people?* And I couldn't stop crying.

REMEMBERING

"I need to ask you a question. Is that okay, Zach?"

I should have had a cigarette before coming into Adam's office. But there I was, staring into Adam's eyes that were blue as the sea but that today looked like they were green as a leaf. I wondered about his eyes. Just like I wondered about Rafael's eyes. And Mr. Garcia's eyes. What was it about their eyes that made me wonder?

"Zach?"

"Yeah."

"When you go away like that, where do you go?"

"I didn't really go away."

"What were you thinking about?"

Like I was going to tell him that I was contemplating eyes. "Nothing important."

"Everything's important."

"Okay," I said. Adam, he knew how to read that I-could-give-a-shit thing in my voice.

"Answer me this, Zach."

"Okay."

"What do you remember about coming here?"

"What do you mean?"

"Do you know why you're here?"

"Everyone seems to think I need to be here."

"That's not what I asked."

"Well, maybe I *do* need to be here."

"You could leave if you wanted. You're eighteen. You're an adult."

"Like that's really true," I said. "I'm still in high school." I looked down at the floor. "Where would I go?"

"Don't you have a home?"

I just sat there for a long time, not saying anything, just looking down at the floor.

"Look at me, Zach."

I didn't want to look at him—but I did.

"What do you remember?"

"I keep telling you that I don't want to remember."

"I get that, Zach. I do. But can you tell me anything about what you remember?"

"I don't want to fucking go there. Don't you get that, Adam?"

"I do. Look, let me ask you another question."

"Okay."

"Do you trust me?"

"Yeah. Mostly I trust you."

"You trust me 100%? 50%? What?"

That made me smile. He liked the percentage thing. I thought that was very cool. I don't know why. Adam tore me up. In a good way. Well, not always in a good way. "I trust you 85%."

"Yeah? 85%?"

"That's not bad."

"How much do you trust the group?"

"60%."

"60%?"

"I thought that was pretty good."

"Okay, how much do you trust Sharkey?"

"Sharkey? I really like Sharkey."

"Okay, Sharkey gets 100% on the like scale. But on the trust scale?"

"70%."

"Just 70%?"

"Look, you know him better than I do. You're his therapist too."

"This isn't about what I think, Zach."

"It never is."

He shot me a look. You know that look that said *I'm not the guy in therapy—you are.*

"And what about Rafael?"

"90%."

"Rafael is 90% on the trust scale?"

"Yeah."

Adam nodded. And then he smiled. "So you like him, huh?"

"Everyone likes him."

"We're talking about you, not everyone."

"Yeah, I like him."

"Why?"

"I just do."

"Okay. Do you talk to him?"

"Sure I do."

"Why do you trust him?"

"He's trying hard to be honest. With himself, I mean."

"Yes, he is."

"I admire that—he's trying to be honest even if it hurts."

"Yes, I think that's right. He's trying to remember everything in his life that hurt him. You're doing the opposite. How can you admire someone who's doing the opposite thing from what you're doing?" He looked straight into my eyes. Adam with the blue eyes that looked green today.

I looked back at him. "Okay," I said. "I'll tell you one thing that I remember."

"Okay."

"Blood."

"Blood?"

"There was blood. That's what I remember. There was blood."

"Where?"

"I don't know. I just know that there was blood."

"And what do you feel when you remember blood?"

"You know damned well how I feel."

"No, I don't."

"Yes, you do."

"How would I know?"

"I know you know."

"I don't, Zach. I don't know what it's like to be you. I don't know what it's like to feel what Zach feels."

"I don't like to feel."

"You say that every session. I get that, Zach, but—"

"But what?"

"Zach, how do you feel when you remember blood? Can you tell me?"

"How do I feel?" I looked at Adam's eyes. They weren't green anymore. They were blue again. "I feel like I died. That's how I feel. Like I died."

GOD AND MONSTERS

Rafael told me that sometimes he feels as though God is nothing more than a set of jaws that bites down on his heart. After Rafael said that, I got this picture in my head of those jaws and I started thinking that if Rafael was right, then God was the monster. Look, I think I know what Rafael's really talking about. He's talking about pain and where it comes from. And me, what I'm trying to do is figure out this whole thing about monsters. I thought I was supposed to get a guardian angel. No guardian angels for Zach. Nope. Look, maybe God *is* the real monster. What the hell do I know?

WHAT DOES THE MONSTER WANT?

-1-

I have a new addiction: I read Rafael's journal.

Okay, this is *not* okay. But the guy leaves it on his desk and it's just sitting there and it feels as though it's calling my name. All right, journals do not call you by name unless you hear voices. There's a woman here who walks around and shakes. She looked me straight in the eye and told me I was suffering. I may be suffering but *I do not suffer from auditory hallucinations.*

This is just the way it is with me right now—I just feel compelled to read what Rafael has written in his journal. Compelled, that would be a Mr. Garcia word. And now that I think of Mr. Garcia, I am absolutely certain that the only thing I really suffer from is intellectual curiosity. Okay, yeah, and the therapists here would call it something else. They would say I was not respecting someone else's boundaries. The real story depends upon your point of view—that's what I'm thinking. We're back to that perspective thing.

This is what I'm thinking: if Rafael's journal was such a private thing, then why was it just sitting there on his desk? It just sits there all the time, *and it's a public space.* Okay, this is all bullshit and I know it and this is a really bad thing to be doing, yeah. Look, I guess I like getting into other people's heads too—just like everyone else. And I especially like getting into Rafael's head. It's cool, the way he thinks.

Reading Rafael's journal—around here it would be classified as a very unhealthy behavior. I mean, we have these sessions on healthy boundaries. Healthy people have healthy boundaries. Unhealthy people, well, let's not get into that. It's like this: some people have walls which means they let no one in. This equals unhealthy. Some people let everyone in and let themselves be stepped all over. This equals unhealthy.

No one has to tell me that reading Rafael's journal is a violation of his privacy, which equals a definitely unhealthy behavior. In group it would also qualify as a secret. We *are not* supposed to keep secrets. Secrets are killing us—that's the theory. And another thing, I am *not* supposed to be talking about *us*. I'm supposed to be talking about *me*. It is not a healthy behavior to speak in universals. I am only supposed to speak for *myself*. And I'm not supposed to use sentences using *you*. I'm not supposed to say things like: "When *you* feel sad, *you* cry." No, no, no. I'm supposed to say: "When *I* feel sad, *I* cry." Adam always corrects us. He's all nice and sweet about the whole thing, but he corrects us all right. Stops us right in mid-sentence. Okay, so I got the point. I, I, I. I, I, I. Okay, *I* am feeling this. *I* am feeling that. Yeah, *I* get it, *I* get it.

Therapy is tearing me up. Am I better? I'm mad. Is getting angry part of therapy? Isn't all this about getting un-angry? What do I know? What I do know is that there's an anger group on Tuesdays and Thursdays. Maybe I'll join that group. Hell, I bet I could run that group.

Sharkey's angry, that's for sure. Worse than me. Okay, this is not a contest. I get that. And even Rafael's angry. This is the thing: life has not been kind to us. I think I'll make a new list: The Reasons Why *I* Am Angry. I am stunned out, torn up, wigged out. I am A-N-G-R-Y. This is why we have no baseball bats around this place. This is why everyone is all concerned about some clients having sharpies. Look, if you're not a windshield, you're pretty safe around people like me.

I'm trying to do the work. And, really, I think that Rafael's journal entries have become part of my therapy. I mean the guy writes really beautiful things. I mean it. *He tears me up to shreds.* Rafael's thinking is very, well, you know, it's thoughtful. The guy writes screenplays for a living and that's very cool, but I'm thinking that Rafael is some kind of poet—just like Mr. Garcia. I'm trying to learn from him. And this *is not* a bad thing.

Yesterday, when I was alone in Cabin 9, my feet took me over to Rafael's desk. There were a couple of sketches on his desk that were probably going to become paintings. I reached over and began leafing through Rafael's journal. I found this very cool story about his monster:

The Boy and the Monster

1.

The boy is reading to the monster. He is like Scheherezade. He will read a story every night—read and read until the monster falls asleep. And the boy will live one more day. He will live this way forever.

2.

The boy's name is Rafael. He is seven. He could be five or six or eight. But right now, he is seven. When he grows up, he will become a writer, though no one suspects this—not even the boy.

There will be many monsters in the stories he will write.

3.

The boy reads the story of his life to the monster but he leaves certain things out of the story. He is afraid of making the monster angry. If the monster gets angry, something very bad will happen. The boy decides that the monster prefers happy stories about happy boys so the boy makes up a happy story about himself. He becomes an expert at telling happy stories. He is certain the monster likes the stories. He is certain.

4.

As the boy grows older, the monster comes to him—mostly at night. The monster is insatiable for stories. The boy, who is now almost a man— but who remains a boy—keeps telling stories to make the monster happy. Somewhere inside of him, the man who is still a boy knows that the monster will never be happy.

But he continues reading the stories he writes for the monster.

5.

Sometimes, Rafael doesn't feel like reading his stories to the monster. He is tired. There are nights when the monster stays away, and he thinks or hopes or wants to believe that the monster has gone away forever. Sometimes the monster stays away for weeks and months and Rafael starts to believe that he is free. He prays that the monster is dead.

But the monster always comes back.

6.

The boy has now become a man (but is really still a boy). Reading to the monster is driving him insane. He begins to drink. He has always liked drinking but now the drinking has become his consolation. He drinks and drinks as he reads his stories to the monster. He knows now that he has always hated the monster. He wonders what would happen if the monster discovered the truth. He feels as if his heart is on fire. The hurt is becoming impossible to bear.

But the drink is good and helps him get through the story when the monster comes.

7.

Rafael, the man who is still a boy, is starting to get old. His hair is turning white and he wears the look of a man who has learned how to whisper the word *suffering* as if it were a prayer. He has forgotten words like *happiness* and *joy.* He laughs but the laughter is hollow. Only the tears are real.

He wonders why he has a monster. He wonders why he has surrendered to him.

8.

He thinks to himself: *What would happen if I stopped reading to the monster? What would happen if I read him a real story—a story about a boy who was damaged and hurt and kept wounds in his body like treasure? What would the monster think about that story? What would the monster say if I told him, I don't want to tell you any more stories about boys. I want to tell you a story about Rafael who wants to cross the border and enter a country called manhood. It is a hard and difficult and beautiful country. Do you understand that, monster?*

Tonight, when the monster comes, he will tell him the story he has wanted to tell all his life.

9.

It is dark outside. The night has come again, but he is not afraid. It is a strange thing for him not to feel the fear. He feels naked. But he thinks it is not such a bad thing to feel his body, to feel his arms and his legs and his chest and his hands and his heart. He is sitting on his bed. He does not need a drink.

He will not drink. He is waiting for the monster to come so he can tell him his story.

I knew Rafael's story had to do with the drawing he brought into the group. The drawing that really wigged me out, the drawing that made me cry, the drawing I thought was about me. I know that. But the thing is that I'm in love with Rafael's story. I think I understand when Adam says that all our stories are different but in some ways our stories are all the same. I never really got that. But when I start to read Rafael's journal, it's as if I can see myself. It's better than a mirror. Even though I'm eighteen and he's fifty-three, I can see myself in the words that Rafael has written. I can. This doesn't make any sense, but this is the thing: *to me* it makes perfect sense.

Adam is not right about everything. No, he's not.

Still, I don't think Adam would get into the fact that I was reading Rafael's journal. But see, it's helping me do the work. Why should anyone have a problem with a guy trying to do the work? Okay, I can just hear myself tell Adam these things. I'm seeing the look that enters into his face. The look that, you know, reminds me that I'm lying to myself. The look that says, Zach you are *not* getting honest.

I'm an addict. There. I've done some work on that and I'm realizing that *yes, I am an alcoholic addict.* So, now I'm addicted to reading Rafael's journal. They say that's what happens—you trade in one addiction for another. *But it is better to read Rafael's journal than it is to drink bourbon and do cocaine.* That's my thinking. Perspective, that's the thing. Okay, yeah, I'm stunning myself out all to hell.

And I've started keeping a journal too. This is what I wrote down this morning when I woke up:

> I think my monster has something to do with my brother. My monster has something to do with my mother and my father. I know that the blood in my dreams and the monster have something to do with each other.
>
> I'm caught between wanting to remember and wanting to not remember. Is it me who wants to keep from remembering or is it the monster? Or maybe the monster wants me to remember. If I remembered, then maybe something really bad would happen to me.
>
> There is something I am keeping inside me that feeds the monster. And I don't know whether this is a good thing or a bad thing. What if I stop feeding the monster? Maybe I'll die if I do that.
>
> Does my monster behave like Rafael's monster? I wonder if Adam ever had a monster. Sharkey, for sure, he has a monster.
>
> Another thought: Normies and earth people probably do not have monsters. But everyone here definitely has a monster. Some people here have more than one.
>
> There are monsters all over the place.

As I'm staring at what I wrote, I'm thinking that maybe God gives us monsters for a reason. I don't have a clue as to why God would do that, but see, I don't know anything about how God works. We are *not* good friends. God and I don't trust each other. Is that my fault? Okay, maybe so.

This is the good thing: I don't really want to die anymore. At least not today. Every day is different. I have good days. I have bad days. That's the way it goes. I don't think I know how to be alive. I'm getting very frustrated and when I get frustrated I get anxiety attacks. I don't like the anxiety. I keep biting my nails and there isn't anything left to bite. I even started chewing on my knuckles but Adam put me on a contract. No chewing on my knuckles. "That borders on a self-harming behavior." I get that. Every day I do something that tears me up. Why am I always screwing up? I guess I'm just a screw-up. Screw-ups screw things up. That's what we do.

I have to stop reading Rafael's journal. It's wrong.

But I don't want to stop.

This is not healthy.

I'll make a list and put it in my journal. On one side of the page I'll list all my healthy behaviors. On the other side of the page, I'll list all my *un*healthy behaviors. But what happens if most of my behaviors fall on the unhealthy side. What happens then?

-2-

"Storytime." Adam smiles, his eyes searching the room. We all know what that phrase means. Someone's going to tell a story. Not just any story. Not just a made-up story. *Their* story. Part of the deal of being here is that we eventually have to tell our stories. It's a part of the healing thing. *Healing.* I hate that word.

Adam looks at me, and I look down at the carpet. I know that I have to tell my story sometime. And I've been here for more than thirty days and most people tell their stories a week or two into their stay. Yeah, well, we're all different. Look, I'm cool with telling the stories. I'm okay with that. Okay, I'm *mostly* okay with the storytelling thing. Okay, so maybe I'm not so okay with the concept as it applies *to me*.

Adam wants to know what's on the carpet that's so interesting. Only he's kinda gentle with me these days. Since the day I sort of lost it when

Rafael brought in the picture of his monster. Since that day, I think Adam looks at me different. I don't like it. It's not as if I'm nuts. I'm just a little wigged out. You know, nervous. Jumpy. I always feel like I've done something wrong and someone is going to catch me. You know, find me out. What's that about?

Adam keeps looking at me like he's expecting me to answer, like he's not going to go away until he makes sure there's someone home. He asks me again. "What's so interesting about the carpet?" His voice is calm and really nice. See, the thing about Adam is that he has an unthreatening voice. That makes me mental sometimes.

"There's a stain," I say, "on the carpet. You see it?"

"Yeah, I see it." He shoots me this smile that's more like a smirk. "Life, it's a little messy. Carpets get stains."

"Yes, they do," I say.

"Carpets get stains and people get scars," he says.

I shoot him back the same snarky smile. "I'd rather be the carpet," I say.

"I get that," Adam says.

"I don't think you do," I say. Some days I get a little feisty. I don't mean the baseball-bat kind of feisty where I smash in windshields. Not that kind of feisty. But, you know, regular feisty.

Adam shrugs. Very calm that guy, doesn't get all bothered about stuff. I worry about him. No one can be that calm around all these non-normies. In fact, sometimes I think we're anti-normies. How can you remain calm in the face of all us anti-normies who are definitely aliens? Look, Adam's not going to get into it with me, but he *does* say, "People step on carpets. You *do* get that, don't you, Zach?"

I hadn't thought of that. "Okay," I say, "so I don't really want to be a carpet."

Adam nods, and gets a not-quite smile on his face. He looks at Sharkey and Sharkey, who's always all set to talk about himself says, "Not today, dude, they're adjusting my meds. I'm feeling all zonked out."

It was true. He looked like crap and he'd been sleepwalking, which was something he did on a regular basis and that sort of had me a little worried. Rafael would guide him back to bed but I would get all wigged out. Not that I said anything. Sharkey was having bad times. Not a good day for him to tell his story.

Adam, he gets these things. "I'll have a talk with your doctor." Adam, now he's got this thinking look on his face. Then he gets a more-focused look on his face, then points that look toward Rafael who looks back at him, like, okay. Rafael smiles that smile of his that doesn't really mean a smile. I mean to say that Rafael's smile can mean a hundred things, not all of them good things. But sometimes it means he's clearing his throat.

"I was born," Adam says. He gets us going that way. It's like "Once upon a time."

"I was born," Rafael says, "on a farm ..." His voice is quiet and soft but he's not hard to listen to. Rafael's voice is like Mr. Garcia's trumpet. It tears me up to shreds. We all sit and listen to his story. The guy's done a lot of things. I mean fifty-three is pretty old. Okay, not like seventy—but still he's not exactly a kid anymore. But, see, there's something about him that *is* like a boy. He wears jeans and Chuck Taylor's and he just doesn't have the look of an old guy. So Rafael has this very serious look on his face as he begins telling his story and his dark brown eyes don't get darker, they get this light in them as he talks.

"My mom named me Rafael because that was the name of a famous painter. She also told me it was the name of one of the angels—San Rafael. I never understood how some of the angels could also be saints. That always confused me. My mom was very religious and she really loved me. I hardly remember my dad.

"They died when I was about five. I had brothers and sisters and we were all farmed out to our relatives. My twin sisters who were eight years old went with my aunt who didn't have any kids. She'd always wanted girls, I think. I don't know if I'm just making that up. I'm not sure. One of my uncles took my two little brothers. They were really little and it was easy to see why anyone would want them. They were two and three. Who wouldn't want them? My uncle and aunt in California took my two older brothers— they were ten and twelve. My uncle owned a garage and I got the feeling that my two brothers were going to be working for him. I was right too. They both became mechanics.

"And me? My uncle Vicente took me. My uncle Vicente was pretty young and I'd never liked him. There was something about him that really bothered me. He wasn't a good man. He wasn't. But he was the only one who wanted me. So, I went to live with him.

"I don't remember how my mom and dad died. I know what I was told but that's different than remembering. It was a car accident. But I never knew the details and no one seemed to want to talk about it. My dad was a serious alcoholic so I always believed that my dad got himself killed while drinking and driving—and got my mom killed too. But that's just an idea that I have. I don't really know whether that's true or not. I think a part of me wants to believe that my father was a drunk who killed himself and my mother. But the whole story of the car accident might not even be true. I don't know what's true. I guess I just made stories up in head. I sometimes hate myself for the not-so-beautiful stories I make up…"

I hated when Rafael said he hated himself. Sometimes he would say something like that. I just didn't like hearing that. Why would he want to hate himself? Okay, people don't really *want* to hate themselves. I get that. It comes from somewhere deep inside and getting to that place is hard as hell. I get that too. This is my theory: the people who *shouldn't* hate themselves, *do* hate themselves. And the people who *should* hate themselves, *don't* hate themselves. The world is all backwards. See, this is one of the many reasons why God and I are not good friends.

I stared at Rafael's face and noticed the lines. They made him look old. And yet, sometimes, it didn't seem like they were there at all and he looked kind of young. I watched him and the words coming out of him were like leaves floating in the air.

"… not long after I went to live with my uncle Vicente, he started sleeping with me. He used to go to my bed. It all started, I don't know, it seemed innocent. Almost nice and normal. He would go to my bed and he would just sleep with me. And he would hold me. And I thought that was nice. I liked that. I was five and I was sad. I missed my brothers and sisters and I missed my mom and dad and I was really lonely. And I liked that he would hold me. But then that changed and he started having sex with me— even though I didn't exactly know what was happening.

"It really hurt and I was really scared. Today, I'd use the word rape, but back then, I didn't know that word and I just didn't know how to name what was happening. I never said a word, nothing, not ever. I felt as if someone had sewn my lips shut. All I knew was that there was something wrong going on and I felt really, really dirty. Sometimes I would spend a lot of time in the shower trying to wash myself off because I wanted to be clean. I remember that. And I thought I'd never ever be clean again. And I hated everything about myself and wondered what it was that I did to make my uncle do the things he did. I knew I'd done something but I just didn't know what.

"I really wanted my uncle to go away, and, after a while, it was as if I wasn't even there. He'd come into my room and take his clothes off and I would just go away somewhere. I would pretend I was a bird that was flying up in the sky and from up there I could see all the trees of the world and all the rivers. I would disappear into a world that didn't exist. But it *did* exist. It existed for me. And I know that the life of the mind helped me to survive.

"I was happy on the nights he didn't come. He didn't come in every night. You know, maybe two or three nights a week. This went on for a few years. Until I was about eight. I was thinking of running away, but I never did. I didn't know where to go. And mostly, my uncle Vicente was nice to me. We didn't talk much. I don't really remember. I just remember that I was really sad and afraid and that I really wished that I could live at school.

"I knew my uncle had a girlfriend and one day he came home and said he was going to get married and that maybe it was time for me to find a new place to live. And then he said, 'You better not ever tell anybody what you made me do. If you tell anybody, they'll know all about you and they won't want you.'

"I didn't say anything. I just nodded. Who would want a boy who let his uncle do all those nasty things to him?

"My aunt took me in, the one who'd taken my sisters. And I was happy. Sort of. She was really nice to me and I tried not to get in the way. The truth was happiness just went away."

Rafael looked around the room and drank from his bottle of water.

I could see the tears running down his face, but he wasn't making a sound.

"I have dreams sometimes, I dream him. I dream that he comes to me. All my life, he's come to me. Everything was okay for a few years. I was okay because I was living with my sisters and I loved them and I know they loved me. But there was something wrong with me—I knew that. I tried to pretend that I was normal. I wasn't. But my aunt and uncle were pretty normal and they really loved my sisters and they did everything for them and I could see that my sisters were happy and smart and that their lives were normal. And me, I had become this very emotionally aloof boy who was distant and didn't trust adults. I didn't want to be that way but I *was* that way. I didn't like talking to my aunt and uncle, and, really, they weren't that interested in talking. Not to me anyway. I understood that they took me in because they felt sorry for me. I hated when people felt sorry for me. I felt like a dog who was pawing at a door.

"But they took care of us and the house was peaceful. My uncle worked at the post office and my aunt stayed at home. She was involved in church things. I don't remember very much about those years. I was bored. I don't remember. I read a lot of books, and I got really good at pretending that I was happy. That was important to my aunt, that we be happy.

"When I was in the eighth grade, my uncle and aunt had to go away somewhere. And we all had to stay with my uncle Vicente for the weekend. I just didn't want to go to his house. But I didn't say anything. I thought my heart was going to leap out of my chest. And everything I was afraid of happened again. Uncle Vicente came to my bedroom at night. There was beer on his breath. He made me kiss him. I could feel myself floating away. That was when I started walking around by myself. It was just something that I did. I got a part-time job at some warehouse, helping to unload stuff three evenings a week. I wasn't old enough to work, but the guy paid me cash. He'd pay me ten dollars every night I worked—which was a lot of money. So I made thirty dollars a week. I gave my aunt ten dollars a week and the rest I kept. She said I should save it, but I hardly saved any of it. I picked up smoking and then I got this idea that maybe I'd like to drink. So I'd hang around outside a liquor store and get someone to buy me pints of cherry vodka. So I used to walk around and drink and smoke..."

I kept thinking that Rafael and I, we were just alike—the whole thing made perfect sense to me. I knew exactly what he was talking about.

"...and all my friends thought I was a very happy human being. Because that's how I acted—like a really happy human being. But all that pretending made me tired. If I had acted the way I felt, then I doubt my friends would have really hung out with me. So the pretending wasn't all bad. The pretending made me less lonely—if that makes any sense. But in another way, it made me more lonely because I felt like a fraud. I've always felt like a fake human being.

"High school was non-eventful. I made decent grades. In fact, I made very good grades. I'd drink a lot on weekends with my friends and I always had some kind of part-time job so I could bring in some money. It's funny, I had a lot of friends. Lots and lots of friends—and no one knew me. One time, this girl who liked me asked me, 'Who are you, Rafael?' And I just looked at her and said, '*I am unknowable.*' It was the most honest thing I'd ever said.

"My uncle and aunt spent money on my sisters, but they didn't spend money on me. My aunt said they gave me a place to sleep and food to eat and that I should be grateful. And I was grateful. I was. When I graduated, my uncle told me that maybe it was time for me to go out on my own. I told him I thought that was a good idea. He said he didn't really like my drinking and now that I was old enough and had a high school diploma, I wouldn't have a hard time making it. But he said if I wasn't careful that I'd drink myself to death. He said I was just like my father.

"I don't think my uncle or aunt ever really loved me."

And there they were again, Rafael's tears. It tore me up to see him cry like that. That was the thing about telling your story, it tore you up. It didn't matter that all those things happened such a long time ago because everything felt like it was happening now. I got that. That's why I didn't want to tell my story. I didn't want to feel those things in the now. Hell no, that's not what I wanted.

I watched Rafael drink from his bottled water. I wondered what his life would have been like if he'd had kids. I mean, I knew he didn't have kids because he'd have told me. And I thought that was too bad because

I think he would've made a good father. Because he was a kind man and even though there was something angry and broken inside of him, there was something very gentle inside of him too. He was hard but he was soft. And the soft side was stronger than the hard side. Maybe that doesn't make any sense. Look, what the fuck did I know? And God, I was hoping that Rafael's story had some happy stuff in it because I really liked Rafael...

"...and hell, I was really scared. I didn't know what to do. I was eighteen, but I didn't know anything about how to live on my own. I got a job at a janitorial service and my uncle let me live with them until the end of the summer so I could save some money. Then I moved out and found a crappy one-room apartment and got a second job—which was good because I didn't have as much time to drink. I worked seven days a week, read books and smoked. That was my life for about two years. I lived in my head. That's really where I lived.

"At the end of two years, I'd saved enough money to go to college—though I didn't know anything about what I should do to get into a university. I'd had really good grades in high school, though I don't know how I'd managed that. I'd hated high school. Look, I won't get into the details, but I finally did get into college and I even got some kind of scholarship. College is a big haze. I drank a lot, went to school, hung out with people who liked to drink and graduated.

"I went out to California and thought maybe I'd like to become a writer. Drinking and writing were the only things I was ever good at. I don't know why I thought of California—but I was twenty-four and it seemed like a good idea at the time. When I got out there, I had very little money and I went looking for a job. I went out to a bar one night and struck up a conversation with a guy who worked building sets at Universal Studios. I told him I wanted to write screenplays though that was a complete lie. The idea of writing screenplays had never entered my mind until that moment. Me and that guy, Matt, sat there and got plastered and talked all night. He told me if I wanted a job working on sets, that maybe he could do something for me. He gave me his number and two days later I gave him a call.

"We got together and things got weird. He said if I slept with him, then he could get me a job. I wanted to know how I could trust him. He said, 'look,' and he took out an application form. 'We're hiring,' he said. 'There's a couple of positions right now.' So he had me fill out the application form and the next day he said he'd show me around the place. But after that, he said if I didn't sleep with him, then he'd make sure I didn't get the job. And he did show me around and he even introduced me to his boss and told him I'd put in my application, so I thought that maybe Matt was being straight with me."

Rafael laughed when he said that. "Straight, well, yeah, much to my great shame, I slept with that man. I didn't feel anything. I just let him do what he wanted to do. It was just like my uncle Vicente. I was just an empty thing that was lying there. I didn't feel. I went away somewhere.

"But I *did* get the job. And when Matt wanted to sleep with me, I'd let him. And I knew that I was nothing but a prostitute but I just didn't give a damn about anything. But that didn't last long. He found a new guy which was okay with me. The new guy seemed to like him and Matt had gotten the idea that I just wasn't ever going to get into being with him. I liked my new job and it paid really well and I thought I was rich. I tried not to drink so much and mostly I was pretty successful at not drinking. I learned on the job and I really liked working there and, after a few years, I got friendly with some people and eventually I worked my way into writing. It took me about seven years, but I *did* become a screenwriter. Not that I've ever written anything important—a movie here and there. But it's how I make a living. And that's the good news and the bad news. Writing screenplays always left me a lot of drinking time. And I was as devoted to my drinking as I was to my writing…"

-3-

Rafael went on for a while, going back and filling in details about his drinking and his work and his one failed marriage and it all sounded really sad to me. But the thing of it was that Rafael had made something of himself. I mean, the guy had read everything. I knew that just from talking to him. He knew stuff—all kinds of stuff. He wasn't just some hack writer who made a living writing shit for a lot of money in Hollywood. Yeah, he made himself sound like that, but he wasn't like that at all. He was real and he sounded like he had always been real lonely. And, okay, the guy was a serious alcoholic. Okay, that was true, and that was a problem. But I didn't see him as just this hurt guy who'd been sexually abused by that bastard uncle of his. I mean it when I say I really hated his uncle. I seriously hated him. But I don't know why, I just didn't see Rafael as some sad beat-up guy. He was bigger than all that pain. That's how I saw him. Maybe that's how I wanted to see him. What the hell did I know?

Look, I know that Rafael had thought about suicide. He'd told me so one night when we'd stayed up talking. Well, I asked him, that's how the topic came up. "Have you ever thought about suicide?"

"Yes," he said.

"Tell me," I said.

He hesitated and then he told me this story—almost in a whisper: "I used to picture myself driving out to the Mojave Desert, parking my car, and then just walking out into that wasteland, then stripping off my clothes and walking. Just walking, the hot desert sand burning my feet. I pictured myself walking and walking until I began to burn—until I felt myself on fire, burning on the inside and burning on the outside. I pictured my body lying on the desert floor, dead. I would hold that picture of me in my head and think, *yeah that's what I deserve. I deserve to die like that.*"

I didn't say anything for a long time—but then I asked him, "So why didn't you do it?"

"I came here instead," he said.

"Why?"

"Because I decided I wanted to live."

And then he smiled. I thought he had the best smile in the world. Sometimes, I just didn't know what was real. But right then I knew that Rafael was the most real man I'd ever known.

I was sitting there, thinking about all the things Rafael and I had talked about. And then I realized Rafael had finished telling his story. The room was quiet. I had it in my head that it was a respect thing. The world beat the crap out of us and we were talking about it—okay, I wasn't talking but Rafael and the others were talking about it—and hell, we all respected that. So that's why we were quiet.

Sometimes, Adam had questions before anyone gave the storyteller feedback. Sometimes, Adam waited. Today, Adam didn't wait.

"Let's go back," he said. "You didn't say very much about your marriage. How long did you say you were married?"

"Almost fifteen years."

"That's a long time."

"Yeah," Rafael whispered. That's when the tears ran down his face again. "I hurt her," he said. "I can't talk about it," he said. "I can't." And then he started sobbing. And I couldn't take it and I wanted it all to be over and I just wanted to tell Adam to call the whole thing off. I was too torn up to keep listening. And I knew I was going to zone out. Adam called it disassociating. I didn't give a damn what you called it, I just knew I had to be somewhere else and I knew how to go away. That was the good part of not remembering. That was the good part about disassociating. It helped me to survive. So what was wrong with that?

But maybe living is supposed to be more than survival.

After group, I just went walking around.

I was supposed to be at another session. Yeah, yeah, okay. I didn't care. I just wanted to be alone and get some air and people could call it isolating if they wanted to, but sometimes I just had to spend some time with myself.

It was strange to walk around sober. Before coming here, every time I went out, I'd take the bourbon with me. And now, I just took myself. I was getting to like that. It was like I could really think. And I wasn't crying as much. The crying thing wasn't working for me anymore.

So I just walked around.

I wanted to be alone. Yeah, I guess the alone thing was a big addiction too.

The grounds were really beautiful and nice with trees and shrubs and stuff. And after walking around a while, I decided I'd walk the labyrinth. See, there was a labyrinth that was supposed to calm you down if you walked it and sat in the middle. I liked the labyrinth thing. It made sense to me. Not like the Breathwork thing everyone was always talking about.

Adam had told me I should do the labyrinth thing. He said I should have an intention when I made my way to the center of the labyrinth.

I thought of Rafael. I knew more things about his monster now. And then I was thinking about my own monster. Rafael, he'd read to his monster all his life. He'd read to his monster to try to keep himself from being swallowed up. And I thought that maybe I was doing the same thing.

I entered the labyrinth and I focused on my monster.

What did the monster want?

What was I supposed to give it so it would go away?

REMEMBERING

I stared at the date on my calendar. February 2nd.

I counted the days I'd been here. *Here*—at this place that's supposed to heal me. I still wanted a drink.

Yeah, well, maybe I *was* an alcoholic.

You know if I wasn't an alcoholic, I wouldn't be craving a drink. Yeah, so maybe I was just eighteen. Maybe I hadn't finished high school yet. But high school and age had nothing to do with addiction. I was thinking that maybe Adam was right.

I'd been here thirty-three days. Whatever my life had been, now there was only this place. There was only Cabin 9.

And what was the past anyway? What was it for? What did it mean?

"You know," Rafael said, "my aunt had Alzheimer's before she died."

It was like I was overhearing a conversation he was really having with himself.

"Did she remember anything?"

"No, Zach, she was sixty-four years old and she didn't even remember she'd had a life."

"That's really sad," I said.

"Yeah, it *was* really sad. It was like she was dead."

"I guess so," I said, "but, you know, maybe that's what we do before we die, we start forgetting."

"Are you planning on dying soon, Zach?"

I knew exactly what he was trying to say to me.

Look, maybe I *was* like his aunt, dead, even though I was still alive.

THE MONSTERS OF NIGHT

-1-

Sometimes the blood in my dreams feels real. Last night I swear I heard my brother's voice floating in the night or in my head and it didn't sound at all like Mr. Garcia's trumpet. There was a crack like thunder. There was a storm. I woke up shivering. I must have been screaming because Rafael and Sharkey were asking me if I was okay.

"Yeah," I said.

"Are you sure?" Sharkey sounded a little freaked out.

"I guess it was just another dream."

"You were talking to Santiago," Sharkey said.

"I don't remember."

"Nights are tough on you, dude."

"Yeah, my dreams are killing me."

"Zach, it's not what's happening in your sleep that's killing you." That Rafael, he always said stuff like that.

"You're full of shit, dude." Sharkey was always so fierce. I liked hearing them talk in the darkness. Their voices made me feel like I wasn't the only person in the world.

"It's the way we live—that's what's killing us. Think about it, Sharkey. That should scare the holy hell out of us."

Sharkey laughed. "Where'd you learn how to think, Rafe?"

God, I loved their voices. They didn't sound like the night.

I fell back asleep listening to them talk.

When I woke, I felt as though I was standing at the edge of something, maybe like the shore, you know right at the spot where the water begins and the beach ends. But I just couldn't bring myself to jump in the water because, well, because I might drown. And that's real to me because I never learned how to swim and the ocean scares me. And I got it into my head that the monster lived in the water. You know, in the water that was my memory. And if I got to remembering everything, then what would happen to me?

The dreams were living inside me now. Rafael's drawing of the monster had made me feel small and scared and really I knew that Rafael had drawn himself in that painting. It was him as a boy and I kept picturing him reading to the monster. I thought that maybe reading to the monster was a way of feeding it. It was like if you fed the monster with stories, then he wouldn't be all that interested in eating you. This is stupid, I know, but the monster feels real to me and I know I'm not nuts because the monster feels real to Rafael too and Rafael is an adult and he's smart and he's not all screwed-up like me. Well, okay, he's sad, but after hearing his story, I can see that maybe his sadness is kinda normal.

I'm thinking too much. Adam says I'm always thinking too much and that thinking too much isn't helping me out. Well, I don't know how to stop thinking.

-2-

And another thing that was bugging me and that had me all torn up was all this Breathwork talk. I mean, I was always hearing how great it was, this Breathwork stuff, and to me, the whole thing sounded pretty screwy. *I was not interested in Breathwork.*

Yeah, so of course, I go to see Adam for one of our sessions. You know, one of our friendly conversations and the first thing he says is, "I really want you to start doing some Breathwork with Susan."

"I don't like Susan."

"Is that true?"

"She's not real."

"She's not?"

"Hell no, she's this white lady who's all about this new age bullshit, you know? You know, I'm not into people who aren't real."

"So you're not into white ladies?"

"You know what I mean."

Adam just looked at me. "No, I don't. Explain it to me."

"Okay, she's real—but not real in the way I like real to be."

Adam nodded. But it was that kind of I-don't-get-you nod. "Can I say something?"

I knew he had a theory. There was nothing I could do to stop his theories. "Sure," I said.

"Is it that you don't trust Susan?"

"I think this breathing stuff is, you know, it's crap."

"How do you know?"

"I just don't like it."

"And you don't like it because—?"

"Because it's crap."

"Okay."

I didn't like the way he said okay. "And do you even know what it is, Zach?"

"I don't need to know."

"What do you know about trauma?"

"Nothing."

Adam gave me this snarky look. Not that I blamed him. I was giving him a snarky look too.

"There's a theory that the body keeps trauma. And Breathwork helps get at the trauma. I'm simplifying, but—"

"Fucking fascinating."

Adam didn't say a word. He just looked at me. I hated that look on his face.

"Look, Adam, if that breathing stuff helps Sharkey and Rafael, that's very cool. But I'm different."

"Terminally unique."

I smiled. "Yeah, something like that." I wasn't liking this conversation.

"Have you talked to Rafael about Breathwork?" He knew Rafael was the only one besides him that I really talked to. He knew that. So why was he asking me stuff that he already knew?

"Yeah, I've talked to Rafael."

"You think Rafael's an idiot?"

"You know what I think of Rafael." I was getting mad.

"What do you think of Rafael?"

"I like him."

"When you say you like him, what does that mean?"

"It means I like him."

"Like a friend? Like a brother? Like a father?"

I really didn't like that he brought this father thing up. I really was getting pissed off. I'm talking seriously, tear me up, stun me out *pissed off.* "Rafael's my friend."

"Rafael's fifty-three. You're eighteen."

"So?"

"So you see yourself hanging out with him?"

"Well, I *do* hang out with him."

"Would you hang out with him if you lived in the same city?"

"I don't know." I looked at him. I didn't like his eyes just then. I didn't. "Look, Adam," I said, "what are you getting at?"

"I'm making up that maybe you see Rafael as a father." Making up. Adam loved that phrase. It meant he had a theory. Like I wanted to hear about all his theories.

"Is that right?" I gave him a look. That really pissed me off. "What's wrong with you?" I said.

"What do you mean what's wrong with me?"

"You know what I mean. Don't play dumb, Adam. That really pisses me off."

"Why are you angry, Zach?"

"Because."

"Because why? You look like you might want to hit me."

"I don't hit people."

"I don't think you do. But you're really angry with me."

"Okay, I'm angry with you." God, I *did* want to hit the guy.

"Do you want me to tell you what I think, Zach?"

I did not want him to tell me what he thought. But I said, "Yeah, sure." But it was a kind of *fuck you* yeah sure.

He shot me back the same snarky smile I shot him. "Okay," he said, "this is what I'm making up. I'm making up that you love Rafael. I'm making up that you'd like him to be your father."

I didn't say anything. And then I said, "I have a father."

Adam was quiet for a long time. He was thinking and thinking. I could see that. Even though I was mad at him, I could see he was having a hard time. I didn't know what that was about. "Have you talked to your father since you've been here?"

I shook my head.

"Why not?" He whispered it. He seemed like he was being very careful and I was really confused.

"I don't know," I said.

And then we just looked at each other for a long time. "Is your father alive?" he asked. He had this look on his face. It was such a soft and kind look. I just kept looking at his eyes—and then I just turned away from them.

"I don't know," I said. And then I started crying. I didn't know why.

Adam didn't say anything. He just let me cry.

And then I said, "Okay," I said. "I'll go. I'll go see Susan. I'll do it. Can we just move on?"

He smiled. God, his smile tore me up. "You don't have to do anything you don't want to do."

"I said I'll go."

"You sound really angry."

"I'm not angry. I'm not. I just need a cigarette."

Adam smiled. He looked at the clock. "We still have twenty minutes. Any dreams?"

"Yeah." Look, I was glad to not be talking about Breathwork. I was glad not to be talking about Rafael. I was glad not to be talking about my father. "Yeah, I always have dreams."

"You want to talk about any of them?'

"Yeah, sure," I said.

We both laughed. God, that Adam, he was fucking relentless.

"I dreamed Rafael's monster."

"Rafael's monster?"

"Yeah, he was in my dream."

"What was the monster doing?"

"He was hanging out."

Adam gave me that you're-being-a-wiseass look.

"I was scared."

He nodded. "I get bad dreams too," he said.

"Any monsters?"

He smiled. "I guess you could say that."

I liked Adam's smile. It was real. And then I asked him. "I'm serious, Adam. Have you ever had a monster?"

He looked at me and his face was serious. Very, very serious. "Yeah, Zach, I've had monsters."

And right then I got that part about getting honest. I mean, Adam was my therapist and he was really honest. He was right about Rafael. I hated that he was right. I *did* love Rafael and I wondered why it had made me so mad when he asked me if I loved him. Why did that make me mad? I *did* want him to be my father. But see, this is how screwed-up I am, on some days I wanted Rafael to be my father and on other days I wanted Adam to be my father. Okay, yeah, I know that these thoughts constitute unhealthy behaviors.

-3-

A few nights later, Rafael was working on a painting in our room. He had all these art supplies he'd bought at the art store on one of our weekly outings. The guy knew what he was doing. He was patient and he could sit there for hours just working on his painting. I'd never seen anyone who could concentrate like that. So I asked him, "When you paint, what goes on in your head?"

"I'm not sure, Zach. Painting, for me, it's not about thinking. When you start working on a painting—" He stopped himself and smirked, "When *I* start working on a painting." We both laughed. We couldn't stop laughing. I mean we were really laughing. And I got to thinking that the whole thing really wasn't that funny, but we were laughing because there was all these feelings inside us and we didn't always know what to do with all the feelings that were like knots that needed to be untied, so sometimes we just, well, we laughed. That's how we untied the knots.

And then Rafael said, "See, painting, sometimes it's like laughing. It's not just about the technical thing. It's not just about the plumbing. I mean, you can learn how to draw and not be an artist. You can memorize the color chart and know how to mix colors and not be an artist." He nodded. "Yeah, I think that's true. For me. Look, I'm not an artist, Zach. I just have this chaos inside me and I just can't live in all that chaos. I tried drinking. I've tried a lot of things and most of those things were killing me."

I walked over and looked at his painting. There was a monster lurking in the background and there were all these things in the painting, things like books and a field of growing crops and the face of a man who looked like he was as large as God and flames in the sky and broken letters that seemed like they wanted to become words. It was like music, like Mr. Garcia's trumpet.

"Rafael, does it hurt?"

"Hurts like hell."

"Then why do you do it?"

"Can I tell you something?"

"Tell me anything." What I meant was tell me everything. And I wanted to yell out that I sometimes read his journal. It felt really bad that I couldn't tell him. I mean, what if he decided that he hated me. I would hate me if I were him. I really would. I mean, I was me and I hated me. Why wouldn't he hate me too?

"I've been hurting most of my life. I tried to pretend I wasn't. I even believed my own lie. I've lived my entire life trying to avoid pain, Zach. That's a terrible way to live. I don't care any more if it hurts."

"Will it ever stop hurting?"

"I don't think so, Zach. If I'm working on a painting, and it doesn't hurt, then the painting won't matter. And if it doesn't matter, then it isn't real—then *I'm not* real."

"But why does it have to hurt?"

"I don't know." And then he got this look and I knew he was thinking and so I waited for him to stop thinking because I knew he wanted to tell me something. "I have a new theory," he said, "and the theory is this: if I develop a great capacity for feeling pain, then I am also developing a great capacity for feeling happiness."

When he said *happiness*, he smiled. And it was one of his real smiles, not one of his clearing-his-throat smiles.

I was confused. The words *pain* and *happiness* stepped into my head. They were words on the pieces of paper lying on the floor of my brain. I didn't know what to think of those pieces of paper. "Rafael?"

"Yeah?"

"Do we all have monsters?"

"Yes."

"Why does God give us so many monsters?"

"You want to know my theory?"

"Sure."

"I think it's other people who give us monsters. Maybe God doesn't have anything to do with it."

"You mean, like your uncle."

"Yeah, like my uncle. And you, Zach? Who gave you your monsters?"

"I don't know."

"I think you *do* know."

"I don't like to think about it."

Rafael was quiet for a while. He kept working on his painting.

All that raw emotion on his face really blew me away. I went back to my side of the room and thought that maybe it was time for me to start working on my own paintings. But painting was like talking. I wasn't sure I wanted to do that.

And then Rafael said, "You know, Zach, I think sometimes we fall in love with our monsters."

How did he know—that I had thought the same thing? "Yeah, I guess so." And then I just blurted out: "I'm going to see Susan tomorrow."

Rafael stopped painting and looked up at me. "Good for you, Zach."

"I don't really want to go."

"Don't be afraid."

"I won't be," I said.

I don't think Rafael believed me. I kept thinking that sometimes God *did* give you a monster. And when God gave you a monster, well, then you were supposed to keep it forever. How could it be right to get rid of a monster that God gave you? How could you hate what God gave you? But the thing is I had to figure out what the monster wanted.

Maybe that was the key to the whole mystery—figuring out what the hell my monster wanted before he ripped me to pieces.

-4-

Two nights later, another storm. The wind was tearing up the night.

I woke up and listened. Rafael was awake. I don't know how I knew that but I could sense him. He liked listening to storms—same as me. I finally got up and looked out the window. It was snowing. Again. I went back to bed and kept listening. I imagined what it would be like to be the wind. I thought of the chart Adam had put on the board. If I were the wind, I could be in charge.

I was awake as a morning bird. I was. I finally decided to get up and go have a cigarette.

"Put on your coat," Rafael whispered.

"I will," I said. Some days, I just couldn't take it that he cared.

As I walked into the cold, I smiled. I liked the cold wind on my face. I liked the way it made me feel. When I got to the smoking pit, I lit up a cigarette. I took the smoke into my lungs and closed my eyes and thought of Susan. I heard her voice: *Okay, Zach, you can close your eyes or you can leave them open. Just breathe deep, just follow my lead.* I heard my own breathing, the loudness of it and the softness of it too. Yeah, it had all been so strange, that Breathwork thing, and I'd cried. I'd just cried. The need to cry had just been too much, too strong to hold back and I'd just howled and my lips had quivered and then afterwards, when I'd finally stopped crying, Susan had whispered: *Okay, just relax the rest of the day. Be good to yourself. And I want you to write in your journal.* It had all felt so weird, even when I was writing in my journal as if the words were water and they were just pouring out onto the page and I just kept writing over and over *Mom, Dad, Santiago, Mom, Dad, Santiago, Mom, Dad, Santiago.* Three pages and I just couldn't stop.

I lit another cigarette and laughed. Here I was at the smoking pit in the middle of the night, in the middle of a storm, smoking cigarettes and remembering. I couldn't decide anymore if remembering was a good thing or a bad thing. What if remembering did nothing? What if I stayed like this forever?

I liked the cold just then.

I liked that I was so sober.

I liked that I didn't have any bourbon flowing through me. And for a moment, just a very small and tiny moment, I felt alive and almost free. It was weird to feel that rush of happiness. It was so strange and beautiful. So much better than cocaine.

I lit another cigarette and noticed someone walking toward the smoking pit. Even before I could make out his face, I knew it was Sharkey.

"Hey," I said.

"Hey, your fucking self," he said.

I laughed and we both hugged ourselves in the cold.

"We're nuts," he said.

"Yeah, we're nuts."

"But I'm really nuts," he said. "Rafael had to wake me up again. I was sleepwalking. I was about to walk out the door in my frickin' undies. That Rafael. He's like a dog on alert."

"I like dogs," I said.

"Me too." He lit a cigarette. "Rafael's going to be okay," he said. "I think he's really going to be okay."

"I think so too."

"Sharkey, when you're old, are you going to get it?"

"Get what?"

"Whatever the hell it is that we're supposed to get."

"Hell, I'm never going to be as old as Rafael."

"Fifty-three, well, that's not so old, not really."

"Well, I'm never going to live to be fifty-three."

That made me sad, to think that Sharkey believed he wouldn't live to be very old. That made me really sad and numbed out. And then I heard Sharkey's voice again. "What about *us*, Zach?"

"I don't know."

"You want me to tell you the truth?"

"Yeah," I said.

"I don't think I'll ever be okay. I don't think I have it in me."

"That's not true," I said.

"*It is true, Zach.*"

"But you're doing all this work."

"I don't think I am, Zach."

"So talk to Adam," I said. "Adam will help you."

"What will Adam do?"

"He'll talk to you. He'll help you."

"No. I'm just a job for Adam. I'm not anything more than that."

"That's not true."

"It is true, Zach."

"He cares about us."

"He gets paid to care about us."

"Oh, like he's getting rich caring about us."

"Oh, so now you're his big friend? What has Adam ever done for you, Zach?"

"He's trying to help me."

"Oh, so he get's all this fucking extra credit because he's doing his job?"

That really made me mad. Sharkey was in a bad space and he was taking it all out on Adam. *And that really made me mad.* "It doesn't matter," I said. "What Adam feels for me or for you and whether he likes or doesn't like us, it doesn't matter."

"You don't know what the fuck you're talking about, dude."

"Yes, I do." I was thinking of Rafael. I was thinking of Mr. Garcia's trumpet. "This is my new theory, dude. It's what *I* think that matters. It's what *I* feel."

"Okay, Zachy, what do you think? What do you feel?"

I wanted to tell him that I loved Adam and that I loved Rafael and that I loved him too. And that was what really mattered. But that's not what I said. Love was just another secret I was keeping. Another secret I would never tell the group or anybody. But at least I was telling myself. Telling myself mattered. "You know what I feel?" I said. "I feel like having another cigarette."

He laughed. We both laughed.

We smoked another cigarette and stood out in the cold.

I hated winter.

Sharkey was thinking his own thoughts and I was thinking mine. I was thinking I was too much in love with the night. It was no good to be in love with the night.

-5-

Sharkey and I walked back to Cabin 9 in the snow. When we entered the cabin, Rafael was awake, writing in his journal. He looked up at us and waved. He looked small and I couldn't decide if he looked like a little old man or a boy. That was a really strange thing to think but that's what entered into my head. I wondered what he was writing. I bet it was something really beautiful. And the thought entered into my head that I would like to be the words on the page that Rafael was writing. I was back to that pieces-of-paper thing and I wondered about my own strange thoughts.

As I lay in bed, I waited for Rafael to stop writing and turn off the light. Sharkey was already asleep and he was tossing and turning and mumbling things. Sharkey never got any rest. Maybe God didn't write *rest* on his heart. I got to thinking about stuff. I was supposed to be asleep. But

I wasn't. I was either dreaming something or I was wide awake. Either way, there was a lot of action going on in my head.

This is what I was writing on the chalkboard in my brain:

> I don't want to dream blood anymore.
> I don't want to live in the night.
> I don't want it to be winter anymore.
> I want to be the brown in Rafael's eyes.
> I want to be the blue in Adam's eyes.
> I want to be Sharkey's laugh.
> I want Rafael to live.
> I want Sharkey to live.
> I want me to live. *Me.*
> I want to be Mr. Garcia's music. Alive. Me.

-6-

I wake up from my dream.

In the dream, I am lying on the side of a road.

I am lying there like a dog who has been hit by a car.

I can see myself lying there.

I keep wanting to wake me up, the me that is lying on the side of the road. I keep thinking that the me on the side of the road is lying there dead.

I keep telling him to get up, get up. And then I hear Rafael's voice.

"Are you okay, Zach?"

I am *not* okay.

I do not know what it means to be okay. I have never known and maybe I will never know.

Okay is just a word I use so I won't have to talk about what's inside.

Okay is a word that means I am going to keep my secrets.

There is something inside me that is killing me.

There is something inside me that wants to let whatever is killing me do its job. I think I could walk into the night and howl like a coyote, howl so the monster could find me and do to me whatever it wanted to do to me. I think I could let the storm swallow me up.

The monster and the night and the storm—they are the same. They want me dead.

"Are you okay, Zach?"

The monster. The night. The winter.

The monster, the night, the winter—they want me dead.

"Zach?"

"It was just another dream." That is what I hear myself whisper.

I wish I was a boy. I wish Rafael really was my father and he could hold me in his arms and sing to me and chase the monster away.

REMEMBERING

Adam looks at me with his blue eyes that see me but don't see me.

Today his eyes look like they have pieces of green in them. Like the leaves of summer. I think this is a strange thing to think because it's so cold outside and the skies are dark. I think of Mr. Garcia's black eyes that were darker than any night but somehow I could see the sky there, in his black eyes and I think that if only the night looked like Mr. Garcia's eyes then I would never be afraid of the night ever again. And I think of Rafael's eyes that are brown and always seem to smile when he looks at me and his soft voice. I am trying to think what color my eyes are and I don't remember. I know the color of Adam's eyes. I know the color of Rafael's eyes. I know the color of Mr. Garcia's eyes. I don't know the color of mine. I wonder what it would be like to be Adam or Mr. Garcia and or Rafael. But I'm me. And even when I grow older I'll still be me. I think of what Sharkey said, that he would never live to be as old as Rafael and I wonder if I will live. Will I live? Will I live? Will I live?

Adam keeps looking at me. "Zach, are you okay?"

Finally I make myself talk. "Yes."

"Where did you go?"

"I was in my head."

"What were you thinking about?"

I don't want to tell him but I promised him that I wouldn't keep any secrets even though I haven't told him about reading Rafael's journal. "I was thinking about the color of eyes," I say.

"What about them?"

I shrug.

"Anybody's eyes in particular?"

"Yours and Mr. Garcia's and Rafael's."

Adam looks at me with a question on his face. "And what about our eyes?" he asks. "Mine and Mr. Garcia's and Rafael's?"

I shrug. "I like them," I say.

Adam smiles. "Why?"

"I don't know. I just like them."

"Is it because we all see you?"

I don't want to cry so I don't. "I guess so," I say.

"Do you love us, Zach?"

I don't know why he asked that question. I am not going to answer it. I am *not*. So I ask him a question of my own. "What color are my eyes?"

"Why do you ask?"

"I don't remember what color they are."

"You don't remember?"

"I don't like looking at myself."

"Why not?"

I think he already has made up an answer.

"I guess I just don't like what I see."

He has a strange look on his face and then he's thinking. He gets up from his chair. "Follow me," he says. I follow him and we walk into the bathroom. There's a mirror there. He stands behind me and puts his hands on my shoulders and points me toward the mirror. "What color are your eyes, Zach?"

"They're a strange color," I say.

"They're hazel," he says. "Sometimes they look dark and brown and sometimes they look green and very bright." He smiles. "Today they look green."

I look at myself. "Green," I say. I think of the leaves of summer. But I know it's winter.

"What do you see?" Adam asks.

I turn my head away. "I don't want to see me," I say.

"Okay," he says. "But can you tell me why?"

"It hurts," I say.

Adam looks sad—like maybe he wants to cry. "It hurts to look at yourself?"

"Yes."

We walk back to his office. I'm glad there aren't any mirrors there.

"Do you want me to tell you what I see, Zach, when I see you?"

"Yes," I say. But I am afraid of his answer.

"I see a young man who is trying to remember who he is. I see a young man who is in a great deal of pain." He is wearing a very kind look on his face. "Has anybody ever told you that you're a beautiful young man?"

I shake my head. "Why would anybody want to tell me that?"

"That's not what I asked, Zach."

"Okay," I say. "I don't remember."

"I'm making something up in my head right now, Zach. Do you want to know what I'm making up?"

I shake my head *yes.*

"I'm making up that the reason you were thinking of my eyes and Mr. Garcia's eyes and Rafael's eyes is that you understand what our eyes are telling you."

"What are your eyes telling me?"

"Our eyes are telling you that you're a beautiful young man."

"Don't say that," I say. "Don't ever say that." And then I'm crying. I'm crying and I'm crying and I can't stop crying. And finally I make myself stop and I sit there with my head down.

And then I hear Adam saying, "Zach, look at me."

And I do. I look at him.

"I see you, Zach. Do you understand that? I see you."

I nod. But I'm not sure.

And then I hear Adam ask me, "When was the last time someone told you that they loved you?"

"I don't remember," I say. "I just don't remember."

THE REASON I HATE WINTER

-1-

Sharkey told his story this morning.

I've been thinking about everything that happened in group all day. It was really something wild. I mean *wild* is the only word that's visiting my head right now. It feels like I'm a passenger in a car and it's going faster and faster and then I look over and there's no one in the driver's seat. And I know I'm going to crash.

And here it is, the middle of the night, and I can't sleep and it's so cold outside that I can't stand the thought of walking straight into the frozen air and making my way to the smoking pit to have a cigarette. So I'm lying here with Sharkey's voice inside me. Sometimes having someone's voice inside you is like having a bullet lodged in your brain or in your heart. Take your pick. Either way, it feels like you just might bleed to death.

Sharkey, he was having some attitude. But I think I'm beginning to understand that attitude comes from someplace. I mean, it doesn't just appear. And if I were Sharkey, I'd have his attitude too.

But this is the thing—I'm really confused and I don't know what's going to happen.

When Adam said with that sort of sweet smile of his, "Storytime," he winked at me, letting me know that he was giving me a pass. He turned his look away from me and then directly into Sharkey's eyes. I could see their eyes meeting for a second. Sharkey was sitting there like he was ready to spit it all out. "I was born..." Adam said.

Sharkey took the ball and ran with it. "I was born in Chicago, Illinois, to a set of parents who would have scared the hell out of fucking Dracula." That Sharkey, he let her rip. He hates his parents. He hates his brother and he hates his sister. If there were more people in his family, he'd hate them too. See, he wanted to play baseball but his mom and dad had other plans. He got piano lessons instead. He also got violin lessons. "Yeah," he said, "see, I didn't get a family. What I got was a father who was a failed musician and drowned his sorrows by getting involved in British banking and spent half his time in London, attending concerts. What I got was a mother who spent half her life drinking very dry martinis at very expensive restaurants with all her friends and part-time lovers—some of whom were not much older than me and most of whom were *not* musicians. What I got was a brother and sister who were more in love with money than my parents. What I got was a babysitter everyone called an *au pair*. I take it she was supposed to love me and teach me Italian. I mean, my parents shipped someone in from Italy to care for me. And when I asked for a dog, my mom said, *absolutely not*. My mom's two favorite words were *absolutely not*. What I didn't get was what most kids have—parents who fucking cared. When I was eight, I got sent to boarding school because I broke my very exquisitely made German violin on my father's equally exquisitely made grand piano." I get this picture in my head, Sharkey as an eight-year-old taking a violin and beating the hell out of the piano with it. I get the feeling that his piano cost more than the house I lived in. I mean, the only thing I ever got to beat the hell out of when I was eight years old was a piñata. Of course, I graduated to windshields. Sharkey and I, we could have hit people but we didn't, so maybe we weren't all bad.

Sharkey's whole life became this series of running away from, well, from his name. I mean the guy was born Matthew Tobias Vandersen IV. I mean, you couldn't make that shit up. I bet it really pissed his parents off when he decided to go by Sharkey. I don't blame the guy. He was way into drugs by the time he was fourteen, and spent all kinds of time on the streets. So one day he decides to turn himself into a pool shark. I mean, this fourteen-year-old kid turns himself into whatever the hell is the opposite of his family. Myself, I think that's very cool. And so that's the way he earned his money. I got to hand it to that dude, he decided to make a life for himself instead of becoming what his parents wanted him to become. That stuns me out in a very cool way.

"Screw my parents." That's what he said. Only when he said that, he fell apart. He cried like a baby. He didn't say it, but I knew what he was crying about. See, this is my theory: Sharkey was crying about what he didn't get. And you know, this is the saddest part, I think Sharkey didn't hate his parents at all. I think he loved them with all his heart. I know. It was the same way with me. I know all about that. That's why we're all screwed-up. Maybe we wouldn't be so screwed-up if we didn't care. But the thing is this: Why do we care? I mean, *that really is all screwed-up*. Why should we care when nobody else cares?

You know, I think a lot of things happened to Sharkey out on the streets. Bad things. You know, sexual things and violent things. He has a scar over his right eye. I think it really screwed him up. And the drugs, shit, I mean that guy has done some heavy-duty drugs. When he rolls up his sleeves, you can see the tracks from where he shot up. It's really a miracle the guy has lived to be twenty-seven. Sharkey should be dead.

He told this story about waking up on some street in Amsterdam and how he just didn't fucking care and how he just wanted to die right then and there. I mean, how did the dude get to Amsterdam? The only reason he didn't die on the streets is that the authorities picked him up. He lived to take more drugs another day. I think a part of him wishes he'd died that day. I mean the guy is rich and even if he hates his parents—the parents that he really loves—he's a good-looking man and hell, he could do something with his life—not that I have any suggestions for him.

Okay, so he wants to be dead. I get that. I can see that his heart is really numb. The heart can get really cold if all you've known is winter. That's how I think about it. It's funny and ironic and sad as hell that he wound up in a group called Summer. No wonder the guy wants to be dead. Summer. Shit.

I get this. I really get all this. I mean, it's the feeling thing, the emotion thing that begins to kill you and when that feeling thing is there in your stomach and in your lungs and in your throat and in your heart, shit, it's better to be dead. I get Sharkey. It's like, when Sharkey was telling his story, all I could see on his face was this look of pain. I mean *real pain*. And I don't think Sharkey could stand it. Who the hell is strong enough to live in the place of all that pain? Rafael, he can live there—but Rafael, well, he doesn't count. I mean, I guess when you're in your fifties, you learn to be tougher or more disciplined. Or something. Maybe if you live with pain long enough, you don't even notice it's there. Maybe that's it. What the hell do I know?

But see, Sharkey's a smart guy. He managed to steal a shitload of money from his parents. "The computer is a wonderful thing," he said. He laughed about that one. "And now, well, my father wants to nail my ass." Man, listening to Sharkey's story made me want to cry forever.

So after Sharkey tells his story, Maggie asks him, "Are you sorry you stole all that money from your dad?"

"Hell no," Sharkey said. "It's not as if I broke the guy."

"Maybe that's not the point."

Man, Sharkey really lost it. "I know where you're going with that, Maggie. I really do. But it's really pissing me off."

"I didn't mean to make you angry, Sharkey, it's just that— "

Sharkey didn't let her finish. "Yeah, this is what I think you're saying, Maggie. You're going to that personal-responsibility-for-all the-crap-we've-pulled place—isn't that where you're going?"

"Isn't that what we're here for?" Kelley asked.

Kelley, she was in graduate school and she was always talking about "being responsible for your own discourse." Discourse? What the hell was that?

Sharkey was really mad. "I don't know why the fuck we're here if you want to know the truth." He gave the whole group a look.

"We're here to be healed." Sheila, she was all about healing. "And we can't be healed if we don't own up to our own stuff."

Adam, he was just watching us. He never stepped in unless he felt he had to. You know, it was like he knew when to step in and when to let us be in charge of our own sessions. I was getting that. Yeah, well, I'd been here long enough to get a lot of things.

Sharkey was sort of quiet for a little while. "Look, I'd rather do a hundred years in jail than to tell my old man I'm sorry. Besides, it's not true. I'm not sorry. And if we're here to get honest, well, I've fucking arrived. Nobody can make me sorry for stealing money from the guy who's been masquerading as my father for the last twenty-seven years. And that's just what he wants—he wants me to say, 'Dad, I'm sorry for being such a screw-up. I'm sorry for hurting you. I'm sorry for being such a bad son.' How come I have to be a good son and he gets to stay a bad father?"

And then Lizzie, who came from roughly the same kind of privileged background as Sharkey, said, "I don't think you should be sorry, Sharkey."

That made Sharkey smile.

"But the thing is, we hate—"

Adam stopped her. "*I* hate."

"Yeah, *I* hated my parents' world. Hated it. And yet I took advantage of all the things their world could buy me. I don't know, I think I wanted it both ways."

"Yeah, well, I don't need my parents' money. And they can stick their lifestyle."

"Then why'd you steal their money?" Adam wasn't letting go of this.

"It wasn't because I needed it."

"Why then?" Adam didn't take his eyes off Sharkey.

"To stick it to the SOB."

Adam had this firm look on his face. "Yeah, well, what if you wind up in prison? Who'd you stick it to, Sharkey?"

"To be Sharkey is to live in a fucking prison. What the hell difference does it make where I'm living? You think I care if I go to prison? You think I care if I live on the streets? Anywhere is better than living with my father. That's what he wants. He wants me to live in his house, play by his rules, dress like him, talk like him, yeah, yeah, he wants me to be Matthew Tobias Vandersen IV. *I say fuck no.* But if I say, yes, yes, yes, then I get to have his money. There's nothing like turning your sons into mercenaries. You think I need his money?"

"So why take something if you don't need it or want it?"

"I took something from him that he loved. And what does he love most? The green stuff." Sharkey laughed—but it looked like he was going to cry.

Rafael kept looking at him. "Sharkey?" His eyes and voice were soft.

"Yeah," Sharkey whispered.

"You deserve better. You deserve better than what he gave you. You *do* know that, don't you, Sharkey? *You do know you deserve better.*"

There were tears falling from Sharkey's face. "Screw 'em," he said. He got this really hard look on his face, this look that said, "*Screw them. Just screw 'em all.*" And then he just got up and walked out of the room.

We all looked at each other.

"Can he do that?" I said. "I mean, shouldn't we go after him?"

Adam shook his head.

"He forgot his coat. It's snowing." I started to get up and go after him.

"You know the rules, Zach. We all know the rules. No leaving group. If you leave group, then there's consequences."

"But—"

"Look, he just needs some time." Adam looked at the group. "We all need to learn how to cope. All of us. We've gone over this. Everyone has to do things in their own way. But we don't do the rescuing thing here. We've talked about that."

I really wanted to tell Adam to go screw himself.

"But aren't we supposed to do something?"

"What, Zach? What are we supposed to do?"

"Bring him back to group."

Adam shook his head.

I really hated Adam. *I hated him.*

I don't remember what went on the rest of group. I just kept looking at the floor and every time I heard a noise, I kept thinking it was Sharkey walking back into the room. But he never came back.

When group was over, we all got in a circle like we always did. We got in a circle and held hands and said the serenity prayer. I was right next to Adam and I had to hold his hand in the circle. And when I was walking out, I watched Adam walking toward his office and I yelled, "Hey, Adam!"

He looked back at me.

I walked toward him.

"I have a secret," I said. "And I know we're not supposed to keep secrets."

"Okay," he said. "You want to tell me your secret?"

"Yup," I said. "When I was holding your hand in the circle, I wanted to break it." I shot him a grin and walked away.

"We'll talk later," he said.

"About what?" I said. And then I just started yelling at him. "You know what your fucking problem is? You keep expecting me to act like an adult. Great. Fucking great! You want me to act all mature and stuff like Rafael, but I never got to be a kid and now you want me to dive into adulthood. Well, I don't fucking know how to swim, dude! I hate you. I hate you. *Do you get that*?" And I know I was crying again and I was really getting sick and tired of those tears that were always scarring my face and screwing up my 20/20 vision. And all of a sudden, I felt myself falling on the ground and I knew I'd tripped on something and I just knelt there crying and I was trying to pick myself up. And Adam was standing in front of me, holding out his hand. "Take it," he said. "It's my hand. Take it. You can break it if you want to."

-2-

Sharkey just disappeared. I couldn't find him anywhere. He wasn't in art therapy and he wasn't at lunch and he just wasn't anywhere.

I went to a breath session with Susan in the afternoon and it was really weird. For no reason at all, I remembered a dream right in the middle of my breathing. My brother and I were in a car and he was telling me how sorry he was for what he did. He had a gun and he kept playing with it. He would point the gun at me and then he would point it at himself and he kept saying, *eenie, meenie, miney, moe.* And then the gun went off—and I started screaming. Susan kept saying, "It's okay, it's okay, focus on your breathing, you're okay." And I felt her hands hovering over me and her hands felt like the wings of an angel.

After the session, I told her I was never going to be okay. She smiled at me and said, "You have no idea how brave you are." But I knew I wasn't brave. I didn't even know how to spell the word. "Is a hug okay?"

Sometimes the therapists thought that hugs were a good thing. I didn't know what to think about that. Hugs, you know, it's not something we did in my family. "Sure," I said. "That would be good."

She smiled at me and I could see her aging face and she combed my hair with her fingers and gave me a hug. "Let go," she whispered. "Let go, brave boy. Let go."

When I walked outside, the sun was out but it was bitter cold. The sky looked wild like another storm was coming up over the mountains. I stared at the pieces of blue in between the black clouds. I felt that way, like the sky, cold and stormy and dark.

When I came back into Cabin 9, I noticed that all of Sharkey's things were gone. I opened his closet door and it was empty—like no one had ever been there.

Gone. Just like that, in an instant. Disappeared.

I could feel my heart and I knew it was panic. That's what it was. I knew that feeling like my heart was about to sink into a cold, empty ocean. I hated that feeling, that feeling that maybe I wouldn't be able to breathe or that maybe something really bad was about to happen to me. *Sharkey? Where was he? Where? Why?* He'd just told his story and he was doing the work and everything seemed to be okay with him and he was writing in his journal and he'd been clean for thirty days and now he was gone and what was it all for and why had he come here if all he was gonna do was leave without finishing the work? I kept breathing in and out. *Breathe, Zach, breathe. Breathe, Zach, breathe.*

I ran out to the smoking pit, but he wasn't there. I asked Jodie if she'd seen him. She took a drag from her cigarette. "He's gone, Zach." She seemed sad. She liked Sharkey. They hung out after dinner all the time and made each other laugh.

"Gone?" I just looked at her.

"Yeah. He must have called for a cab because he got in one about half hour ago."

"Did he say anything?"

"See you out on the streets."

"That's what he said?"

"Yeah, that's what he said. He was smiling. Sharkey's got a helluva smile."

"But how could they just let him go?"

"They can't make you stay here, Zach."

"Why not?"

"That's not the way it works."

"But, he's—," I stopped. I didn't even know what I was going to say.

"He's what, Zach?"

"He's not okay yet."

"He never will be, Zach. None of us will ever be okay."

She just looked at me and took another drag from her cigarette.

"Then what's it all for, Jodie?"

"God, you're just a kid."

"Fuck you, Jodie." That's all I said before I walked away. God, I wanted some bourbon. I wanted some real bad. Real, real bad. I walked around like a nervous cat. Man, I was nervous. The anxiety had me all wigged out and I swear I was going to go completely mental. I kept chewing on my finger nails, not that I had any left. I started gnawing on my knuckles. God, I'd never been this wigged out. I didn't know what was happening with me. I don't know, I was walking up and down the grounds like a crazy man. And then all of a sudden I felt a hand on my shoulder and that hand scared the crap out of me. I made a fist and turned. I found myself staring into Rafael's brown eyes. My fist was aimed at him.

"You okay?" I hated that his brown eyes were so soft.

"No, I'm not okay. If I was okay would I be hanging around this place?"

"What happened?"

"What happened? Fucking life happened, Rafael. That's what happened."

He kept his hand on my shoulder.

"This is a no-touch facility. Didn't you know that?"

He kept his hand on my shoulder.

I pushed his hand away.

"You want to tell me what happened?"

"Sharkey left."

The news hit Rafael like a punch to the stomach. I could see that. But he just stood there. "That makes me sad," he whispered.

"He was gonna make it. He was gonna make it, Rafael. And now what's gonna happen to him?"

"There's nothing we can do about it, Zach."

"Why the fuck not?"

"We can't live other people's lives for them, Zach. You know that."

"Adam just let him leave."

"It wasn't Adam's choice."

"Screw Adam."

"This isn't Adam's fault. Don't do that, Zach. This is about Sharkey. Sharkey, he just couldn't take it."

"Why?"

"I don't know."

"I can't take it either."

"Yes, you can."

"No. *I can't*. I don't want to be here anymore."

"Let's walk," he said. I don't know why, but I walked with him. Not that we said anything. I just sort of walked next to him. And then, as we're walking, he pointed to a tree. "See that tree?" It was a stubby cypress tree, all bent and twisted.

"Yeah, I see it."

"It's my favorite tree."

"It's not that great a tree," I said.

"That's it. That's exactly it. It's like me. The wind beat the holy crap out of it when it was just a sapling. Never could straighten itself out again." He sort of smiled at me. "But, Zach, it didn't die." He looked like maybe he wanted to cry. But he didn't. "It's alive."

"Maybe it should have just given up."

"That tree didn't know how to do that. It only knew how to live. Crooked. Bent. Taller trees dwarfing it even more. It just wanted to live. I named it, you know?"

He was waiting for me to ask what he'd named it—but I decided I didn't want to ask.

"Zach," he whispered. "The tree's name is Zach."

"Stop it," I said. "Just stop it!" I knew I was starting to cry and I was so sick, sick, sick to death of all those sad damned tears I had inside me. How could I have so many tears living there, in my body? How could they fit? When was it going to stop? When?

We just sat there, Rafael and me. We sat there for a long time.

Then I heard Rafael's voice and his voice was asking me a question. "You love Sharkey, don't you?"

I nodded.

"I love him too."

"Then why didn't he get better?"

"Love doesn't always save people."

"Then what's it good for?"

Rafael smiled, then laughed—but I thought that his laugh was more like crying. "If I knew the answer to that question, I'd be God."

We sat out there until it got dark. It started snowing again.

We walked back to the cabin in silence.

There weren't any more words living inside us.

-3-

So I'm lying here trying to figure out this day.

I just can't figure it out.

Everything is a knot.

I can hear the wind outside.

I wonder if Sharkey is out there somewhere, walking around, stoned out of his mind. This cold could kill him. I hate winter with all my crooked heart. The only thing that winter can't kill is the monster.

The monster will live forever.

REMEMBERING

When I woke up this morning, there was a note on my desk:

> Zach,
>
> You told me that remembering was the monster. I think you're wrong. I think it's forgetting that's the monster. I just wanted to tell you that.
>
> Love,
>
> Rafael

I kept staring at his note. And then I just kept staring at the word *love*. I was trying to remember if that word had ever been pointed in my direction. I couldn't remember. Was that because I had amnesia or because nobody had ever told me they loved me? Maybe to be loved you have to have something written on your heart that tells other people something good about you. Maybe there's nothing good about me. Maybe there is no monster. *Maybe I'm the monster.* Maybe that's what God wrote on my heart: *monster.* God and I will never be friends. Not ever.

I took a shower, and everything seemed to be moving in slow motion. As I walked to the smoking pit, I saw people waving, "Morning, Zach."

Yeah. Morning.

At the smoking pit, I kept expecting to see Sharkey.

But he was gone.

HOW CAN YOU LIVE WHEN YOU DON'T KNOW HOW TO SING?

I keep thinking about the song I was writing when I used to get wasted with my friends. What's wrong with me? Why would I want to write a song? I don't even know how to sing. I don't even believe that I have a song inside me. But there has to be something else inside me besides really bad dreams.

WHEN RAFAEL STOPPED SINGING

-1-

Cabin 9 was a lot quieter with Sharkey gone. So was the smoking pit. Sharkey took up a lot of space. I guess I liked that about him. Now there was just more empty space in the world I lived in. Two days after Sharkey left, I was lying in bed. Thinking about my dream. All I could remember was my brother's face. He must have been in my dream. I don't know why but I spelled his name in the air.

The air can hold a lot of things. But it couldn't hold my brother's name.

I sat up on my bed and studied the familiar room. Rafael had put up one of Sharkey's drawings on the wall. It was a drawing of a boy on fire playing a piano. Rafael had told him it was a beautiful drawing. "Imagine a young man who could draw such a beautiful thing." I don't think Sharkey heard what Rafael was trying to tell him.

I walked over to Rafael's desk and stared at the painting he was working on. It was a self-portrait in different shades of blue. His hair was a little wild and he was crying. It was the saddest painting I'd ever seen. I just stared at it for a long time. I think I was looking for all of the things that were making Rafael sad. But there were so many things in the world that could make a guy sad. The list was like this winter—it just went on forever.

Then my eyes fell on Rafael's journal. *It was right there*. I'd seen him writing in it the night before. He always wrote something in it—even if it was just a few lines.

Then I found it in my trembling hands. It was like I just found it there. I read the words he'd written on the cover: *And here I am the center of all beauty! Writing these poems.* It was from a poem. He'd read the poem to me. He told me the poet's name but I didn't remember the name of the poet. He'd laughed when he read the poem. "He's being ironic and sincere all at the same time." I got that. Rafael would have gotten along with Mr. Garcia. They would have understood each other perfectly.

Rafael had so many words living inside him. I guess he just had to empty them out sometimes. At first I thought I was just going to stare at the words, you know, like they were paintings on the walls of a museum. I wasn't actually going to read the words. I was just going to look at them. But that's not what happened. I knew it was wrong. My heart was beating faster, but I couldn't help it. I just couldn't. I turned to the last entry:

> I just finished painting my first self-portrait. I don't think I intended to paint myself. It just happened. Not that anything just happens. Adam believes that everything happens for a reason. I think he may be right about that. The problem is that most of us are too lazy or too scared to think about all of the reasons for the things that "just happen."
>
> I don't really know what I was thinking when I started painting. But then I realized I'd painted a face. And it was me. At fifty-three maybe it was time to paint myself. I didn't even have to look in the mirror. Now that I think about it, I've never really enjoyed looking at myself in the mirror. Sometimes it just hurts too damned much to look at yourself, to see what you've become. To look at me. To see what I've become.
>
> I just sat here and painted myself from memory, trying to remember what I looked like. It's strange, how the hands and fingers remember. They take a brush and paint and remember and your face appears on the blank sheet of watercolor paper.
>
> Maybe I'm just trying to re-invent myself or re-create myself. Maybe I'm just working on another piece of fiction. I'm good at fiction.
>
> This is what I'm telling myself right now: This is you. Rafael, this is you. I'm trying to tell myself who I am. I lost myself somewhere. And that's a very sad thing. Losing yourself is sad and heartbreaking. Fucking sad and fucking heartbreaking. Losing yourself isn't like losing

a key to your house. It isn't like losing an expensive pair of sunglasses or even the only copy of the greatest screenplay you've ever written.

I've been talking to myself a lot lately. That doesn't bother me much. I have a feeling I'm trying to talk myself into existence. I'm trying to listen.

It's time I start listening to my own voice.

Sometimes I find myself laughing.

Sometimes I find myself crying.

Friday night, I was at an AA meeting and I was in the back of the room and I started crying. I didn't bother to think about why. But I just let it happen. The great thing about a room full of alcoholics is that people emote all over the place. Crying is the least of it.

So my first self-portrait is of me crying. Maybe that's not a bad place to begin.

I wanted to sit there and get drunk on Rafael's writing. That's what I really wanted to do. I looked around the room, you know, like guilty people do when they're stealing something. I put the journal back. *I have to stop doing this I have to stop doing this.*

I was beginning to understand what Adam meant by addict behavior.

I took a quick shower. I kept thinking about that idea of talking yourself into existence. I wondered if that was possible. I didn't know how to do that. Maybe Rafael didn't either. He seemed sadder than ever and I wondered if he was really going to get better. But, at least, he was trying to get at what he felt. Maybe he could do that because he was so at home with words. I mean, he worked with them. They were the tools of his trade. Mr. Garcia had always told me I was good with words too. But I felt inarticulate—and reading Rafael's journal, I don't know, it made me feel even more inarticulate.

But it wasn't as if words healed us. What good were Rafael's words? What good were Adam's words? What good were anybody's words? I kept thinking about what Jodie said. *None of us are ever going to get better.* The thought entered into my head that maybe Sharkey had lost his faith in words. Who could blame him?

On my way to the smoking pit, I walked by the labyrinth. I saw Rafael walking it. His steps were slow and deliberate and I wondered what was in his head. I watched him for a little while. I was hiding behind some trees. I guess I just didn't want anyone to see that I was watching him. I felt stupid. Why was I hiding? Who was I hiding from? I hated myself sometimes.

I saw Adam walking toward me. I pretended to act normal—though I wouldn't know normal if it bit off my private parts.

I waved *hi*.

He waved back *hi*.

As he passed me, he stopped and said, "New guy today. He just came in early this morning. So you and Rafael will be getting a new roommate."

"Great," I said. But there must have been something in my voice because Adam didn't keep on walking.

"You want to tell me what that *great* meant?"

I shrugged.

"Not having a good day, huh?"

"I don't want a new roommate. That's all."

"Where do you suggest we put the new guy?"

"I don't really care."

"What's this about, Zach?"

Adam, he loved to ask that. I hated all the questions he had inside him. "It's not right," I said.

"What's not right?"

"What if Sharkey comes back?"

Adam didn't say anything. He just, well, he was just thinking. "Can you come in to see me today?"

"Like I have some place to go."

"After group. Let's have a session. Me and you."

"Yeah, okay."

"Still mad at me?"

"Like it matters."

"It might."

I think I gave him a snarky smile. "See you in group," I said.

I headed for the smoking pit. Jodie was there smoking up a storm. I liked the way she held her cigarette. She was really into smoking. She smoked like maybe her life depended on it. Well, hell, she was a *for real* addict. Jodie, she had a couple of other people living inside her. Sometimes, those other people showed up. When one of those other people showed up, I made like a scared rabbit who'd just heard a rifle go off. I just couldn't deal with that. Adam said it was good to know our limitations. Embrace them. Sure, embrace, embrace, embrace. I wish Adam would get out of my head.

I smiled at Jodie. I knew by the look on her face that the two other people living inside her were gone today.

"Hi," I said.

"Hi back," she said. "I'm giving you a big hug right now."

"No touch," I said.

She laughed. "I can hug beautiful boys with my eyes. You know that, don't you?"

"There's a lot of things you can do with your eyes," I said.

"Except have sex."

"No talking about sex," I said. "We're all on contract."

"Who needs sex?" she said. "All I need is coffee and cigarettes—and a new therapist." She hated her therapist. She'd gone through two of them. She said she'd love to have Adam. She said Adam was "easy on the eyes." I knew what she meant. But I got the feeling she wouldn't have liked Adam as a therapist either. She was too rebellious. That's what I liked about her.

We both laughed.

"You been to breakfast?"

"Not hungry."

"Gotta eat, sweetie."

"Don't want to."

"Finish that thing."

I took a drag off my cigarette. "You're acting like a mother," I said, "making me eat breakfast."

"I'm not making you do anything. Besides, you could use some mothering."

"Think so?"

"Yeah, I *do* think so."

"So now you're a part of my therapy?"

"Of course I am, sugar. Didn't anybody tell you we're all part of each other's therapy?"

"Maybe that's why we're all screwed."

"You may be right about that, sugar."

Sugar. Sugar. I liked that Jodie called me *sugar*.

"Nice smile," she said, "very sweet. C'mon, put that thing out and let's go see if there's anything exciting happening at breakfast." There was always someone acting up or acting out or having a breakdown or crying or emoting or yelling or something. Breakfast seemed to be a good time for throwing your emotions around. Jodie said that at this place emotions were like Frisbees—people just tossed them around all day long like they were at a park.

My theory was that conflicts at this place were unavoidable. When you get a lot of people with issues in one big group, well, there were going to be serious explosions. Jodie loved to watch the explosions. Me, I don't know. It sort of embarrassed me to see people engage in unhealthy behaviors in such a public way. I liked to keep my unhealthy behaviors to myself. You know, like secretly reading Rafael's journal. Or like drinking bourbon all by myself.

When Jodie and I walked into the dining room, Rafael was sitting there reading the newspaper. He had a way of ignoring all the commotion. Not that he wasn't social, but sometimes, well, he just wanted to read his newspaper. Jodie and I sat next to him. "What's new?"

Rafael looked up and smiled at Jodie. "The world's falling apart. It says so right here." He pointed at the headline.

That made us all laugh.

Jodie looked up, her eyes surveying the room. I mean, she loved studying all the other clients. That's what we were—*clients*. I wondered why we weren't patients. Sharkey said we were clients because we could leave anytime we wanted. "Patients can't leave. Clients can." Sharkey had an answer for everything.

Jodie nudged me and pointed her chin at Hannah and called her over. "Where's the bus?"

"What bus?"

"The one that ran over your ass. You look like crap."

That made me laugh. Hannah sat next to me and gave me the eye.

Rafael just kept on reading.

Hannah reached over and tugged at the newspaper. "What is it about newspapers that you like so much?"

"There's a world out there, Hannah. Anybody ever tell you that?" Rafael smiled at her.

"That world almost killed me."

"Oh, so it's the world that's doing you in?"

Hannah shot Rafael a fake smile. "You should smile more."

"I'm working on it."

"What was your favorite drink?"

Hannah was sort of flirting with Rafael. I could tell. But, well, in a good way. I mean, I could tell she liked him. "You planning to take me out to some bar?"

She tapped her temple. "In my dreams, sweetie."

"Red wine," Rafael said.

"What kind of red wine?"

"Always liked a good cabernet."

"Ever hit the hard stuff?"

"An occasional Manhattan. What about you?"

"Very dry Martinis. About ten a night."

"How could you tell how dry they were?"

Hannah and Jodie broke out laughing.

Hannah shook her head. "God, I miss drinking. Miss it like hell."

"Me too," Jodie said. "Sometimes, I just wanna scream."

"Me too," I said. I don't know why I said that. Not that it wasn't true. I did want to fucking scream.

Hannah studied my face. "I have a son your age." Her voice got real soft and that really tore me up because she could be so tough. She patted me on the cheek. "I know, no touch. No touch." She laughed. "Bourbon. Wasn't that your drink?"

"Yeah," I said.

"I hope you never touch it again." Then she burst out crying. "Or you'll wind up worse than us." She took a deep breath. "This place is making me sad. God, we're all so sad."

"That's not true," Rafael said. "We're just sorting things out, that's all."

"You're a sweet man." Jodie was wearing a crooked smile.

"Am I?"

Rafael smiled. And right then he looked old and beat-up and I knew he was going through something and I wanted to ask him about that. He had to make it. Somebody had to make it. Rafael seemed like maybe he would be the one. Sharkey, he'd given up. *Rafael had to make it. Please, God, please.* I was praying to a God I didn't get along with.

-3-

I could tell it was going to be different in group. I don't know what it was, but the anxiety thing was visiting me again and it was really making itself at home. I had the urge to go away. Numb out. Disassociate. I seriously wanted to do that. But I was trying to make myself stay focused.

Sharkey was gone and I kept staring at his chair. He always liked to sit on the same chair. The new guy, Amit, was doing his paperwork so Adam said he wouldn't be in group. Sheila and Maggie were out sick and Kelley, no one knew where she was. Sometimes, she just isolated, didn't want to go near anyone, see anyone, talk to anyone. I knew what that was like.

So it was just me and Rafael and Lizzie and Adam.

Adam handed the Check-in card to Rafael. Rafael took it. Today he didn't smile. He always smiled—even when he was feeling bad. But not today. "I'm Rafael. I'm an alcoholic." And we all said, "Hi Rafael." He paused for a moment, then looked at the card, then set it down. "I've been keeping a secret," he said.

Adam didn't say anything. He just waited.

"I killed my son."

Adam got this very serious look on his face. I could see a look of surprise—then it was gone. "When you say you killed your son—what do you mean, Rafael?" His question was soft, not like an interrogation.

Rafael had his eyes pasted to the floor. "He was seven—" He stopped and hit his chest softly. He kept hitting it.

"Breathe," Adam said. "Just breathe."

Rafael took a few deep breaths. In and out. Inhale. Exhale. It was like I was breathing with him.

"Rafael, it's okay. Take your time. You can do this."

"I can't."

"You can. Rafael, *you can.*"

Rafael nodded, then shut his eyes. He spoke just above a whisper. "I was driving. I wasn't paying attention. I was thinking about the screenplay I was working on. I had my son in the car and I didn't keep my eyes on the road. And then, all of a sudden, something hit the car and I went skidding out of control and then—I don't know. Everything was spinning and—Joaquin screamed, he screamed—and the next thing I remember is that I woke up in a hospital room. And I kept asking for Joaquin. *Joaquin? Joaquin? Where's Joaquin?* I knew by the look on my wife's face that he was—." He stopped. It was like he just couldn't say the word *dead*. He just couldn't.

"My wife, she didn't even have to say the words. I killed him. He was seven years old and I killed him." He kept whispering *Joaquin* between his sobs. And he kept hitting himself in the chest and he was more like a wounded animal than a man. And I hated it, seeing him like that and I was torn up to hell and I just couldn't take it. *Joaquin, Joaquin, Joaquin.* I don't know, it was like he'd let go and there was nothing but his pain and he was living in that pain now. All of him, his heart and his mind and his body and he fell on his knees and he kept hitting himself and I looked at Adam and my eyes were telling Adam to make it all stop and I don't know, I just grabbed hold of Lizzie's hand and I could see that tears were rolling down her cheeks and I wanted it all just to stop.

I never knew that hurt in a man could sound like that. It was the saddest song in the world. And I knew that Rafael was broken, that he had fallen and reached the very bottom of a dark hole and I wondered if he had it in him to climb back out.

And then I saw Adam reach for Rafael and pull him up from the floor. He stood him up and sat him back down on his chair. I don't know how long Rafael cried. The whole world had gone quiet and there was nothing in the entire universe except for the sound of a man breaking in half. And finally, Rafael grew quiet and still. I could tell that he'd gone away and now he was trying to come back. He reached for the box of tissues that was always in the center of the circle. He took a deep breath, then looked at Adam. "I couldn't tell you."

He looked at the floor, then looked back up into Adam's face. "I haven't spoken his name since his funeral. Eleven years."

He looked at me.

"He'd be eighteen." He gave me a crooked smile.

And I wanted to say, *I'll be your son if you want. I will be. I'll be a good son.* But I didn't say anything. I just tried to smile back at him.

"My life fell apart after he died. He was adopted. My wife, I don't really think she wanted to go through with the whole adoption thing. But she went along. I guess she could see how much I wanted to have kids. I think she knew I loved him more than anything in the whole world. She felt left out. She *was* left out. When he died, she moved on. I think I hated her for moving on. She hated me back for *not* moving on. She grieved too. But she couldn't live in all that sadness. Me, I just drank. After a year, she left me. But I'd left her long before that. I don't forgive myself."

Rafael's tears were like little rivers. And then Adam did something I'd never seen him do. He took Rafael's hand and held it. Then he just looked at Rafael. Looked him right in the eyes. "I think you *can* forgive yourself. I think you know it's time."

Rafael looked down at the ground, but Adam didn't let his hand go. "I used to sing to him when he was a baby. All the time. I stopped singing the day he died."

There were tears falling from Adam's face. That was the first time I saw Adam as a man, as a human being. Before that instant, I'd only seen him as my therapist. He was only a guy whose job it was to help us. To help *me*. But he was more than that. Everyone in the world was more than anything I ever imagined. I felt small and stupid. We all sat there quietly, the four of us. And finally Adam let go of Rafael's hand and nodded at me and Lizzie. "What's coming up for you, Zach? Lizzie?"

"It was an accident," Lizzie said.

Rafael nodded. He wanted to believe. But he didn't. Not quite. Almost.

Adam looked at me, a question in his eyes.

"I want to remember," I said. I didn't even know I was going to say that. "I think the monster will go away if I remember. It's like—." I stopped and looked at Rafael. "It's like you saying your son's name again. It hurts. But it's not stuck inside you anymore."

Rafael gave me a smile. I swear it was the most beautiful smile in the world.

And then I heard myself say: "Don't hate yourself anymore, Rafael. Please don't hate yourself."

-4-

After group, I sat on the steps outside Adam's small office and waited for him. I wondered what he and Rafael were talking about. For some reason I remembered the conversation at breakfast. When Jodie had said *I have a son your age* Rafael had winced. Almost as if someone had punched him in the stomach. Now I knew why he had winced. Now I knew why he was so kind to me. Because I was his son's age.

I thought maybe Rafael didn't see me.

Maybe all he saw when he looked at me was his son.

That thought really tore me up all to hell. See, that was the thing about my mom and dad. I think that most of the time they didn't see me. My mom and dad, they didn't even see themselves. I hadn't thought about them in a long time. I wondered why.

I heard Rafael's voice as the door opened. "Your turn," he said. He was smiling and the sun was out and it wasn't so cold outside. Not today. He sat down next to me. He didn't say anything. "Are you okay?" he asked.

"Yeah, I guess. What about you?"

"I'm good, Zach. I really am." He took a deep breath, held it, then let it out. "God, sometimes I wish I still smoked." He laughed. I think he was laughing at himself. He did that a lot, laugh at himself. I thought that was a good thing. You know, a healthy behavior. "Have you ever been in a summer storm in the desert, Zach?"

"Yeah," I said.

"They just come up on you—the wind and the thunder and the lightning and the rain begins to pound. And you think that the world is going to end. It's this overwhelming apocalyptic moment. And then, just like that, it's over. And the world is calm again. And the air smells clean and new. And smelling it, you want to be alive again."

"Yeah, it's like that," I said.

"That's how I feel, Zach. Like the desert after a storm."

-5-

Adam was on the phone and his door was open. He motioned me to sit down. When he hung up the phone, he nodded and asked, "How you doing, buddy?"

He liked the word *buddy*. I liked it too. "I'm kind of stunned out," I said.

"You mean about group this morning?"

"Yeah. That was a big secret Rafael kept."

"Yeah. You know, the secret thing, I know you guys think it's just this little bullshit thing, but secrets are killing you guys. That's why it's on the list. You have to let them out. They really *are* killing you guys. They're killing all of you." Then he looked at me. "You have a lot of secrets you don't talk about."

"Guess I do."

"When are you going to let them out?"

"I'm not as brave as Rafael."

"I'm making up that you're as brave as they come."

I wanted to tell him that God didn't write *brave* on my heart. "You're giving me a lot of credit."

"You don't give yourself *enough* credit, Zach. You never have. You know, it was a beautiful thing, what you said to Rafael, that he shouldn't hate himself. You should take your own advice."

"Yeah, sure," I said.

Adam shot me a snarky smile. I knew about those smiles of his. "You said you wanted to remember."

"I do."

"I'm going to ask you a question, Zach."

"Sure."

"Why haven't you ever asked about how you came here? How long has it been—sixty days?"

"Fifty-three days."

"Fifty-three days and you still haven't talked about what got you here."

I looked at him blankly.

"Your first day here you told me you didn't know how you got here. And since then you've never asked. You've never asked who's paying for your stay here. You've never asked why you have money in your account, the money you buy cigarettes with and buy your soap and shampoo and shaving cream and all those things." He stopped, almost as if he wasn't sure, but then he got this determined look on his face. "And you've never asked about your family."

All of a sudden I felt numb and frozen. You know, I felt like one of those windshields I used to take a bat to. I couldn't speak. I didn't know what to say.

"Zach?"

Adam was looking at me, studying me. I looked back at him. I know I was holding a question in my eyes. He was holding a question too.

"Adam, I don't want to know."

"You don't want to know or you're afraid to know?"

"I told you I wasn't brave."

"You *are* brave, Zach. Didn't I tell you once that you've already survived the worst? You're here. You're alive. You've survived all the bad things already."

"I'm not alive," I said.

"Yes, you are."

"I don't feel anything. I hate feeling. I've told you that."

"But you *do* feel, Zach. When I didn't go after Sharkey, you were furious with me. I'm making up that the reason you were so angry with me was because you love Sharkey. And you love Rafael. I saw the look on your face this morning when Rafael was talking about his son. You looked at me and I thought I saw this look. I'm making up that you wanted me to stop his pain. You wanted Rafael to be free of pain and you wanted me to do something. Am I right?"

"Yeah, something like that."

"I can't stop his pain, Zach. But you love him. You love Rafael. I can see that. That's a beautiful thing. That's feeling, Zach."

"It hurts like hell, Adam."

"Yes, it does, buddy."

"I hate that."

"But love doesn't always have to hurt, Zach. Didn't anybody ever tell you that love could feel good?"

Nobody had ever said anything about love to me. Not anything. Not one word.

-6-

Amit, our new roommate, had chocolate skin and black eyes. He was sort of a big guy and he was a lot like Sharkey in some ways. He liked stuff. He had lots of sunglasses and watches and stuff. And lots of different kinds of expensive tennis shoes and lots of clothes. He was around thirty and just like Sharkey, he took up a lot of space. Rafael kept smiling and I knew what he was smiling about. He was thinking the same thing I was thinking: already this guy was taking over Cabin 9. Not that either of us cared.

Amit wasn't very talkative. He seemed a little far away. I was reading a book and Rafael was working on another painting and as soon as Amit finished putting away all his stuff, he put a pack of cigarettes in his pocket and was out the door.

"I guess people just come and go here," I said.

"No one comes to stay, Zach."

"I guess not." The thought entered my head that maybe Rafael wouldn't be staying for very much longer. I had this feeling. You know, it was like he said, he felt like a desert after a storm. And then I sort of got this thing inside me. You know, when he left, what was I going to do? And me, how long was I going to stay? That anxiety thing was going at me again. Shit.

I got up from my bed, put my book down and walked over to see what Rafael was painting. It was a moon right in the center of the night sky. And he was drawing a figure to the left of the moon. "What's that going to be?"

"A coyote."

"Why a coyote?"

"A coyote howls. It's his way of singing."

But the coyote didn't look like he was howling. I looked closer. Rafael wasn't finished with the coyote, but it looked like he was going to be leaping through the air. You know, like he was happy.

"I'm sorry about Joaquin," I said. I sat down on the chair next to his desk like I always did when I wanted to talk to him.

"I think that's one of the reasons I came here. To let him go. His memory, that's one of my monsters. Beautiful Joaquin. I can't carry all that stuff around inside me anymore, Zach." I think I knew what he was trying to say.

"Last night I couldn't sleep. You were having a bad dream. You were talking to Santiago. You kept saying, *don't don't don't*. I went and sat on your bed. And you know what I did, Zach? I sang."

"You sang?"

"I sang, Zach."

"But you said you'd stopped singing after Joaquin died."

"Until last night."

"What did you sing?"

"A song. I used to sing it to Joaquin."

"You sang it to me?"

"Yeah. And you got quiet and calm. And I guess I thought you were safe again. And then I got up and got dressed and walked to the tree named Zach. And I stood there and I sang. I sang that song and I swear it felt like that song was coming from my heart like a fire."

I looked into Rafael's eyes and whispered, "Sing it."

It was like Rafael saw something in my eyes. Or maybe heard something in my voice. So he did, he sang it...

One of these mornings
You're going to rise up singing
Then you'll spread your wings
And you'll take to the sky.

But till that morning
There's a'nothing can harm you
With daddy and mamma standing by.

I swear Rafael looked like an angel. I remembered the day Mr. Garcia had played the trumpet for me. The song he played had been the most beautiful thing I'd ever heard. Until now. And I knew that Rafael had found a way to tame his monster.

I knew right then that Rafael would be leaving.

I wanted to keep him.

I wanted him to stay forever.

I wanted him to teach me to sing that song.

How can you live when you don't know how to sing?

REMEMBERING

I can't sleep.

Rafael just finished leading Amit back to bed. He sleepwalks just like Sharkey. Rafael, he really is like a watchdog. He's the sentry of Cabin 9.

I'm running through a list in my head of all the things I'm worried about. I'm worried about Sharkey. I'm worried that he's not going to make it. I'm worried about me, about what I'm going to do when Rafael leaves. I heard him talking on the phone after dinner. I don't know who he was talking to, but I heard him say that he would be back home in a week or so. Home. That was a strange word. I hadn't thought about that word in a long time.

This is the thought that's entering my head right now: Adam knows what happened to me. He knows how I got here. So why doesn't he just tell me?

I already know the answer to that question.

I'm fighting myself. I know I am. One minute I want to remember. The next minute I want to live in the land of forgetting. One minute I want to feel. The next minute I never want to feel anything ever again. One minute I want to learn how to sing. The next minute I want to hate Rafael for reminding me that there are songs in the world.

I'm beating the crap out of myself.

I'm living in a space between day and night.

I want to move. I want to stay still.

I want to sleep. And I want to be awake.

I want to be loved. And I want to be left alone.

I know that I'm better because I can name things now. I can place myself on the map of the world. I can. I can talk about myself to myself. I can be honest about a lot of things. But I don't want to think about my mom or my dad or my brother.

I know that something bad happened.

I'm thinking that a memory *can* kill a guy.

I wake up. I look at the clock. It's four in the morning. I get up and turn on my desk lamp. I get my sketch pad out. I haven't sketched anything since I've been here. I don't know why, but I have to sketch. I just have to sketch because if I don't, I know I'll die. I just know I'll die. Anxiety is back. I can hardly breathe. If I just sketch, I'll be able to breathe again.

I'm sketching. The pencil is moving on the white pad. I can see what I'm drawing.

I feel like I'm standing outside my body. Watching. My hand is moving across the paper.

I'm sketching. I'm remembering.

THE WAKING

-1-

This morning, I felt a hand on my shoulder shaking me awake. Then I heard Rafael's voice. "Okay, Zachariah, it's time."

I kept my eyes closed. "I'm too tired."

"Time to get up."

"Screw it. I'm staying in bed."

"No can do, dude. Up. C'mon. Hit the shower."

The guy wasn't gonna let up. "Okay," I said. "And fuck you."

"Nice mouth. Very nice mouth."

"I mean it, Rafael. Fuck you. And why didn't you tell me you were leaving?" I sat up on the bed. Rafael just looked at me.

"Guess you're awake now, huh?"

"I thought we were friends."

"We *are* friends, Zach." He popped his knuckles. Sometimes he did that. "My days are up, Zach. I thought you knew that. Fifty-eight days I've been here." He shot me one of those Rafael smiles, the kind that made you unsure of what the smile meant. "Fifty-eight fucking days."

"Nice mouth," I said.

"Yeah, nice mouth. Look, Zach, it's time."

"You should've have told me you were leaving."

"It wasn't a secret, Zach."

"Fuck you."

"Hit the shower, kid."

"Don't call me a kid. Fuck you."

Rafael didn't say anything. He just sort of smiled and looked at me. I'm not sure what the look meant. I watched him as he left the cabin.

I sat there in bed staring down at the floor. What was that about—staring at the floor? Why did I always do that? I really hated myself sometimes. I got up and looked at the sketch. It was a scene from my life, the part of my life I had wanted to forget. But now I was remembering. Not that it made me feel any better. All it did was make me feel bad. I held the sketch in my hand, then put it down. I had the urge to tear it up. Tear it up to pieces.

I wondered what it was like to feel whole, to not feel torn up or stunned out or wigged out or any of those things. I wondered what it was like to walk around the world looking up at the sky instead of searching the ground, eye to eye with things that crawled.

I walked toward the shower, but as I walked past Rafael's desk, I saw his journal sitting on his desk. It was open. I walked up to the journal and picked it up. I held it and told myself to just put it back down and walk away. But that's not what I did—I stared at the words and began reading:

I feel like I've been driving down a road for a long time—and I'm the only traveler. I don't really know where I'm going—and the problem isn't that I'm alone. Alone is good. I've never really minded being alone. But sometimes I just want to stop traveling down wherever the hell the road is leading to. I just want to stop the car and remember where this trip began and why I'm taking it.

I want to talk to someone and I want to ask them to point to the place of the pain. I want to say: "Show me where it hurts." And then I want to touch them there. And then I want to show them where *my* hurt is and I want them to touch *me* there. Letting someone touch you in the place where it hurts the most, if I could do that, if I could just do that, well, that would mean I was alive.

I'm thinking that if I can touch other people's hurt and they can touch mine, then something might happen. Something really beautiful. I don't mean that the hurt would disappear. I just mean that it might be possible to continue on the road toward a place called home.

Home. There was that word again.

I stared at all of Rafael's words. God, there was all this chaos inside me. It was like all these memories were having a riot inside my heart and my brain and maybe that was why I was all torn up. Was there a word that could save me?

I kept thinking about my sketch as I took a shower. The thought entered my head that it had all been a dream and that what I'd sketched wasn't a scene from my past at all. It was just a dream. It was just another dream.

Nothing was real—except for the words in Rafael's journal. I felt the hot water hitting my body. Hitting wasn't the right word. Hitting was what my brother had done to me. Hitting was what I had done to windshields and parked cars. The water was soft and my brother, there was nothing soft about him. His fists were hard, his eyes were hard, his voice was hard, his heart was hard. He was the hardest thing in the known universe. In *my known* universe.

I closed my eyes and let the water rush over me and I wondered what it would be like to be as soft as water, to make people clean, to quench people's thirst. That would be a beautiful thing, to be like water. And then all these photographs started entering my head, my brother hitting me, my father's head on the kitchen table, the empty look in my mother's eyes, me roaming the streets like a wounded dog, me lying down in Susan's office, breathing, crying, Rafael sitting on my bed singing, Adam's voice, *"When was the last time someone told you they loved you?"* Then there was a gunshot. I kept hearing a voice, *"No no no please God no."* The voice was mine.

I don't know how long I stood there in front of the mirror, hugging myself. My eyes were dark today. I stared at them. Adam had told me my eyes were hazel. Sometimes they looked green. Green, as if there flecks of leaves in them. Like summer.

Today my eyes were dark as winter.

I looked at my calendar.

This was my fifty-fourth day—in this place.

Fifty-four days.

I was thinking that I had been here all my life.

"What's that?"

I turned and saw Rafael looking at my sketch. He was studying it.

"Did you say something, Zach?"

"I was just talking to myself."

"A habit you share with most of the denizens of this place." He seemed only halfway in the conversation. "This is wonderful, Zach. I didn't know you were an artist."

"It was one of two classes I loved."

"What was the other one?"

"English."

"Ah," he said, "Mr. Garcia."

I looked at him. I wondered how he knew about Mr. Garcia. I'd never told him about Mr. Garcia.

"You talk to him in your sleep."

"You shouldn't listen in on other people's dreams."

"I'll try not to. Just keep it down. People are trying to sleep." He kept staring at my sketch. "Are you bringing this into group?"

"I wasn't planning on it."

"Bring it in."

"I don't want to."

"Storytime," he said.

"I don't—."

Rafael stopped me dead. "People tell their stories on their second week."

"I know that."

"It's time, Zach."

"Adam will tell me when it's time."

"Adam's not going to tell you shit, Zach. Adam's not here to tell you what to do. He's not a cop. The work we do is not for Adam, Zach, it's for us."

"I thought you liked Adam."

"I love Adam. He's a beautiful and gifted man. But what does liking or not liking Adam have to do with you telling your story? This is up to you, dude. *You.*"

Rafael didn't say dude. It wasn't a Rafael word. When he said dude, it meant he was starting to get mad.

"You're no expert on what I should do."

"So what? You think anybody's an expert? No one's an expert on human behavior, Zach. Especially fucked-up human behavior."

"Are you saying I'm fucked up?"

He grabbed me by the shoulders and looked right into me. *"I'm saying it's time, Zach."* He was wearing this very serious look in his eyes. "You can't just hang out, Zach. You can't just loiter. There's a reason you're here." He took his hands off my shoulders.

"I can't."

"You can, Zach." He smiled. "You want me to try guilt?"

"Guilt?"

"You want me to leave this place without hearing your story?"

"Fuck you, Rafael."

"Nice mouth."

"Yeah, nice mouth." I gave him a snarky smile.

He looked at his watch. "We got twenty minutes."

"To do what?"

"Let's you and I walk the labyrinth."

-2-

I don't know what made me follow Rafael to the mouth of the labyrinth.

We stood there for a moment. There was something still and quiet about the labyrinth. It always made me want to whisper. "Close your eyes," he said. "Take a breath—then open your eyes and walk." I heard Adam's voice inside me: *Walk the labyrinth with intent.*

Remember remember remember. That was the word that came into my head. It was almost as if *remember* was a wind blowing through all the sad and dark corners of my body. That wind blew and blew and blew until I reached the center of the labyrinth.

Rafael was there.

Don't be afraid. It felt as though his voice was coming from my heart.

-3-

After Check-in, Adam asked if anyone had something to work on
during group. I found myself raising my hand. Not that the hand-raising
thing was something we did in group. It wasn't like school. Well, I think it
was a school. The subject here was our pain.

Adam pointed his chin toward me. "Zach? You have something?"

"I was born," I said.

Adam kept himself from smiling but I knew he was smiling inside. "I
was born," Adam repeated.

My heart was beating as fast as a hummingbird's. I took a deep breath.
"I was born," I whispered, "in Las Cruces, New Mexico on August 16th,
1990. I'm a Leo." I smirked. Like I cared what sign I was. I looked down at
the carpet, then tried to look up. "My mother once told me that the day I
was born was the happiest day of her life. That sounds like something she
made up. My mother was never happy. I wish I had a picture of my mother
holding me—me and all her happiness. I'd like to have a picture of that." I
told myself I wasn't going to cry. I was sick and tired of all the tears around
this place—especially mine. I took a breath and kept talking. "My mother
was depressed. My father drank. My brother was a drug addict. And I fell in
love with bourbon the first chance I got..."

I spilled the whole story out. Everything I could remember about
my mom and my dad and my brother Santiago. I told them about the
windshields and Mr. Garcia and how he'd played the trumpet for me.
I told them about my friends and about the song I was writing, the one
about the monsters of night. I told them about all my father's bottles of
bourbon and my brother and how he'd hurt me and how he'd managed to
own the house we lived in, control it with his angry eyes and his angry fists
and how my dad and mom just let him. I talked about all the sadness in
our house and about my mom and how she wanted me to touch her in ways

that wigged me out and made me go mental. I told them everything I could remember and I felt like a storm dropping wind and rain on the earth and even though I just couldn't stand it, I kept talking. I must have talked for a long time because I looked up at the clock and an hour had passed by. "I should stop," I said.

"You need a break?"

"No," I said. "I'm okay."

"Then why do you need to stop?"

"I don't know. I think that's all I have to say. I've been talking for a long time."

"Can I ask you a question, Zach?" I looked over at Rafael.

Adam was about to say something but Rafael kept going. "Does that sketch—?" he was holding something in his head and was trying to push that thought out into the world. "Does that sketch have something to do with your story?" He pointed to the sketch that I'd pushed under my chair.

I don't know if Adam had noticed the drawing. Probably he had. He noticed everything. "Let's have a look," he said.

I pushed out the drawing and placed it in the middle of the circle.

There was a lot of quiet. The group just sort of studied it—though really there wasn't much to study.

"It's lovely," Lizzie said. "I didn't know you were an artist."

"I'm not."

"Yes, you are." Sheila said. "*You really are.*"

I looked at my sketch and tried to see what everyone was seeing.

"You want to tell us about it?"

I shrugged and looked at Adam.

"It's all there," I said.

"What's all there?"

"My whole life."

I knew what Adam was saying with his eyes. I knew the words were there, but it was so hard to pull them out. "That's me, lying on the side of the road. And that's a dead dog lying next to me. I'm like the dead dog. And the road, it's just going somewhere like roads do. They go on forever, but see, I'm not going anywhere. I'm dead, like the dog."

"Why a dog?"

"I love dogs. I had one once. Did I talk about the dog in group? I don't remember."

I saw everyone shaking their heads.

"My dog's name was Lilly. She used to sleep with me. I used to talk to her and it seemed like she always knew what I was saying. When I was around five, she died. I found her in the backyard. She wasn't breathing. I ran and got my dad. He was drunk. 'Dogs die,' that's all he said. And then he went back to his drinking. I buried the dog in the backyard."

"By yourself?" Adam was wearing a strange expression on his face. He looked sad. Like what I said made him sad.

I nodded.

He nodded back.

"So maybe I was thinking of Lilly. I don't know. Really, I wasn't thinking anything. I just sketched it. I had a dream and I couldn't fall back asleep so I just got up and sketched this, this—."

"Self-portrait." Rafael finished my sentence.

"Yeah, I guess that's what it is."

"Why a desert?" Adam always asked all these questions when it came to our artwork. I mean, that was his thing.

"That's where I live. I live in the desert. That's where I've always lived."

"Do you like the desert?"

"It's quiet there. And things grow. People don't think that there's anything in the desert. People think that it's just this waterless and dead place, but that's not true. It's like a forest really. I mean, there aren't any trees, but there's all kinds of things growing there. It's amazing really. The desert really tears me up. If you've ever spent time in the desert, you'd know how amazing it is. Once, I went hiking with my father in the desert. He knew the names of all the things that were growing there. It was the best day of my life."

"So," Adam said, "you're there—dead—along with a dead dog—in the middle of a desert where all sorts of things are growing. So there's death. And there's life."

"I guess so."

"You think you can tie this sketch to your story?"

"Okay," I said. All kinds of things were entering my head. "I think maybe I always felt like this in my family. You know, like I might as well have been dead. I was just a body on the side of the road. That's all I was. That's how it felt."

"But you're not dead, Zach." Rafael's voice was quiet but there was something very stubborn in it.

I looked down at the floor. "It feels like I am. Most of the time."

"I see you, Zach." Adam's favorite expression.

"I see you too," I said. I gave him a look.

He shook his head and smiled. "When was the last time you felt you were alive? *Really alive?*"

I knew the answer to that question as soon as Adam asked. Only I didn't tell him. I didn't want to tell the group. I didn't want to tell anyone. My lips were trembling and I couldn't make them stop. And there were salty tears running down my face and I couldn't see. I just closed my fists tight until I could feel my lips stop trembling. Then the tears stopped. And then I took a breath and then I unclenched my fists. I looked down at the floor. I could feel the words coming out of my mouth, could feel them, the words I didn't want to speak. "The last time—the last time I felt really alive was when Rafael sang to me."

"What did he sing?" I could tell Adam was looking across at Rafael even though I was looking down at the floor.

"Well, I didn't even know he was singing to me. I mean I was having a bad dream and he came over and sat on my bed and sang to me until I was calm."

"So, if you were asleep, how do you know that Rafael sang to you?"

"He told me." I looked up at Rafael. I tried to smile but it wasn't working, the smile thing. I hated talking about things that I felt. I hated it. It tore me up. I took another breath. "He told me the story and then he sang the song, the song he'd sung. He used to sing that song to his son." I stopped. I couldn't talk anymore. My lips were trembling too much. I just couldn't talk.

"That was a very beautiful thing. Don't you think so, Zach?"

"But I don't want to feel alive. Don't you understand! Don't you get that? How many times do I have to say it?" I was screaming so hard my voice was cracking. "I don't want to fucking feel alive." I didn't know I'd run out of the room. I just wasn't in control of my own movements and everything was spinning. The only thing I knew was that when the world stopped spinning, I found myself sitting in front of Rafael's tree—the tree named Zach.

-4-

I was tired.

God, I was tired.

Everything seemed so dull and hollow and far away. I knew that if I didn't rest I would just die, so I lay down on the ground and went to sleep and started dreaming. In the dream, I was waking up and it was summer and my eyes were as green as the leaves on the trees. I was so happy but I was so tired so I kept going back to sleep. Then I would wake again and look around at the summer world. The sky was blue and cloudless and the air was so clean and I could hardly stand it, all the happiness. So I would fall back asleep. Then I would wake again. I would sleep and wake and sleep and wake. But it was all a dream.

When I really woke, Rafael was shaking me. "Wake up, Zach."

I got up slowly. I looked around. I was a little confused and I was trying to figure out where I was.

"You okay, Zach?"

"I guess so."

"It's getting cold again. Let's get inside."

"How did you know where to find me?"

Rafael just looked at me like I'd just asked a really stupid question.

"I thought you weren't supposed to come and rescue me. I thought those were the rules."

"I'm not rescuing you."

"What are you doing then?"

"I'm bringing you in from the cold."

"I think that's still rescuing. Rescuing isn't allowed."

Rafael looked up at the looming clouds. "It's gonna pour, I think."
He looked at me. "You don't even know enough to come in from the rain."

"I need a cigarette."

"Jesus, kid, get a coat first. Crazy guy, Zach. You're a crazy guy."

-5-

Amit handed me a cigarette, then gave me a light.

"Thanks," I said.

"You okay?"

"Yeah."

"Thanks for the story."

"Yeah, well, that's what we do around here. You're next."

"Fucking swell."

That made me laugh.

"You've had it rough."

"That's why we're here."

"Yeah, well, I hate your brother."

"You don't even know him."

"He beat on you, dude. I hate him for that." That's when it started
to rain. Amit and I watched the storm in silence. Maybe we were addicted
to storms. Maybe so. I finished my cigarette. Amit offered me another. I
took it. "I feel like this fucking weather."

"Me too," I said.

"Rain wakes the world up."

"Where'd you get that idea from?"

"My sister. She always said that to me."

"Is she nice, your sister?"

"Yeah, she's more than nice."

"That's great, that you have a sister."

"She hasn't given up on me. Not yet anyway."

"Maybe she never will."

Amit didn't say anything after that. It was like he'd gone away. He was thinking of something, maybe his sister, maybe something else. I could see someone walking up toward the smoke pit in the rain. I could see the umbrella and as the figure moved closer, I could see that it was Lizzie. When she got inside the smoke pit, she kept her umbrella open, then tried to reach for her cigarettes in her pocket.

"Need help?" I took the umbrella and held it above her.

She took out a cigarette and lit it. "You asshole," she said. "Leaving group. We didn't even get to give you feedback. You owe us all an amends."

I shrugged and looked down at the ground.

"Well," she said. "I'm waiting."

"I'm sorry," I said. "I just—I don't know what happened."

"You know exactly what happened. You got scared. And you ran. Been there, done that." She laughed. "Just don't do it anymore, okay?" She shot me a smile. It was really beautiful, her smile.

"I won't."

"I'm watching you," she said.

"Yeah," I said. "I see you too."

"Do you?"

"Yes, I do."

And then at the same time we both said, "I see you. *Yes, I do.*" We laughed and laughed. But what was so funny? *I see you, Zach. I see you.*

REMEMBERING

"What does the road represent?"

"What does any road represent?"

Adam shot me that famous snarky smile of his.

"I know, I know. What does the road represent *for me*?" I stared at the picture of his two kids. They looked happy. I thought of Santiago.

"Staring at that picture of my sons again, huh?"

"Yeah." I tried to concentrate on our conversation. Sometimes that was hard. "The road? I don't know, Adam. I mean that. I mean, it's a road. It's going somewhere. But I don't know where."

"In your other drawings, the ones you do at school, do they have people in them?"

"No."

"What do you draw?"

"Cityscapes. That's what Mr. Drake calls them. Buildings and alleys and streets."

"Empty streets?"

"Yeah. But sometimes lots of cars."

"Any drivers in those cars?"

"No. Just cars."

"No people in your cityscapes?"

"Guess not."

"Guess what cities are full of?"

"Yeah, okay, they're full of people."

"But no people in Zachland."

"I don't know, maybe I don't like people."

"I don't think that's true. I'm making up that you like people a lot.

You like Rafael. You liked Sharkey. You like Mr. Garcia. You like Amit—I think you do."

"Yeah, I like him."

"You liked Mark. You like Lizzie and Sheila and Kelly and—is there anyone in Group you don't like?"

"No. I like our group."

"Any of the therapists you don't like?"

"Just one of them. He's a prick."

"Fair enough. So out of all the therapists here, you only dislike one?"

"Yeah, I guess so."

"You like people, Zach. That's not your problem."

"What is my problem?"

"Well, let's get to that."

"You know what my problem is?"

"Not exactly, no."

"But you have a theory?"

"I have a lot of theories, Zach. My theories don't matter a damn."
And then he took the conversation to exactly the place he wanted to take it.
Like I didn't notice. "Where did that sketch come from?"

"That's where they found me," I said. "By the side of a road."

"Do you remember which road?"

"Yeah. There's a road that leads to Carlsbad. An old highway going east out of El Paso. That's where they found me."

"Do you remember anything else?"

"I was shivering."

"Were you cold?"

"I was dying."

"Were you?"

"Yeah. Alcohol withdrawal. Really bad. It can kill you, you know?"

"Yes, I *do* know. Do you remember who found you?"

"A cop. I don't remember anything much after that. I was in a hospital. I dream it a lot." I took my eyes off the floor and looked at Adam. "I almost died."

I HATE THEM FOR LOVING ME

-1-

Every hour or so, I'd wake up and look around the room. It was just one of those nights. I'd stare at the clock. 12:45. 12:46. 12:47 and then I'd fall back asleep. But then I'd be at it again. 1:48. 1:49. 1:50.

Rafael was reading. When he couldn't sleep, he'd just read. Around 3 o'clock in the morning, Amit was up. *Let me out*, he mumbled. *Let me out*. He looked like he was headed toward the door. It was raining and thundering and being out there in your underwear didn't seem like a good idea. Sleepwalkers didn't bother Rafael one damned bit. He got up and gently led Amit back to bed. But Amit didn't stay put. He sat up on his bed and mumbled, "I didn't do it. Just let me out."

"Okay," Rafael said, "we'll let you out as soon as the sun rises."

"Now. Let me out now." He looked like he was about to get up and out of bed again so Rafael walked over to his bed and shook him awake.

Amit looked up at Rafael, confused.

"You were talking. You were going to get up again, so I thought I should just wake you up."

Amit nodded. "I didn't do anything—I didn't do anything, did I?"

"No."

"Good. Sometimes I do things that I'm embarrassed about."

"Like what?"

"I urinate in corners of the room. Embarrassing things like that."

"You were saying *Let me out*. From where? Do you remember?"

"No, I don't remember." He stared at Rafael. "Don't you sleep?"

"Yeah. Just not tonight."

"I hate this fucking place," he said. "They're overmedicating me. That's why I walk in my sleep."

"Maybe. Maybe not. You might be sleepwalking anyway—even if you weren't overmedicated."

"What the fuck do you know?"

Rafael smiled one of his clear-your-throat smiles. "Sleepwalking can be a symptom of PTSD."

"You a fucking therapist or what?"

He picked up his book. "Nope. It's called reading. You should try it."

"Fuck you." And then Amit got real quiet. "Are you serious? Sleep-walking? It can be, you know, a part of this trauma thing?"

"The guy before you, Sharkey, he was a serious sleepwalker. So I read a book about it."

"You still have the book?"

"Yeah."

"Will you let me borrow it?"

"Sure."

"Will you teach me how to paint?"

"Just paint."

"I'm not any good."

"Do it for therapy. You can go to art school later."

"You're a wiseass, you know that?"

"Yeah, I know that."

I don't know why I didn't join the conversation. I just liked listening. I think a part of me was trying to memorize Rafael's voice. So I could carry it around with me when he left.

"Can I ask you question, Amit?"

"Yeah."

"How many of these places have you been in before?"

"Does it show?"

"I guess it does."

"Three or four."

"Three? Or four?"

"Four. These places don't work."

"Then why are you here?"

"I got into some—."

Rafael finished his sentence. "Legal trouble."

"Yeah."

"Drug of choice?"

"Cocaine, heroin, booze. Take your pick."

"When did you start?"

"Oh, I don't know. I was probably fourteen. Some guy called me a nigger. A few days later, someone spray painted our garage with that nice word on it."

"So you decided to get wasted."

"It hurt."

"I bet it did."

"Not that you'd know."

"Not that I'd know." Rafael took a deep breath, almost like he was smoking a cigarette. "So you got wasted."

"So I should have wasted him instead?"

"Those your only options?"

Amit laughed, you know one of those smartass laughs that sort of said *fuck you*. "You like to screw around with people's heads?"

"Not really. Sometimes, I just like to ask a lot of questions."

"It's a wonder you haven't gotten your ass kicked."

"How do you know I haven't?" Rafael was laughing at himself. Again. "What kind of crowd do you hang with that people get violent when you ask questions?"

"Normal people."

"You hang out with normies?"

"Guess I don't."

"Sometimes, when people ask questions, that means they care."

"You one of those people?"

"Yeah. I'm one of those people."

Amit didn't say anything.

"You know, Amit, you can make this place work for you. How long have you been clean?"

"Eighteen days."

"Eighteen days is good. Eighteen days is great. You know what they say—if you can stay clean for a day, you can stay clean for a lifetime."

"Who says that?"

"I say that."

"Bet you were a wine drinker."

"Bet you're right."

"Bet you drank nice wine too."

"Real nice wine."

"Bet you drank alone too."

"The only way to drink. That way there aren't any distractions." Rafael laughed. I could tell it was one of those laughs that meant sad. "I quit for a day."

"A lifetime, huh?"

"I know you're pissed off at the world. For all I know, you've got a right."

"I live in a fucking racist world."

"Yes, you do."

"You live in that world too, dude. And what are you fucking doing about it?"

"I'm talking to you."

That made Amit laugh. It was a nice laugh. A good laugh. I don't know how I knew that, but it just seemed that way to me. I didn't know I was laughing too.

"Are you awake over there, dude?"

"Yeah," I said.

"You're pretty quiet."

"Guess I am."

"You like it here, Zach?" I let Amit's question just hang there. In the air. "It's good."

"What's so fucking good about it?"

"The food is good." That made Amit and Rafael laugh. I mean they were laughing. And, well, I just laughed with them.

I don't know how long we laughed, but it seemed like a long time. And then everything was quiet and still. The only light in the room came from Rafael's lamp. As I looked across the room, everything seemed like it was a painting. A quiet and strange painting that told a story—and you had to look at the painting a long time in order to figure out what the story was about.

-2-

I liked weekends. This place was a lot like school. Group was homeroom every morning. Then two classes, then lunch, then two classes in the afternoon.

We were angry, so we had anger classes.

We were addicts, so we had addiction classes.

We were co-dependent, so we had co-dependent classes.

Twice a week, we had art therapy. Other kinds of classes too. The ones where we had to act things out, play roles—I hated those. Hated those. In the evenings, meetings three days a week. "Hi guys, I'm Zach, I'm an alcoholic." Weekends. Time enough to do our homework and hang out and smoke and read. Weekends were good.

When I woke up on Saturday morning, Rafael and Amit were gone. I took a breath and then another and then another. That reminded me that I had another Breathwork session with Susan in the afternoon. I was tired. I wanted to crawl back into bed and just sleep. I looked at the clock. It was 8:20. On weekends they let us sleep in until 8:30—then we had to get up. If I went back to bed, one of the counseling assistants would knock and come in and smile politely and say, "Time to get up." I hated that.

I couldn't decide if I wanted to smoke a cigarette first or take a shower first. I decided to take a shower. When I was drying myself off, I looked at myself in the mirror. I stared at my scar just underneath my right nipple. I touched it. The whole scene came flooding into my head, my brother holding me down, a piece of glass in his hand. *I could cut you I could cut you* and then the piece of glass moving across the lower part of my right chest. I see myself, a boy of six, screaming. I see my father coming into the room and picking me up.

My dad didn't take me to the hospital. He cleaned my wound, put gauze and that suture tape that worked just like stitches. He gave me one of my mother's pills. And I slept.

-3-

I knew what I was going to do next. I was going to engage in my new addiction. I was going to read Rafael's diary. He was leaving. He would take his words and his voice with him, and I would be left with nothing but my own thoughts. I picked up his diary and read his last entry:

> I believe that there are defining moments in every human life. In each of those defining moments we experience a death. I died here. It doesn't matter anymore why I thought I came here. But I did something more important than die here. I don't know how to say this exactly except to say that I have never felt more alive. Not ever. I have never felt at home in my own body until now. My body is my home. I keep repeating that to myself. To me, those words sound like a miracle.
>
> I don't know what the exact shape of my life will take—and what the days to come will bring—except I know that I am happy and my heart is still. I know that I have fallen in love with the word surrender and know too that I can no longer live in disappointment. I have lived in disappointment all my life. I refuse the medicine of alcohol. I have taken a crooked road to arrive at the country of manhood. It will take time for me to find myself in the world again. I have a great many difficulties I have to confront. But I'm not running anymore.
>
> I feel whole. I *am* whole.
>
> Before I came to this place I wanted to walk out into the desert and die. Now, I want only to live. I want to write those words again and again. I hear those words and understand them in all their beauty and awesome weight. I want to live. That is all I know today. I want to live.

I knew I was a thief for reading these words, for stealing them. I was ashamed of myself. And yet, I wanted to keep Rafael's words, take them and keep them and put them somewhere inside of me so maybe I could have what he had.

Rafael had come here nearly broken. And now he wasn't so broken anymore. Sharkey, he'd left before he could do the work. Maybe it was too hard and too painful and too impossible to do what Rafael had done.

I wondered if I had it in me. I wondered if I could say with conviction what Rafael had written: *I want to live.*

I knew I wasn't letting go. I knew I was still living in a small and dark room. But there was a door to the room. And a window. And I could see that there was a sky out there.

-4-

On Monday morning, I waited for Rafael and Amit to leave the room before I got up out of bed. I walked over to Rafael's desk to look for his journal—but it wasn't there. It was like looking for one of my dad's bottles of bourbon, and discovering that all the bottles were gone. I didn't know what to do, and, for an instant, Mr. Anxiety was back. I hated that guy. I couldn't breathe and everything in my head was racing. I sat at my desk and forced myself to breathe. Susan said I could calm myself down if I concentrated.

So I concentrated.

I breathed in and then breathed out. I tried to pull my breath out from my feet up into my head. And after a few minutes, I could feel myself calmer. I took out my notebook and began writing:

> Rafael is leaving tomorrow. He's going back to wherever he came from. He lives in LA though he made a joke saying that nobody really lives in LA. Everybody just drives there. It wasn't that funny a joke. Rafael is leaving tomorrow. Rafael is leaving tomorrow. Sharkey is gone. Maybe he's dead by now. Mark went back to a sad marriage. Sharkey went back

to the streets. Rafael is going back home. He's going be sober and he's going to keep writing. He told me he was going to write a novel. I asked him about what. About this place, he said. But I knew that he was only joking. But I wish he would write a novel about this place because if he did, he would keep me in his head and I wanted to live in his head, to stay alive there.

I shut my notebook. I was too sad to write anymore.

At Group I didn't say anything. My Check-in was easy: "No lies," I said. That was a lie. "No secrets," I said. That was a lie. I don't know what went on in group. I just kept staring at the floor. Adam asked me if I wanted to give Lizzie feedback about something. I shook my head *no*. I was vaguely aware of the fact that Amit's drawing of his addiction was being discussed. Adam asked if I had any feedback for Amit. I shook my head *no*.

At the end of group, we held hands in a circle like we always did. When Rafael reached for my hand I shook my head *no*. No. *I don't want to fucking hold your hand.* That's the look I gave him. I crossed my arms and locked them in place and looked down at the floor.

I didn't go to any groups the rest of the day.

I hung out in Cabin 9 and stared at the calendar.

I lay in my bed and tried to make my brain go blank. I could do that. I could be blank. I could make myself numb. I knew how to do that. It was a skill. It was an art. One of the counseling assistants came into the room. "You should be at sessions," he said. His voice was firm. He waited for some kind of response.

I looked at him blankly.

"You know there are consequences for missing sessions."

The thought entered my head that I could attack this guy like I attacked the windshields of parked cars. I didn't need a baseball bat. Hell no. I could just go for the guy. They'd throw me out. I could leave and— and then what?

The guy finally left the room.

I was glad. I knew that none of the therapists would bother me. I closed my eyes and took a breath, then another, then another. Somewhere along in my breathing, I fell asleep. When I woke up, it was night. Amit was at his desk working on a painting.

Rafael was packing.

I watched them in silence. Rafael looked up and noticed I was awake. "Hi," he said.

I waved.

"You wanna talk about it?"

"What?"

"You know what I mean."

"No."

"Can I tell you something?"

"Can I stop you?"

"You're acting like a five-year-old."

"Like you'd know."

"I *would* know. I *do* know." He had this fierce look in his face. "Refusing to talk—that's what five-year-olds do when they're mad."

"I'm not mad."

Amit peered over his desk. "Yes, you are. You're one pissed-off dude."

"Fuck you, Amit."

Amit laughed. "Fuck you too, Zach."

Rafael shot us both a look.

"Talk, Zach. Talk to me."

"You are not the boss of me."

Rafael shook his head. "I'm leaving tomorrow, Zach."

I turned and faced the wall. I wanted all the words in the world to disappear. I wanted all the faces that had ever made me feel anything to disappear too. All of them.

I fell back asleep.

I dreamed that Rafael was sitting at the foot of my bed. He was singing softly and I had my eyes closed. But when I opened my eyes, I was awake. And Rafael wasn't there.

I got up, put on my shoes and made sure I had cigarettes in the pocket of my coat. I walked out to the smoking pit. The wind had picked up and it was cold and I wondered if there were more storms left in this year's winter. I wondered where Sharkey was and wondered if he'd gone back home or if he was going to jail for stealing his father's money or if he was out in some pool hall, conning some poor sucker into playing him a game of pool.

I wondered where Rafael was going.

I wondered why I couldn't make myself talk to him.

As I reached the smoking pit, I noticed someone was standing there. For a second, I thought it was my brother and my heart started beating faster. I stopped, then moved a little closer. It was Amit. My heart grew calm again.

I took a cigarette and lit it. "You're up late."

"Yeah, couldn't sleep. So you're talking now, huh?"

"I'm not much of a talker."

"You did okay when you told your story."

"I don't like to talk. I'm, well, you know, inarticulate."

"That's bullshit, Zach. You're killing me."

"It's not bullshit."

"Yes, it is. You just don't want to talk about what's fucking inside."

"Oh, like you're really good at that."

"I suck at that. I suck at talking about what's inside of me. But you don't, Zach. You just—I don't know. You just don't want to, I guess. Ah, what the fuck do I know?" He lit another cigarette. "You want to know what I think? I think you don't know how to say goodbye to Rafael. I think that fucking scares you to death, Zach. That's what I think."

"Thanks for the feedback."

"Don't be an asshole."

This is what I wanted to tell him—these are the words I wanted to say, *I'm a five-year-old boy who doesn't know how to sing and the only songs I have ever heard, the only real songs I've ever heard, came from Mr. Garcia's trumpet and Rafael's voice and they didn't teach me how to get at my own song. They didn't. And I hate them. I hate them for loving me. I hate them for leaving me. They sang to me. And now I'm more alone than I have ever been. Yeah, Amit, I'm fucking scared.* "I'm sorry," I whispered. "I don't mean to be an asshole."

We smoked the rest of our cigarettes in silence.

REMEMBERING

I have been keeping another secret.

I have imaginary conversations with people.

Sometimes I talk to my mom. I ask her why she's so sad. I ask her if she ever tried not being sad. I ask her if there was a time before the sadness came and stayed. I ask her if she and Dad ever had a normal life, if they laughed and held hands and took walks. I ask her what it's like just to live inside her head. I ask her if her head is big place or a small place, a scary place or a beautiful place. I ask her why she wanted to touch me like a husband. I ask her if she knew what she was doing or if it was the medications. I ask her if she loves me and I always feel bad when I ask her that because it makes me sound so desperate. I ask and ask and ask.

She never answers.

I talk to my dad. I say, "Hi, Dad."

He is sitting in a chair with a drink in his hand. "Hi," he says. His voice sounds dull and far away.

I ask him, "What would it be like if you didn't drink every day? What would it be like inside you?"

He just looks at me.

He doesn't answer me either.

And I talk to Santiago. "What made you have all that hate inside you?"

"Mom and Dad are all fucked up—haven't you noticed?"

"Yes," I say. "Are you getting back at them?"

"Something like that."

"But what about me? Why do you *hate me*? What did I do?"

And then I hear him say, "You were born."

I am remembering having all these imaginary conversations. If they're not real, why do they make me so sad?

ANOTHER SEASON

I've lived eighteen years in a season called *sadness* where the weather never changed. I guess I believed it was the only season I deserved. I don't know how but something started to happen. Something around me. Something inside me. Something beautiful. Something really, really beautiful.

THE MONSTER OF GOODBYE

-1-

Adam took the copper medal out of a small box. Time to say goodbye. To Rafael who'd been here for sixty days, Rafael who had been my
roommate, Rafael who had calmed me down from all my bad dreams
and sang to me, Rafael who had stayed alert for Sharkey and Amit, the
sleepwalkers.

I stared at the medal that Adam was dangling from a string. And then
Lizzie took the medal and started talking. "I press into this medal all my…"
I couldn't listen. I was half aware that people were talking. I kept staring at
the floor. I felt Maggie nudging me, handing me the medal. I kept my eyes
on the floor.

I looked at Rafael. Then I moved my eyes back to the stain on the carpet.

The room was quiet. I heard Adam's voice but the words were
jumbled and I could hear a distant echo in my ears. And then his voice
disappeared and I felt alone, like I was in a dark and silent room and there
was nothing in the world except the darkness. I was a just a shadow. But
Adam's voice pushed itself in the room. The voice felt like a hand that was
tugging at my arm. "Zach? Zach?"

I was in the room again even though I knew I'd been there all along.
I looked at Adam, then at Rafael. And then I heard myself say, "Do I have
to say something?"

"Don't you want to?"

"I can't."

"Why can't you?"

"I can't." I kept focusing on the stain on the carpet. I wanted to find a bat and a windshield. That's what I wanted.

"I'll miss you, Zach." Rafael's voice was softer than it had ever been. I wondered why he was speaking because that wasn't in the goodbye rules. The goodbye rules were that you listened to what everybody was pressing into the goodbye medal. Rafael was breaking the rules and I wanted to yell at him and I opened my mouth to speak but it seemed like it had been sewn shut. Rafael smiled and whispered, "I love you, Zach. You know that, don't you?"

He said that in front of the whole group and it just wasn't right and my lips kept trembling and then I swallowed real hard and made myself talk because I wanted my voice to be stronger than my trembling. "You don't. You don't love me."

Rafael's face was calm. "I do, Zach. I want you to know that."

I placed my hand over my eyes and shook my head.

Do not feel. Do not feel.

I knew what Adam was going to say. He was going to say, "I see you, Zach." But he didn't see me. No one saw me. No one in the whole fucking world saw me.

-2-

I went to all my groups. But I wasn't there. I could make myself not be there. It wasn't a trick really. It was, well, normal. Normal for me. In the middle of the afternoon, I was too tired to keep my eyes open. I told Jennie, the afternoon therapist, that I felt sick. She studied my face. I don't know what she was seeing. "Give yourself what you need." I decided to give myself a nap.

I went to Cabin 9 and stared at Rafael's packed bags. I lay down on my bed and looked up at the ceiling. I couldn't fall asleep. Maybe I didn't want to fall asleep. The thought entered my head that Rafael would be coming to get his things and I knew that I couldn't handle seeing him. Goodbye was a monster that was swallowing me up. That monster was too strong for a guy named Zach. I had to leave Cabin 9 before Rafael came back. *I had to leave.* I couldn't breathe and the thought entered my mind that I was never going to get better, not ever.

I was going to live forever in this in-between space, somewhere between the living and the dying. I was stuck there.

I don't know how I managed, but I scrawled out a note to Rafael and placed it on his desk, next to his journal: *Don't hate me.*

Then I ran out of the room.

No one sees me no one sees me no one sees me.

I found myself sitting in front of the tree named Zach.

The sky seemed so dark. I lay down on the ground. I had another strange dream. I was walking alone in the desert and I saw two men coming toward me. One of the men was my father and the other man was Rafael— and then all of a sudden Adam was standing right next to me and he said to me: "You have to choose, Zach." And I knew I wanted to pick Rafael because that's what my heart was telling me, but I didn't. I didn't pick him. I picked my father. And then me and my father were walking together in the desert and when I looked close, I could see that we were both holding pints of bourbon and we were drinking and there was blood all around us. Father and son. Blood.

When I woke up, it was dark and I was shivering from the cold.

I thought about the dream. I thought about the bourbon and the blood. I knew that I was trembling and I didn't know if that was from the cold or from the dream. I picked myself up from the ground and made my way to the smoking pit.

I smoked a cigarette. And then another. And then another. I was numb. I wasn't feeling. That was okay. I concentrated and held on to the numbness. This is what I really wanted, not to feel. I wanted to be like an ice cube that refused to melt. If I could just stay exactly like this, then I would never be sad again, not ever—if I could just hold on to this numbness. If I could just do that, then the name Rafael couldn't hurt me. The name Santiago couldn't hurt me either. And the memory of my father and mother, that would mean nothing.

I looked up at the stars and envied them. God didn't make them feel things.

I walked into Cabin 9. Amit was working on a painting. He looked up at me. "I'm really pissed."

"So what?"

"I don't get you, Zach."

"You don't have to get me. It's not part of your work here."

"That's really shitty, dude, you know, how you treated Rafael."

"Rafael will live."

"You're a piece of shit, you know that?"

"I don't want to talk."

"What's wrong with you?"

"Me? What's wrong with me? Nothing's wrong with me."

"Then why don't you just leave?"

"Shut up, Amit."

I threw myself on my bed and looked up the ceiling. I was holding on to the numbness. It was almost like drinking. I swear it was just like that.

I heard Amit get up from his desk and heard him as he put on his coat. "Rafael left something for you, asshole. It's on your desk."

I pretended not to hear him.

I heard him leave the room.

When I fell asleep, I had the dream again, the dream with Rafael and my father and Adam in the desert. I saw Rafael walk away when he got close to me, but my father offered me a drink. I woke just as I reached for the bottle he was handing to me.

4

I didn't go to Group. I pretty much just hung out in Cabin 9. The only place I went the whole day was to the smoking pit. People said hi. I didn't have the energy to say hi back to them. In the afternoon, I kept staring at Rafael's journal—that was the gift he'd left for me. There was an envelope with my name written on it. I didn't open it. I picked up the envelope and studied it. I tossed it back on the desk.

When Amit came back in the room, he glared at me. I looked back at him blankly.

The dreams got worse. I woke up screaming but I didn't want to think about the dream. I heard Amit's voice. "I can't stand to watch you, Zach. You're dying, dude."

I heard me answer him. "They're just dreams."

"They're killing you."

What do you know? That's what I wanted to say. But I didn't say anything at all.

-5-

I went to Group. I didn't interact, but I went. I stared at the floor mostly. During the break, I figured maybe I should just go hang out in Cabin 9. But before I reached the cabin, I heard Adam's voice. "Two o'clock, Zach. Can you come see me?"

I shrugged.

"Is that a yes?"

"Yeah, okay." And then I looked at him. "What's the point, Adam? I'm just wasting your time."

He started to say something—but he stopped himself. "Two o'clock, Zach?"

"Yeah, okay."

I walked into Cabin 9 and stared at Rafael's journal. I flipped through the pages and stared at the neat handwriting. I found myself reading one of entries:

> In the dream, all the trees were bare and leafless, the winter
> night dark and starless. I was wandering around without a coat. I
> don't remember what I was desperately searching for. I knew my life
> depended on finding whatever it was I was in search of. But I was
> exhausted and hungry and my only thought was how cold I was. I had

never been that cold. I woke up and it was still dark, the blanket on the floor. I covered myself up and wondered about my search.

I was a wanderer on the earth. A nomad. That was my last thought before I fell asleep again.

The next morning when I woke all I could think of was leaves. I had this image in my mind as I walked the labyrinth: I was standing in the sun and green leaves were floating down from heaven.

It was snowing leaves. And I was young again.

I ran my fingers across the words. Little pieces of paper filled with words.

I pictured Rafael standing at the center of the labyrinth, the sun shining and the leaves of summer raining down on him. I pictured him smiling and laughing. I tried to picture myself standing right next to him.

-6-

"What's going on up there?" Adam tapped his temple with his finger.

"I don't know."

"Okay, what's going on here?" He tapped his heart.

"I don't know."

"Yes, you do."

"I didn't say goodbye to Rafael."

"I know."

"I couldn't."

"I get that."

"Do you?"

"I guess goodbye can be a monster."

"Yeah."

"It's not bad to love someone so much that it hurts."

"You don't know. You're not me."

"Strange as this may sound, Zach, I *do* know something about pain.

And I *do* know something about love. And that's a fact."

"But you don't know anything about me. You say you see me, but you don't. You don't." I felt my lips trembling. *No no no no no don't cry, Zach, no don't cry don't cry* but my body wasn't listening to what I was telling it. I got up to leave but I when I stood up, I couldn't move. I felt Adam's arms around me. I leaned into his shoulder and cried. "I'm lost," I whispered. "Adam, I'm lost." And then I started saying things that I didn't know I was going to say, words stuck inside me. "I want my father, Adam. I want him. I don't know where he went. It hurts. It hurts. Adam, it hurts."

-7-

I kept staring at the envelope with my name on it. I took a breath and opened it. And there they were, Rafael's words:

Zachariah—

There are a good many things that I want to say to you and yet I don't know exactly what those things are. I've learned over the years that if I just begin writing, then I somehow manage to find the right words. I think you already know that I'm a true believer in words. I believe in their power, in their ability to hurt and their ability to heal. Maybe that's why I'm leaving you my journal—because writing in these pages was an important part of the work I did here. Maybe that's why I'm writing to you right now—because I want to say something that might help you. I don't mean that in a condescending way either, Zach. I'm fifty-three and you're eighteen but that doesn't mean I'm smarter or even that I'm somehow more enlightened. The only thing I really know is that I'm finally getting to know myself. I hope, Zach, that you get there before I did. I hope you don't wait.

You once confessed to me that you had imaginary conversations with people. I have those imaginary conversations too. Here's one I had with you:

Me: Are you going to say goodbye?

Zach: I can't.

Me: Will you do me a favor? Will you stop looking at the floor and look at me?

Zach: You're making me feel like a little boy.

Me: Then don't act like one.

Zach: You're going to give me a lecture as a parting gift?

Me: Will you just look at me?

Then you, Zach, you look at me. And I hold out my journal to you and say: I have this gift for you.

Then you, Zach, say: I can't take that. They're your words.

Me: Maybe I want you to have my words.

You, Zach, shake your head.

Me: Take it. Then I place my journal in your hands.

Zach: I have a confession to make. I read your journal. You look away, afraid to see the expression on my face.

But I'm smiling and say: I know.

Zach: You know?

Me: Yes, Zach, I know.

Zach: Why didn't you tell me you knew?

Me: For the same reason you didn't tell me you were reading it. Maybe we're both a little too in love with keeping secrets. Maybe we should stop.

You, Zach, hold the journal in your hands and nod.

And then I look around the room one last time before I leave.

And then you, Zach, say: I guess I have to say goodbye.

Me: This isn't goodbye, Zach.

Zach: When someone leaves, it means goodbye.

Me: Not always.

Zach: People come here—and then they leave. And after they leave, they want to forget they've been here.

Me: Some people, maybe so. I'll see you again, Zach. I'll see you again because I want to see you again. And because I want to see you again, it will happen. I will make it happen.

And then you walk me to the van that's waiting to take me to the airport and I say: You're the sweetest boy in the whole world.

Zach: I'm not.

Me: Don't argue with me, Zachariah. And then I look into your face one last time, smile and get into the van and leave.

That's my imaginary conversation.

Zach, I knew you couldn't say goodbye to me. It hurts. If it hurts a fifty-three-year-old man, then how much more would it hurt an eighteen-year-old boy? But here's the problem, Zach. If you want to be alive, you can't avoid pain.

I know something about avoidance—I was an expert at that. But avoiding pain, Zach, isn't possible. Just because life has hurt me or you or all the people that are here doesn't mean we have to live in pain all the time. I lived in pain because I chose to live in pain. Somewhere along the line, I fell in love with the idea of tragedy, the idea that I was destined to live a tragic life. I had this romantic idea about the life of a writer and what he was supposed to suffer. I was Rafael, the artist, the superior being who created beauty out of his own misery. Somehow, I made my own pain a kind of god. I worshipped that god with all that I was. As Sharkey would say, *That is so fucked up, dude.* Inexplicably, though, and this is the part that *really is inexplicable,* I somehow avoided the real pain—the pain that was killing me. I avoided it altogether.

I think you're like me, Zach. I think you live in pain even as you don't want to feel. You're beautiful and brilliant and in love with words and yet, like me, you remain in an inarticulate space where words are stuck somewhere between your heart and your throat.

Speak, Zach.

Do you know the story of Zachariah in the Bible? I think you should read that story. God struck him dumb for his lack of faith. He was unable to utter a single word. He regained his ability to speak when his son was born. And he sang. Zachariah sang! Sing, Zach. If I could sing to my monster, then you can sing to yours.

Rafael

I read the letter over and over and over. And then I opened his journal and I saw he'd written his cell phone number and his address. I thought of the imaginary goodbye scene that Rafael had written. *I will see you again because I want to see you again.*

For a moment, I thought of the word *happy* and it was a word that just, well, it felt like it was visiting me. I knew it wouldn't last for very long and I'd be sad again and then it would be worse because it's one thing to be sad and it's another thing to be sad once you've been happy. Being sad after you've been happy is the worst thing in the world.

I must have been smiling because Amit asked me, "What are you smiling about?"

"I was just thinking."

"Well, I don't know what you have to smile about after the shitty way you treated Rafael in group. I mean, dude, that really sucked."

I didn't know what to say. "I'm sorry I behaved like a five-year-old. I'm sorry."

Amit smiled. "Yeah, just like Rafael said."

"Yeah, just like Rafael said. I'll make amends to the group."

"I'll remind you. In case you forget."

"Okay."

"Okay. Good." Amit studied his painting. "What do you think?" He held up his painting. It was a road. It didn't look like my road. Well, why should it? It was *his* road. There were tepees and cacti and all kinds of stuff on either side of the road. His painting was a lot more complicated than mine.

"You want to tell me what it means?"

"I'm taking it into Group."

I was glad Amit wasn't mad at me anymore. It was weird, but I felt like talking. Maybe I was tired of my internal life. My sad internal life. "Amit? What's the worst thing that's ever happened to you?"

He got this look on his face, like maybe he didn't want to answer. But he *did* answer. "In prison—well, bad things happened."

I think I knew what he was telling me. "Do you think about it a lot?"

"Sometimes, I have dreams."

I nodded. I didn't know what to say. "I'm sorry those bad things happened."

He nodded. "Sometimes I wish it would all go away."

"Yeah."

"But I guess things don't go away just because we want them to."

"Guess not."

"What's the worst thing that happened to you?"

"I lost my parents." I didn't know I was going to say that. I didn't even know if that was true. But I knew it *was* true. I'd never said it before.

"You wanna talk about it?"

"No," I said. "I can't." I thought of what Rafael had said, that I should be put on contract regarding the two words *I can't.*

"That's cool." Amit kept staring at his painting as if he were trying to analyze himself. "You wanna go have a cigarette?"

"Yeah," I said.

When we stepped out into the night air, I could hear Amit talking to me. I mean, it was good to hear a human voice. It was good that the voice was right there next to me. But I wasn't really listening to what he was saying. I thought of Rafael and I kept seeing him as he sang to his monster. I kept seeing Adam's face and it was a kind face, a good face, and I kept seeing tears on Lizzie's face and I thought she must have been really pretty when she was young and I wondered where I was going. I thought of the road in my drawing.

As we reached the smoking pit, I heard Amit say that the weather was changing. "It's like you can almost feel winter going away."

That was a nice thought. A good thought. A beautiful thought.

Summertime. It was a song. It was a season. I wondered if that season would ever live inside of me.

REMEMBERING

"I keep having this dream. You're in it, and Rafael's in it, and my dad's in it."

"What's the dream?"

So I told him all about the dream.

"Are you mad at me in the dream?"

"Why would I be mad?"

"I'm the guy that's making you decide. Is that how you see me—as the guy that's making you choose between—," Adam stopped. He looked at me. "Let's forget about me for just—tell me, what does your father represent in the dream?"

"He's my father. My father represents my father."

"But you said you really wanted to go with Rafael."

"I do. I mean, in the dream I do. In the dream, I want to choose him. But I don't. I wind up going with my father."

"You choose drinking."

"Well, no, I choose my father. But, well, yeah, I guess I mean that's how it turns out."

"You choose your father. You choose drinking. Your father represents what, Zach?"

"My old life."

"And Rafael represents what?"

"My new life, I guess."

"Yes, I think so. And in the dream you choose your old life over your new life. How does that make you feel?"

"But he's my father. I'm supposed to pick my father."

"Are you?"

I just looked at Adam. "Yes."

"Zach, the last time you were in my office—"

"When I sort of fell apart."

"Yeah, when you sort of fell apart. You said you missed your father. You said it hurt."

"Yeah."

"Can I ask you a question?" He didn't wait for me to answer. "Do you believe you'll see Rafael again?"

"Yes. I guess I do. I hope so. I'd like to."

"What will stop you from seeing him again?"

"Nothing—I guess."

"You guess? Don't you know how to get in touch with him?"

"Sure I do. I can reach him if I want."

"Do you want?"

"Yes."

"Okay. And do you believe you'll see your father again?"

I couldn't answer his question. I didn't know how to answer it.

Adam was studying my face. "You avoid questions about your family."

"I guess I do."

"Yeah, I guess you do. Can I ask you something, Zach? Can I be really honest with you?"

"Yeah, you can be honest."

"How much longer are you going to put off dealing with what got you here?"

"I'm trying."

"The sketch was good work. It was, Zach. And the work you did with Rafael, that was good work."

"What do you mean the work I did with Rafael? Rafael's my friend."

Adam looked at me. He had that careful look on his face and then he said, "You let yourself love him. That's good work for someone who doesn't like to feel."

"Yeah, I guess," I said. "But I didn't say goodbye to him."

"I know. Can you tell me why?"

"Don't you have a theory about that?"

"I don't care about my theory."

"It hurt too much—to say goodbye."

"Why?"

"Because."

"Because why?"

"Because—"

"Will you do something for me, Zach?"

"Sure."

"Repeat after me. *I*."

"I."

"*Love*."

"Love."

"*Rafael*."

"Rafael."

"*I love Rafael*."

"I love Rafael."

Adam nodded and looked straight at me. "That's hard for you to say, isn't it?"

"Yeah, it's hard."

"Even though it's true, it's hard."

"Yes."

"It's normal to love people, Zach."

"I'm not normal, Adam."

"I get that. But I think you fight—." He stopped and searched for a word or a thought. "You fight yourself, Zach. And you keep fighting yourself. And it's killing you because you're fighting the best part of yourself."

"I—." I didn't even know what I wanted to say. I was staring at the floor again. I was back to that.

"Do you believe that Rafael loves you? Do you think that's true?"

"That's what he said. But what does that mean?"

"Could it mean he cares about you? Could it mean that he thinks what happens to you matters?"

"Yes. I guess so."

"You guess so? Let's just say Rafael loves you. Why? Why does he love you? Does he have ulterior motives? Does he have selfish or unhealthy intentions? Is he some kind of pervert?"

"Is that what you think?"

"No. That's not what I think. I want to know what you think, Zach. Why does Rafael love you? What's your theory?"

"Because I remind him of his son. Because he could be a father to me. And he always wanted that—to be a father."

"Yes. Yes, I think that's true. But you think that's the only reason?"

"I don't know."

"Is it possible that Rafael sees you?"

"Yes. It's possible."

"You know what I'm making up? I'm making up that Rafael left you his journal because he believed that you'd find something in there that would help you." Adam got this look on his face, the look that said an idea had just entered his head. "The road in your sketch—it's going somewhere. You don't know where. I don't know where. No one knows, Zach. And Rafael's journal, that's his map, that's his road. Do you understand what I'm trying to tell you?"

"Yes, I think so."

"That road, where you're lying next to your dead dog Lilly, that road led you here, Zach. And it's going to lead somewhere else after you leave. You gotta get up, Zach. You're not dead. The road is waiting for you."

THE LAST STORM

-1-

"Keep breathing, Zach, you're doing just fine." Susan's voice was firm but soft as I breathed. I focused on bringing the air out of my feet to the top of my head. When I'd brought up all the air out of my body, I'd let it out. Not too fast, not too slow. Steady. My arms and hands were numb but that's what always happened in Breathwork, parts of my body began to feel tingly, numb and other parts felt heavy. I had my eyes closed and thought of nothing else but my breathing. I was vaguely aware of Susan's presence. During our sessions, she only spoke when she sensed I needed encouragement.

And then something happened that had never happened before. There it was right in front of me. My brother with a gun, a grin on his face. And then I could see blood on the floor, like spilled water. Santiago pointed the gun at me, then laughed, then pointed the gun at himself, then laughed and then the whole scene turned blank and all I could see was red. I felt Susan's hand lightly running over my arm. "It's okay, Zach," she whispered. "It's okay. Do you want to stop?" I kept breathing, just kept breathing.

My mother's eyes were open. They were as grey as a cloud. My father was still, motionless. The world was quiet. And there was an explosion. And my brother was wearing a strange smile. I heard Susan's voice. "Let's stop now, Zach. What's your body telling you?"

"There's something pushing down," I said, "on my chest. On my arms, on my hands, on my legs. I can't move."

"You *can*, Zach. Move your legs."

I opened my eyes and lifted one leg, then the other.

"Now move your arms, Zach."

I lifted my arms toward the sky, then let them drop. "I guess I *can* move."

"Are you okay?"

"I have a headache."

"How bad? Scale of 1 to 10? How bad?"

"10."

"Okay, Zach, close your eyes." I did what she said. God, my head felt like it was going to break in half.

"I can tell you're in pain. Just relax your face, Zach. Take a breath and relax your face."

I took a breath and let the muscles of my face relax. And then something happened. There was a slight breeze that moved through my body and left through my temples. And then I saw a gun lying on the floor.

The headache was gone. I opened my eyes.

-2-

I walked back to Cabin 9 after my breathing session with Susan. I walked slowly, unsteady on my feet. I felt as if my whole body was trembling. The ground beneath me felt like a cloud and I thought I was going to fall through the earth. I managed to get to my room.

I sat at my desk. *Write whatever comes to your mind when you get back to your cabin, Zach. It's important.* I could still hear Susan's instructions, the serious look on her face, the concern. It was odd, how the therapists cared. I wondered about that. I wondered about myself. I wondered about everything. My life had been so strange since coming here. Nothing was the same. It was like I was changing. But it was odd, so odd and weird and I felt lost but not in a bad way.

I took out my journal and began to write in it. I didn't want to think. I just wanted to write whatever came out of me.

I felt a little weak after the session with Susan. It's strange, all this Breathwork. I've grown to really like it which is really weird. Weird and amazing and fantastic. The Breathwork makes something happen inside me. It makes my body feel different. And it's like, I have a body and I like having one. Imagine Zach liking the fact that he has a body. Fucking wow. I keep hearing Susan's voice inside me.

I remember telling Adam that I didn't think Susan was real. I was wrong about her. I'm wrong about a lot of things. I think I'm mostly wrong about me. I'm going to write this down so I can see the words: I don't hate myself anymore. I'm going to write it again: I don't hate myself anymore.

Zach doesn't hate Zach. Zach, I see you. Zach sees Zach.

I felt so calm. The anxiety had left. I knew it had only left for a little while, but it had made a home inside me for so long that I'd gotten used to it. But right then, as I sat in front of the words that I'd written, I felt a new word rising up inside me. Only I couldn't make out that word yet. I don't know why, but I decided I wanted to walk the labyrinth. I had this urge, this feeling inside, and I decided to trust the feeling.

I headed toward the labyrinth.

The nice day was turning cold and the wind was starting to come alive again.

As I stood at the entrance of the labyrinth, I thought of Rafael and Adam. I pictured both of them walking the labyrinth quietly. I pictured the stillness in them. I pictured their eyes. I pictured them seeing me as I watched them. I pictured me waving at them *Hi Rafael Hi Adam.* I was happy that Adam and Rafael were there with me. Even though they were only there in my head.

The wind was picking up, getting angry. I zipped up my leather jacket. I thought of my dad. It had been his when he was younger. I could almost smell him. I placed my hands in the warm pockets. *Summer.* That's the word that came to my lips. *Summer.* That was my intent—even though I didn't know exactly what that meant or why that word had come up. *Summer.* I began walking slowly toward the center of the labyrinth.

I tried to clear my head of all thoughts. At first, my mind was free of all those pieces of paper that were lying on its floor. My ears and face were getting cold and the wind seemed like it was my enemy now but I didn't care. I just kept walking and repeating the word *summer*. All I had to do was put one foot in front of the other and follow the path. I could trust the labyrinth. It would lead me to the center. I could hear the wind blowing through all the trees and the earth was moving and I knew that it would be smarter for me to stop and go back to Cabin 9 where I would be warm and safe but I didn't want to be warm and safe. I wanted to go to the center of the labyrinth. I knew I had to go. I don't know how I knew that I had to go there, *but I had to go there.*

The wind grew colder and colder.

I kept walking. I made myself stay calm.

I closed my eyes. It seemed that I could see the path, even with my eyes closed. I kept them closed and kept walking. Step by step, I walked, eyes closed. *I'll get there I'll get there I'll get there.* I pictured the large stone in the center of the labyrinth. I pictured me standing on the stone, my arms stretched out toward the storm.

Then the images started entering my head like some kind of disconnected movie. Mr. Garcia's hands on the valves of his trumpet, Sam's face as he watched me in a movie theater, Rafael's voice as he sang *Summertime*, Adam's eyes as he said *I see you, Zach* and then I saw my mother's eyes again, sightless and gray, and my father's motionless body and Lilly, the dog I loved lying dead on the ground, and Santiago whispering *eenie, meenie, miney, moe* and laughing, a gun in his hand, the gun pointing at me, then the gun aimed at his own temple and then *eenie, meenie, miney, moe* and then the sound of the gun. There was an explosion in my head as I reached the center of the labyrinth. I opened my eyes. They were there, my brother, my mother, my father. They were lying there, blood spilling on the ground.

And then they were gone.

I sat on the stone.

The snow started falling. Not a kind snow, not a lovely snow. But a harsh, cold snow that felt like pebbles flinging themselves at me.

I sat there with my brother and mother and father.

I sat with them. And then I screamed. Sometimes when I screamed or cried, it was as if it was someone else doing it, as if I were only watching me doing something from the outside. But this time I was inside of myself. I screamed. I screamed. And then I knew why I had come. I knew what I was doing. I was singing.

It was night now.

I was singing.

I was in the middle of a storm.

I screamed.

I howled.

And then I sang. I sang to the monster.

-3-

When I got back to Cabin 9, Amit asked me if there was something wrong. I didn't like the way he was looking at me. "You don't look good, dude."

"I'm tired." I was wincing. My head was throbbing.

"Where'd your color go, dude?"

I gave him a crooked smile.

He looked a little worried.

I fell into bed. I know I was trembling and my teeth were chattering. I was cold and it felt as though the storm outside was living in my body. Everything hurt and my head felt as if it were on fire.

I sensed Amit standing over me. I felt his hand on my forehead. "Dude, you're really sick."

The world I'd carried around inside me had left me. Everything was far away and I wanted to keep my eyes open because if I shut them then maybe I'd never see the light again. But then I was so tired that I just didn't care. I wanted to let the storm or the sickness or whatever just take over.

Before I fell asleep, I kept seeing my mother's gray eyes. They had always been as gray as a cloudy day. There had never been any sun in them.

I called her name. If I called her name, maybe she would come to me and sing all my sadness away. I fell asleep calling her name. *Sarah.*

My dreams went on forever. There were oceans and my father and mother and brother were swimming there. I watched them and they seemed happy and then things turned bad, my brother trying to drown my father, my mother just watching. Then the dreamed changed and Mr. Garcia was playing his trumpet and the whole world was dark and he was crying. I could see his tears and I wanted to say *don't cry don't cry* and then the dream changed again and I was alone in a place that had no sky and I knew I would never find a way to get out of that dark and skyless place. I woke up soaked in sweat. I was shivering in the cold. I dried myself off with a towel and changed into a clean t-shirt. I stumbled around and somehow managed to change the sheets. I fell into bed again.

I slept. I slept and slept and slept.

I was aware that people came and went. I heard voices. I was confused and thought I was in that hospital where everything had been white. Once, I found myself sitting in the chair next to my bed as Michael, one of the counseling assistants, changed my sheets. I watched and watched him as if he was a movie. I remember him handing me a clean t-shirt and clean underwear and asking me if I could make my way to the bathroom and change into them. I remember staring at my pale and colorless face in the bathroom and thinking that maybe I was going to die and wondering why Michael was being so kind to me.

I remember asking Amit, "Am I going to die?" He handed me a glass of water. "Drink it," he said. "Pretend it's bourbon, dude."

I drank the water.

I kept whispering my mother's name. If she would only have sung *Summertime* to me. *Sarah, Sarah,* who never had a song inside her. My dreams were heavy and I thought they'd never cease. I dreamed Sharkey, I dreamed his voice, I dreamed I found him and took him home with me. I dreamed Amit's arms. His scars were the same as Sharkey's. I dreamed I was trying to rub the scars out of their arms, trying to erase the tracks from all the needles. I dreamed I was sitting next to Sam at a movie theatre and I let him hold my hand and I whispered to him not to let go. *Don't ever let go.* I dreamed I was a boy and I was in a park and I was crying and Rafael picked me up and held me in his arms and he whispered, *Don't cry, sweet boy*. And I took my little hands and ran them across his face and he smiled at me. I dreamed my father and I were walking through the desert and I leaned into him and said *I love you, love you, Dad. I love you, love you, love you*. I dreamed Adam. He was standing at the entrance of the labyrinth and he was smiling and I wasn't afraid of his eyes and I said *Adam, I'm having a good day*.

-4-

The room was quiet and full of light. I wondered if I had died. But then I laughed. Heaven wouldn't look like Cabin 9. I sat up in bed. I felt weak but I couldn't help but smile. I felt the tears falling down my face and I wasn't ashamed of them anymore. *Look at me, I'm feeling*.

I took a shower and studied my face in the mirror. I was a little washed out. As I looked at the rest of me, I decided I was getting a little too skinny. I checked to see what color my eyes were today. They looked more green than dark. Maybe it was the way the morning sun was coming through the bathroom window. "Hi, Zach," I whispered. "I see you." And then the idea entered into my head to read something in Rafael's journal. I sat on the floor and leaned against the bed.

I flipped through the journal but then I decided to read the letter instead. I don't know why but I just needed to read it again. I kept thinking about Rafael. And I wanted to tell him that I had survived the last storm of winter. *Rafael, I sang. I sang to the monster*.

-5-

I looked up and saw Amit walking through the door. "Hey, you're alive."

"Yeah, I'm alive."

"You were down for a few days, dude."

"What's today?"

"Sunday."

"I guess I was really sick."

"Yeah, dude, you got a home visit from a doctor and everything. They almost put you in the hospital. You know, you said a lot of things in your sleep. I mean you were talking to everybody in the book—Rafael, Adam, me, Sharkey, Santiago, your mom, your dad. You were even talking to your dead dog, Lilly."

A part of me wanted to ask him what I said, but a part of me already knew. A part of me was embarrassed. And a part of me wasn't. I shot Amit a snarky smile. "So what did I say to you?"

"It was nice what you said. You kept telling me that maybe you could rub out all the tracks on my arms. I thought that was a really great thing to say."

I laughed. It was good to laugh. "I'm screwy," I said. I was tired, but I felt clean after my shower and I changed the sheets again and I spent the afternoon reading sections of Rafael's journal to Amit. I didn't think Rafael would mind. Amit was like a kid. He really liked being read to.

So that's the way we spent Sunday afternoon, listening to Rafael's words.

What a strange thing—to fall in love with Rafael's words. To fall in love with storms. To fall in love with your own life.

-6-

On Monday morning, I missed group. I had an appointment with the doctor. I hated that. I really wanted to go to group—which was strange and great all at the same time. And going to the doctor's office was a pain because I had to be taken in one of the vans by one of the counseling assistants. But it was Steve who was taking me to the doctor's office and Steve was okay. Yeah, he was a pretty good guy, I think. On the way to the doctor's office, he smiled at me and said: "Hey Zach, you're singing."

"Am I?"

"Yeah. You're singing."

"I guess I am."

"I never took a guy like you for a singer."

"Really?"

"Yeah, really."

"Well, I guess people change." That's what I said. People change. If Adam had been in the van, he would have given me a snarky smile and said, "People?"

And I would have returned his snarky smile and said, "Me, Zach. Zach changed."

And then we both would have given each other a real smile.

See, I hadn't changed that much. There I was in the van, exchanging a real conversation with Steve for an imaginary conversation with Adam.

-7-

"Zach?"

Adam looked a little confused when he saw me standing in front of his office.

"You were maybe expecting to see Amit?"

"That's exactly who I was expecting to see."

"We traded."

"You traded?"

"We switched appointments."

"Your idea or his?"

"Mine."

Adam had this very quiet smile on his face.

"What's that smile, Adam?"

"It's just that I'm surprised."

"Why are you surprised?"

"In the past, you've skipped two sessions with me."

"No, no, that's not true. I just didn't show up. I was sick one of those times."

He sort of grinned at me. "I always made up that you came to our sessions under duress."

"Not everything you make up about me is true."

He nodded but I could tell he was still smiling on the inside. "So, you're alive?"

"Yeah."

"Well, I gotta say that you're looking pretty good for someone who's spent the last four days in bed."

He motioned for me to come into his office. I sat in *my* usual chair and he sat in *his* usual chair. Everything was the same but *everything felt so new and so strange.*

"How do you feel?"

"Is this a Check-in?"

"Yeah, it's a Check-in."

"I feel spiritually connected."

"You're a wiseass, you know that?"

"Yeah." I smiled. I just kept smiling. I don't know. I was happy. "I feel good, Adam."

"I was worried about you."

"That's nice," I said.

"Are you eating?"

Yeah, I knew I was looking pretty skinny. "The doctor says I'm fine. He says I'm underweight but that I'm healthy. And I got the results to the blood work they took last week. My liver is great. No damage."

Adam nodded and then studied me. "You look different."

"I feel different."

"You want to talk about that?"

"There was a storm," I said, "and I sang to the monster."

"So now you're singing to the monster?"

"Yes."

"Explain that to me."

And so I told him about what happened in Breathwork and how I walked the labyrinth and the storm and how Rafael was there with me and how Mr. Garcia's trumpet was with me too. "And you were there too, Adam, and you told me *I see you, Zach."* I told him everything that happened. I didn't keep anything inside, and it was like I was letting out all the secrets that had been living inside me. "The secrets were killing me, Adam. They were."

"So you remembered?"

"Yeah, Adam. I remembered."

"You want to talk about it?"

"Yes."

"Are you sure?"

"Yes. I'm sure." I caught myself staring down at the floor and lifted my eyes up toward Adam. "I trust you."

"I know you do."

"Okay. It was a Saturday night. I went out with my friends. Antonio, Gloria, Tommy, Mitzie and Albert. Well, Albert and Gloria were supposed to come but they didn't make it. I don't remember why. So it was just the four of us, Antonio, Tommy, Mitzie and me. We went to this party but there wasn't much going on. And then Tommy said he knew this place out in the desert where people partied and he said there was gonna be some big bash. I'd come prepared. I'd gotten some wino on the street to buy me two bottles of Jack Daniels."

"Pints? Half-pints?"

That Adam, he always had questions.

"No, you know the bigger bottles."

He gave me that look. "Guess you *were* ready to party."

"Yeah. So we go to this place out in the desert and there's like a hundred kids out there. I mean, maybe more. And they had this fire going out there which was cool because it was December and it was cold as shit and we just partied. I mean, most people were just drinking and there was some pot being passed around."

"Did you do any pot?"

"Yeah. Some. And it was really weird because I ran into Sam."

"Who's Sam?"

"Guess I didn't tell you about Sam."

"No, guess you didn't. Who is he?"

"He's this guy who wanted to kiss me."

"When? That night?"

"No, no. See, he was this guy at school and he was kind of a jock and we hung out one night. You know, we drove around and went to a movie. And the guy was watching me more than he was watching the movie. And when he drove me home, he wanted to kiss me."

"And what did you do?"

"I asked him why he wanted to do that."

"That's what you asked him?"

"Yeah," I said. 'Why would anyone want to kiss me?'

"That's what you said?"

"Yeah."

"And did you want him to kiss you?"

"No. I just got pissed off and grabbed one of my dad's bottles and took off walking."

"Did you get real drunk that night?"

"Yeah."

"And did you think about Sam when you got drunk?"

"Yeah."

"What were you thinking?"

"I was thinking that it really made me mad that he wanted to kiss me. Why would he want to do that?"

"So you were really angry?"

"Yeah, I was."

"Didn't you do the same thing when Mr. Garcia played the trumpet for you?"

I had to think about that. "Yeah," I said. "I guess I did."

Adam nodded. He was about to say something, but then he didn't. Then he thought a moment. "Anyway, you were at this party with your friends out in the desert getting plastered and you ran into Sam."

"Yeah, I ran into Sam. Which really wigged me out because in the first place, I saw him as this really straight jock—I mean straight in the sense that I didn't figure him for a guy who liked to get high. He wasn't straight in the other way. I mean, he wanted to kiss me. So, anyway, I'm half trashed but I'm feeling really good. You know, there's this part when

I'm drinking that I feel really happy and at peace and there isn't any sadness in me. I was at that part of my high and I was so happy. And I ran into Sam and I said, 'Hi.'

"And he said, 'Hi.' And then he said, 'Are you as drunk as I am?'"

"And I said, 'I'm just feeling really good.'"

"And he laughed and said, 'I'm feeling really good too.' And then he said, 'I'm surprised you're talking to me.'"

"And I said, 'Why wouldn't I talk to you?'"

"And he said, 'Because I wanted to kiss you.'"

"'Yeah, well,' I said, 'that really wigged me out.'"

"'I thought you knew I was gay. It's not a secret.'"

"'Wow,' I said, 'really? Like everybody knows?'"

"'Yeah, everybody but you, Zach. I guess I thought you knew.'"

"And, I didn't know. I guess that made me feel really bad. I don't know why. And he kept looking at me and I just, hell, I just took a drink from my bottle of Jack and smiled and we talked some more and then he asked me if I was sure I didn't want to kiss him and I said I was sure."

"And were you sure, Zach?"

"Yeah."

"You sure?"

"Yeah."

"And then what happened, Zach?"

"I don't know. I don't remember that much. You know, I think I drank too much."

"You *think* you drank too much?"

"Okay, I drank too much. Later, I remember waking up. I was lying on the hood of Antonio's car. I remember throwing up and everything spinning and I felt really bad. And there weren't as many people around and some girl asked me if I was all right and I said I was just a little sick. And she was really nice and she gave me a bottle of water and I drank it all down and she just smiled and said there was an ice chest in her car if I wanted more. And she pointed to the car and I walked over there and drank another bottle down and then I got another bottle and poured it all over my face and I went looking for Antonio and Mitzie and Tommy but I couldn't find them. I figured they must have gone into the desert to shoot up or something. I just didn't know, but I felt really bad and I don't know why but I was scared."

"What were you scared of?"

I looked at Adam. I wanted him to know what I'd felt. "I had this feeling. This really bad feeling. And I just wanted to go home."

"And so you went home?"

"Well, I didn't have a ride and I was in the middle of nowhere—but then I see Sam. And he's talking to some guy and I walk up to him and ask him if he could take me home. And he says, 'You won't kiss me but you'll take a ride from me.'

"And I said, 'I see your point.' So I just walked away from him. But he caught up with me and said, 'Sorry. That was really mean. I'm not mean. I'm sorry. Look, I'll take you home. You look like shit.'"

"So he took you home?"

"Yeah. I slept most of the way. But it was really a nice thing to do, to take me home. He didn't have to do that. And when we got to my house, he woke me up. 'Zach, you're home.'

"I nodded and thanked him. And I told him it was a really nice thing that he did and then I told them that maybe next time I saw him, maybe he could kiss me."

"You said that, Zach?"

"Yeah, I said that."

"Did you mean it?"

"I don't know. I just wanted to thank the guy. You know, he did me a favor."

Adam didn't say anything. "So what happened then?"

"Sam smiled and he said he'd hold me to it. And I smiled back. And then he drove away. And that's when the nightmare began." I didn't fight the tears that were falling from my face. I guess I'd decided to stop fighting a war with my tears. See, the tears always won anyway, so I just went with it. "When I walked into the house, Santiago was sitting in my father's chair and he was holding a gun. And my parents—" My throat was dry and swollen and the words were stuck in me again. They were stuck but I knew

I had to say this. *I had to say this.* I had to tell Adam what had happened. Because I was telling myself too. I needed to hear the words. I needed to hear myself say them. I hadn't noticed that Adam had walked out of the room and had come back in with a cup of water. He handed me the water.

"Take your time, Zach."

"Is our hour up?"

"Don't worry about the hour, Zach."

I drank some water. I kept moving my palms over my cheek, but the tears kept coming. And I knew I just had to make myself talk. I had always stopped. I had always let the words stay dammed up inside me. And I wanted to blow up the dam so that the words would just come out of me.

"Breathe, Zach."

I took a breath like Adam told me to.

"Again."

I took another breath.

"Now let it out slowly."

I did what Adam said.

"Good. Just keep breathing."

I nodded. And then finally, it seemed that the words were there. They were there and I just pushed them out. "My mom and dad were lying on the floor. There was blood everywhere. And Santiago was just sitting there." I didn't care if the sobs were trying to get in the way of my words because *I was going to talk.* I was going to tell my story. The words, those awful words weren't going to stay inside me anymore. *No more no more no more.* "And, Adam, I didn't know what to do. I couldn't move. I just saw my mom and dad lying there in their own blood and I knew they were dead and Santiago kept looking at me and smiling and then he said *I've been waiting for you.* And he pointed the gun at me and then pointed the gun at himself and then at me and then at himself, back and forth like that and he was singing *eenie, meenie, miney, moe.* And I thought he was going to kill me and I guess I just didn't care. I closed my eyes and I heard the gun go off. And then I opened my eyes and saw Santiago. He'd stuck the gun in his mouth and—" That's when the words stopped. That was all I could say.

I don't know how long I sat there. But the tears had stopped and the world was very quiet.

"I ran, Adam. I just ran."

"But you're not running now, Zach."

"I think...I think...I think that—"

"You think what, Zach?"

"A part of me wished Santiago would have pointed the gun at me, you know? Do you know what I'm saying, Adam?"

"I know."

"I wished I would have died along with them."

"A part of you *did* die, Zach."

I looked at Adam who was sitting across from me. There were tears rolling down his face. "But look, Zach, another part of you lived. You lived, Zach."

"You're crying," I said.

"That happens sometimes," he said.

We both sat there for a long time, not saying anything.

"When Rafael was talking about his son, you cried then too."

"Yeah, I cried."

"Do we hurt you?"

"No. You move me, Zach."

That's a beautiful thing. That's what I wanted to say, but I didn't say that. I didn't say anything.

We just sort of sat there and smiled at each other. That was really nice. I wanted to tell Adam that I loved him. I don't know what was stopping me. *I was stopping me.*

And then I heard a cell phone ringing. Adam looked at me like he was really sorry. "I don't normally keep my cell phone on—but—I have to take this. Is that okay?"

I nodded. Adam was a real pro. If it wasn't important, he wouldn't have kept it on. I was making up that it had something to do with his family. I got that.

He stepped out of the room and motioned for me to just wait.

I nodded.

So I just had this imaginary conversation with Adam. You know, I was really into imaginary conversations.

"I guess you know, but I wanted to say that, well, I really love you. I mean—"

"I know, Zach. I know what you mean."

"I guess that happens—patients love their therapists."

"Yeah, it happens."

"You don't mind?"

"No, I don't mind."

"Good," I said. "Because I think I might love you forever."

Adam smiled. And then he laughed. And it was a really nice laugh, a laugh that made me feel really, really good.

"Sorry about that." Adam walked into the room again. "It's one of my sons."

"Is he okay?"

"Yeah, he's okay."

"Good," I said. "He's lucky."

"Yeah. I'm lucky too." He thought for a little while. "You've been through a lot, Zach. You didn't deserve all that, Zach. You didn't. I told you that you were brave. Remember that?"

"Yeah. I remember."

"I was right."

"I know what you're going to say next."

"What's that?"

"Give yourself some credit, Zach."

"That's exactly what I was going to say." He got this really serious look on his face. "I'm happy for you, Zach. You have no idea how happy I am for you."

"I think I'm happy too."

"You think?"

"Yeah. I guess I'm just wondering why Santiago let me live."

"Maybe he loved you."

"I thought of that."

"Do you believe that?"

"I only want to believe it if it's true."

"We won't ever know, Zach. Can I tell you a secret? Sometimes, Zach, all we have is what we make up."

"I'll have to think about that one."

"Me too."

I looked into his eyes. No gray in them. Not at all like my mother's. I could have stared at his face forever. "Adam?"

"Yeah, Zach?"

"Remember my dream, the one where I go off drinking with my father?"

"Yes, I remember."

"I know what my father represents. He represents death. And I know what Rafael represents. He represents life. In the dream I choose death. I want to choose life, Adam. I loved my father. But I have to let him go. Is that okay, Adam?"

"Yes, Zach, it's okay. *You do have to let him go.*"

"But it makes me feel bad—that I don't choose my father."

"Your father's dead, Zach. And you know what else? You loved your father. That's why you feel bad for wanting to choose Rafael in your dream. But that just means you have a heart, Zach. And it works. Your heart works. Imagine that, Zach."

Adam. His smile tore me up. In a good way. In a good and beautiful way.

REMEMBERING

This is the problem with addicts. They find new addictions all the time to take the place of their old addictions. So this is my new addiction: *remembering*. I'm serious about this. It's so strange and odd and weird to *want* to remember. It feels bad and it feels good all at the same time. It feels bad for the obvious reason that, well, bad things happened. It feels good because remembering is helping me to dump those bad things out of my body. See, this is my new thinking: my whole body, my brain and my heart included, was just this dumping ground for a lot of trash. And now, well, I'm dealing with cleaning it all up.

Not that it doesn't hurt.

I still keep thinking: how many tears does a guy have inside him?

It's all good. I keep telling myself it's all good.

So I'm remembering. Remembering, remembering and remembering.

When the gun my brother was holding went off, my heart stopped. And when I opened my eyes, and saw the whole scene, I just went away. I remember running out of the room and I don't really remember that clearly, but I remember downing a bottle of bourbon. And then rummaging through a closet and finding another bottle. I remember running out of the house. And then I remember turning back and running back into the house and kissing my mom and dad, just kissing them and I was really crazed, and I knew I'd lost it, and I just didn't know what to do.

I ran.

I just ran.

I don't remember how many days I walked around lost. Drunk. I remember finding myself walking on the side of a road. I remember feeling that I wasn't even living in my body anymore. The sun was coming up and there weren't any cars and it was cold. God, it was so cold. I remember feeling really sick and there was an earthquake in my body and I swear I thought I saw a monster. So I just lay down on the side of the road.

I remember a hospital.

And then I was here. In Cabin 9. Bed 3.

I keep staring at my hands. These are my hands. I keep pressing my palms into my heart. This is my heart.

I didn't die.

Didn't die means I'm still breathing.

I'm still breathing means my heart is still beating.

My heart is still beating means that I'm alive.

THE WORD *CHANGE* ON MY HEART?

-1-

Group was great. I was the first one to Check-in and I confessed to keeping two secrets: "I read Rafael's journal when no one was around and my other secret is that I hated my family. I know I said I loved them and that was true but I also hated them. Those are my two secrets. Oh, and I have a third secret—I really miss Rafael." And I didn't even look down at the floor.

Sheila and Maggie and Lizzie and Kelly all started clapping. You know, like a little applause. And I said, "Hey, what's with the applause?"

And Lizzie said, "You've never admitted to having any secrets."

"I have lots of them," I said.

"Yes, you do," Lizzie said. And we both laughed.

And then I said: "I'm sorry I've been such a shit in group."

Adam was real quiet but when I looked at him he was smiling. That guy could smile.

That was the first time I had a really good time in group. *A really good time.* I had never had a good time in group. Not ever. Maggie brought in a bunch of drawings and I really liked them and I guess I was talking a lot, you know, giving her feedback. And it was good. It was a good group. We all talked and laughed and made jokes and Adam went to the board and wrote HAPPY MOMENTS.

I kept trying to think of a happy moment and I began thinking about things, my friends I used to get shitfaced with and the good times we had and I thought that they weren't really such good times. I saw their faces in front of me and their names ran across the messy floor of my mind, that floor that was still cluttered with little pieces of papers, *Antonio, Gloria, Tommy, Mitzie and Albert*. Maybe I'd loved them. I guess maybe I did in my own way— not that I knew anything about love and how to go about handing that love out to people.

But the thing is, I didn't make my friends happy and they didn't make me happy. All we did was get stoned out of our minds. That didn't have anything to do with happiness. I'd never thought of that before, how I just didn't have that many times when I was really happy. I tried to come up with a list and these are the things that entered in my head:

> My seventeenth birthday when my dad and I went hiking in the desert
> The first time Mr. Garcia played the trumpet for me
> The night Rafael sang *Summertime*
> The day I told Adam my whole story

Those were the four things on my list of HAPPY MOMENTS. Four things. I was only eighteen so maybe I was doing okay.

Okay wasn't great. I knew that.

I looked at the list Adam had on the board about HAPPY MOMENTS. No one had a long list. But everyone had something. Everyone knew what happiness was. Even sad and torn-up people know what happiness is. And then Adam looked at the list and sort of smiled. "Okay," he said, "let's do some numbers." That Adam, he was a real numbers guy. "Scale of 1 to 10 on the happiness scale. How happy are you? Ten being very happy, 1 being, well, not very happy." He looked at Amit.

"Let's see," Amit said, "I'd say a 4."

Adam put a 4 next to his name.

"Lizzie?"

"7."

"7? Good job. Kelly?"

"Depends on the day."

"Fair enough. What is it today?"

"6."

"Is 6 a good day for you?"

"6 is an excellent day for me."

Adam nodded and put the 6 next to her name. "Maggie?"

"4."

"4? You working on that?"

She shrugged.

"Annie?"

"An even 5."

"5? Okay, 5."

"Zach?"

"I'm not sure. I'm getting better I think."

He waited.

"6. Yeah 6."

6 went up next to my name.

"You notice something?" Adam asked with that sort of snarky smile on his face. "No 8's, no 9's, no 10's."

"Well, we're in here, dude. What did you expect?" Amit said.

"*Yes, you are in here*," he said. That kind of made us all laugh. And then he wrote across the board: WHAT DO I NEED TO GET HAPPY?

"Good question," Lizzie said.

"I didn't come here to get happy," Amit said. "I came here because I'm an addict."

"If you were happy, would you be an addict?"

"I don't know."

"I'm making up that you *do* know."

"No one's happy." Everyone looked at Kelly.

"What do you mean no one's happy?" Adam waited for an answer.

"I mean just that. No one's happy. Why should we be any different?"

"So happiness is impossible?"

"Happiness isn't in the cards. Not for me."

"You know that, do you?"

"I don't care about happiness."

Adam was thinking. "Anybody else not care about happiness?"

I held the question in my head. "I care about happiness," I said. But I didn't say it out loud. And then I wanted to say, "I used to be a 1. Now, I'm a 6. I'm better."

I thought about Rafael. I wondered how he would have answered the question. I pictured him saying "9. I'm a 9 on the happiness scale." And then I pictured him telling Kelly, "It's not true what you're saying about happiness. Happiness is the most important thing in the world." I wondered why I was having an imaginary Rafael talking to the group. Change is hard.

-2-

I took a walk and found that my feet had taken me to Rafael's tree. The tree he'd named Zach. I studied the tree. Crooked and scruffy as hell. But really beautiful. I got an idea. I walked back to Cabin 9, got my sketch pad. I spent all morning in front of the tree, sketching and sketching. And then it was done.

I would send it to Rafael. That's the thought that entered into my head.

I lay down on the ground and looked up at the sky. I was happy and I didn't even know why. But I was scared too. Maybe happiness was scary. Or maybe I was scared because I didn't know where I was going after I left this place. Where would I go? Back home? By myself? I didn't know how to live by myself.

I had one aunt. I remembered that. She was my mom's sister and she suffered from agoraphobia, same as my mother. She had a really nice house but she never went out. I didn't know anything about her except that she didn't much like people. I'd only met her once. We went to visit her when I was a boy. She looked at me, then looked at my mother and said, "Well, at least he doesn't have fleas." That's what she said.

I knew my aunt would never take me in. I thought of Rafael who said his uncle and aunt just took him in because they felt sorry for him. I didn't want anyone to feel sorry for me. Besides, I was eighteen. I was a man. Yeah, okay, like I was really a man. I hadn't even finished high school. My plan about going to college was all shot to hell. God, I was working myself up. I could feel my friend *anxiety* entering my body again. *Breathe, Zach, breathe.*

I painted a self-portrait. In the painting, I was standing in front of the tree named Zach. I was looking up at the sky and I was singing. And there was a coyote right next to me. The coyote and I had become friends—and he was singing too. In the corner of the painting, you could see that a monster was going away.

I liked my painting.

I took out my journal and wrote:

These are things that I know to be true. Or, as Adam would say, these are things that fit under the category of THINGS I KNOW:

- My brother killed my father and mother
- I miss them, my mother and my father and Santiago
- I am definitely an alcoholic
- I'm scared of leaving this place
- I wish Rafael was my father
- I wish Adam could be my therapist forever
- I love being sober
- I want to let myself be touched
- I wish Sharkey would come back and do the work
- I want Amit to get happy
- There are beautiful words inside me
- Winter is not the only season
- I didn't die
- I am alive

And these are questions I have. Maybe they fall under the category of THINGS I DON'T KNOW. Maybe they fall under the category of THINGS I DON'T KNOW THAT I KNOW or maybe they fall into the category of THINGS I'LL NEVER KNOW. The last category is not Adam's category but my category. See, this is what's entering my head right now: I NEED TO HAVE MY OWN CATEGORIES. So these are the questions I have:

- Why did my parents allow my brother to own our family?
- Why did Santiago kill my mother and my father?
- Why did Santiago let me live? Was it because he loved me?
- Did God write *change* on my heart?
- Did Adam write *change* on my heart?
- Did Rafael write *change* on my heart?
- Was it me who wrote *change* on my own heart?
- What am I going to do about this thing called *touch*?
- Is Sharkey alive?
- Will Amit stay? Or will he find a reason to leave like Sharkey?
- Is Rafael happy? Is he sober?
- Why are so many of us so fucked up?

-4-

"So, Zach, you've still never asked about how you got here."

"I've been thinking about that," I said.

"So tell me about what you're thinking."

"Well, I have this idea that maybe my aunt is involved." I was trying to see if I could read anything in Adam's eyes.

"Tell me about your aunt."

"Well, I don't know that much about her. She's my mom's sister. Her name is Emma Johnson. She lives in a big house. It's really a nice house. She's rich, I think. She's the opposite of my mother, in some ways. She runs some kind of business and she has an office in her house and she has a secretary. But she never leaves the house. She's an agoraphobic—just like my mother. I guess there were some bad genes on my mom's side. I think their mother killed herself."

I glanced at the floor—then looked up. "Let's see, what else do I know about my aunt? She doesn't really like people—but she really loved my mother."

"How do you know that—that she loved your mother?"

"She called every week. Like clockwork. Every Wednesday evening at 7 o'clock sharp. Weird, huh? And I just knew that she wasn't the kind that called people. I got the feeling that, aside from her business, she just didn't call anyone."

"Did she love you?"

"No. I was her sister's son. You know, that's how she saw me. I mean, I don't think she hated me. She was, you know, indifferent. She hated my brother, I'll tell you that."

"How do you know?"

"When my mother couldn't talk, she'd ask me things. Talk to me a little bit. She said my dad should throw him out of the house. I told her maybe he could go live with her. I remember she just laughed and said, 'Where did you get that sense of humor, young man?' Really, that's all I know about my aunt." I looked at Adam. "Did she send me here?"

"Yes."

"She paid for it?"

"Well, in a way. Apparently, she took care of some financial matters for your mother. And she was your parents' executor. Your mom and dad had some money."

"A lot?"

"No, not a lot. But some."

"Enough to pay for this place, I guess."

"Apparently. Your aunt handled all the arrangements."

"So she got me here?"

"Yeah, Zach. She got you here."

"How did she know about this place?"

"She's been here."

"As a client?"

"Yes."

"When?"

"I don't know. Years ago."

"Were you here then?"

"No, I don't know your aunt."

"I need to thank her. She saved my life."

"Well, she helped."

"So, Adam, what happens now?"

"The million-dollar question."

"I know my aunt Emma isn't going to take me in."

"She's indicated as much."

I sort of smiled. "She has her limitations. Around here we call them boundaries."

Adam was trying not to smile. "Yes, I see that."

"I come from a long line of unstable people."

"That's true, Zach. But—let me ask you: Do you think you're unstable?"

"I don't know. Maybe I'll wind up like my brother or my mom or my aunt."

"I don't think so. I don't think you're mentally ill, Zach."

"You don't?"

"No. I *do* think you'll wind up like your father if you decide to drink again."

"Yeah, well, that sounds about right."

"Do you want to end up like your father?"

"No."

"Good." He smiled as he handed me a file. "Homework."

I took the file. "What is it?"

"It's a relapse prevention plan."

"What's that?"

"You have to come up with a plan to stay sober."

"Okay."

He pointed at the file. "The paperwork is pretty self-explanatory. You just go through it and answer all the questions honestly. And I mean *honestly.* And then come up with a plan."

"Okay. But—," I just looked at him.

"You have a question, Zach?"

"I know I'm eighteen. I know I'm supposed to be an adult. It's just that I don't feel like one. I mean, where will I live?"

"That's a very good question."

"You look like maybe you have a suggestion."

Adam smiled. "I do. There's a place in California."

"What place?"

"A halfway house. You know what those are?"

"Yeah. Aren't there any in El Paso?"

"You want to go home again?"

"Yeah, I guess so."

"What if you go back to hanging out with your friends?"

"I get you," I said.

"Listen, Zach, I think you should try this place. I think it's really got your name on it."

"Yeah?"

"Yeah. Look, if it doesn't work out, I'll help you find a place closer to home. Will you think about it?"

"Yeah. Okay, I'll think about it." I was trying to keep my eyes off the floor. It was such a hard addiction to break. I opened my journal to the page where I'd written my lists. I handed it to Adam.

He took his time reading it. He got a really big smile on his face and then he just looked at me. "Zach, do you believe in miracles?"

"I don't know, Adam."

"I do."

"Really?"

"Zach, I'm staring at one right this very second."

-5-

Last night I walked around the grounds.

The moon was full and the night was cool, but the cold had gone away. I found my way to the tree named Zach. I wrote my name on the ground. And then I wrote Rafael's name, and Amit's name and Sharkey's name and Lizzie's name. I wrote everybody's name. Everybody's name I had said goodbye to. Everybody's name that had ever been in Group. Everybody's name I could remember ever having met here.

In this place.

In this beautiful place.

I took out my goodbye medal from my pocket. I stared at the angel. I decided that I would give the angel a name. Santiago. My brother. The man who had let me live. I decided that he had let me live because he loved me. Maybe it was a lie. But it was a very beautiful lie.

I stared at all the names I'd written on the ground.

The earth had room for all our names.

I wondered if the earth was another name for God.

-6-

Amit walked me to the front building where I was supposed to wait for the van.

I was flying to Los Angeles. Someone would be waiting for me. Someone who would take me to the halfway house. I remembered Adam's words: *Keep it simple.*

I knew what he meant.

One day at a time.

One sober day at a time.

I had the phone number of a man named Brian. He was going to be my sponsor. I was going to meet with him when I got settled in.

Amit hugged me goodbye. I hugged him back. I was trying to get more comfortable with this *touch* thing. "I'll miss you," he said.

"I'll miss you too, Amit." I shot him a snarky smile. "Do the work."

"Yeah, yeah. Do the work."

He waved—and left me there.

I watched him walk away.

Amit had a hard time with goodbyes. He was like me. We were all like each other. We were all the same.

"I'll miss you!" I yelled. I wanted him to know that it was true, that I was being honest.

He turned around and smiled. People were so beautiful when they smiled.

I had my last session with Adam yesterday. He told me to call him once I was in Los Angeles. He gave me his cell phone number. We went over my relapse plan—even though I had no intentions of relapsing.

"Everyone swears they'll never use again, never drink again, Zach. Do you want to go over the statistics again?" That guy Adam and his numbers.

I took out a piece of paper from my notebook and wrote the word *change.* "Someone wrote this on my heart," I said.

"Have you figured out who?"

"Everyone."

"Everyone?"

"Yeah, everyone. You and Rafael and Sharkey and everyone in Group. Everyone."

"What about your higher power?"

"God? He wrote *change* too. I guess he helped."

"Still having a hard time with God?"

"Well, he made you and Rafael, didn't he?"

"Yes, he did."

"Then he's okay in my book."

"Just okay?"

"It's a start."

It *was* a start. Yes it was.

I said goodbye to Adam. There were still words left inside us. But you could never say everything you wanted to say. I knew that. Before I left his office for the last time, I looked at him and said, "I think I'll take a hug. Is that all right?"

I felt his arms around me. And for a moment, there was only me and Adam in the world. Only me and Adam.

This is the thing that I hated about hugging Adam: I had to let him go.

I took a deep breath when I got into the van. I felt my pocket to make sure I had my goodbye medal with me.

Goodbye, labyrinth.
Goodbye, tree named Zach.

Goodbye, group named Summer.

Goodbye, Adam.

Adam who sees me.

Adam whose eyes are blue as the sky.

-7-

At the airport, I had an imaginary phone call with Adam. I was calling him on my cell.

I heard his voice.

"It's Zach," I said.

"Something wrong, Zach?"

"No. I just forgot something."

"What?"

"I never told you. I kept a secret."

"What, Zach?"

"I love you. I thought you should know."

"I think I already knew that, Zach."

"Oh, okay. I just wanted to hear myself say it. Is that okay?"

"Are you embarrassed, Zach?"

"Yes."

"Well, you'll have to work on that, won't you?"

"Yeah, I guess so."

Imaginary conversations. They tore me up.

-8-

I mostly slept on the way to LA.

It was strange not to be at that place anymore. I felt free of it. And yet I didn't want to be free of it—not ever.

I wanted that place to stay alive in my head.

I thought of the monster and how it might always be there. But that was all right, because the monster didn't scare me anymore.

Adam said that there would always be monster days. I would have to stay alert. Rafael, he had stayed alert. I would have to become like him. I wondered about him—and wondered if he was still living in LA. I'd gotten a postcard from him. He'd sent it from Italy. I guess he'd decided to travel.

I knew I'd see him. *I'll see you again because I want to see you again.*

I knew he'd come to visit once he found out I was staying in LA.

But what if he didn't?

What if Rafael had only been my friend at that place? What if he wanted to forget and move on? That's what people did—they moved on. I started to get a little anxious thinking about that. Okay, working myself up was not good for my sobriety. Not good. *Breathe, Zach, breathe.*

I knew exactly what to do when my plane landed in LA. There would be someone at baggage claim with my name on a sign. Adam had told me it was a man who would be picking me up and that I should trust him.

Okay.

Everything was all planned.

Okay.

I had all my paperwork. The name of the place. The address. The brochure. The phone number. The name of the director.

Okay.

When I stepped off the plane, all the panic was back. I couldn't breathe. I hated the racing thoughts, hated them. It entered into my head that I had done the wrong thing. It hadn't been the right time for me to leave that place. I'd been wrong to think that I was ready to live in the world with a lot of normies and earth people. What was I going to do?

The thought entered into my head that I should get on the next plane and head back. The thought entered into my head that I should call Adam and tell him that I wasn't going to make it if I didn't get back there.

I'm not safe.

I'm lost again.

I sit down and rock myself and breathe. I make myself relax. I think of Susan and her voice and how she called me *brave boy*. I remember I have Adam's cell phone. That makes me feel calm. If something goes wrong, I can just call him.

Okay. I'm okay.

I make my way to the baggage claim. I don't walk fast. I feel the beating of my heart. I know *scared* is written there, on my heart. *Breathe, Zach, breathe.*

I am picking up my luggage. I am looking around for the man who is supposed to pick me up.

I see a sign waving in the air that reads ZACHARIAH.

I see the face of the man who is holding the sign and I feel my feet running toward the man, running and running, not running away, but running toward. Running forward. I feel my arms reaching toward the man and embracing him and holding on to him. I am the owner of the happiest heart in all of God's universe. "Rafael! Rafael! Is it really you? Is it really you?"

I feel his arms around me. I hear him whispering, "Yes, Zach. It's me."

REMEMBERING

The first thing I did when we arrived at Rafael's house was call Adam. I don't remember all the details of our conversation. He did ask me if I felt okay about living with Rafael. I heard something in his voice. "You think it's a bad idea?" I asked.

I remember his answer. "I don't know." It was an honest I-don't-know. That confused me.

Later I asked Rafael about that.

"Look, Zach," Rafael said, "Adam isn't responsible for what happens to us once we leave that place. He has to let go of us. He knows that. I think he understood that I was going to find you one way or another. And I also think he understood that you might not make it on your own. Adam, he's a very ethical guy. And he knows there aren't any guarantees in life. He knows the odds and they're not in our favor. This may not be the best thing for either one of us. We'll just have to see."

That was six months ago.

I had a choice. I could go live at the halfway house or I could live with Rafael. And it was me who had to decide.

There are rules in our house. Not a lot of rules but a few.

I can't stay out past eleven unless I check in with Rafael.

Everybody picks up after themselves.

Nobody drinks.

Nobody smokes—not in the house.

I guess you could say I have my own smoking pit in the back yard. Sometimes, when I go out there I think of Sharkey. I think of Amit. I think of Lizzie. I sometimes have imaginary conversations with them. I am addicted to having imaginary conversations. I haven't decided yet if this is healthy or unhealthy behavior.

Rafael is helping me to stay articulate. As in speaking. As in talking. As in expressing what I feel. Sometimes, as a joke and not a joke, Rafael looks across the table at me as we eat breakfast and says, "Check-in." We both laugh and then I say something like this: "I'm Zach. I'm an alcoholic. No bad dreams and I'm going to make this a good day."

Rafael looks at me and says. "I'm Rafael. I'm an alcoholic. And I am in love with my sobriety."

We smile. We laugh.

We discuss things in our house. That's another rule. Things must be discussed. For example: school. We discussed my predicament. We discussed the plan I had about going to college. Then, after all the discussing, Rafael asked me this one simple question, "When are you going back to school?"

"How about now?" I said.

It was my job to make all the arrangements. Part of that I-am-responsible-for-my-life thing. I still have this thing for A's. Not everything has to change.

College. Wow. That thought really tears me up. It makes me want to cry. I guess there will always be a lot of tears inside me. Rafael wants to know why I think that's such a bad thing. One day, when I was leaving for school, I found a note on the kitchen table from Rafael. And this is what it said: *Tears are for girls.* Then he'd crossed that out. And then he'd written; *Tears are for boys.*

School. Wow. Who knows what college I'll be going to. I'm making a list of schools. I was going to apply to twenty-five. Rafael looked at me with the same kind of snarky smile that Adam used to give me. Maybe Adam sent Rafael that smile—wireless.

"Okay," I said, "I'll apply to ten."

Rafael said ten schools sounded reasonable.

Sometimes, when I look at my list of schools, I get that old feeling inside, that old feeling that says: *They won't want you.* And then I have an imaginary conversation with Mr. Garcia and he says: *They'd be damned lucky to have you, Zach.* Yeah, I'll go with Mr. Garcia.

The house we live in is full of books and art and a kitchen that really stuns me out. Rafael has everything. A real kitchen gadget guy. I mean, the guy is all about cooking—which is really great because I really like to eat.

I like to watch him cook. "Watch and learn," he says. So that's what I do.

Rafael goes to meetings. He paints. I love his paintings—because they make me want to feel things. He's writing a novel and he's also working on some screenplay that his agent sent him. When he gets a script like that he calls himself a doctor. He gets a screenplay with problems and he fixes them. He turns a bad screenplay into a good one. Sometimes he doesn't even get the credit. I don't think that's fair but Rafael doesn't care. "I get paid, Zach. I don't need my name on a screen."

I go to meetings too. There's a meeting for younger people. I like those meetings. But some of the guys in there are pissed-off as hell. I don't think some of them are going to make it. But we're all doing the one-day-at-a-time thing. And I think of what Rafael said when we both lived in Cabin 9, "If you can quit for a day, you can quit for a lifetime." You know, sometimes I think that maybe these guys wouldn't be so mad if they had an Adam or a Rafael or a Mr. Garcia in their lives. That's the thought that enters into my head.

Rafael, he's pretty calm these days. He listens to jazz. He hums, he laughs a lot. He sings.

Me too. I'm calm too. Except I don't really sing.

Rafael and I, we're both addicted to coffee and movies. We both like really serious movies.

At school, I always recognize the guys that are into drugs. One day, I really wanted to go up to a group of guys—and, you know, join them. But I didn't. No use in looking for trouble.

Sometimes I get to thinking of all my old friends. It makes me sad to think of them. I have their numbers in my cell phone but I never call them. It makes me sad that I had to let them go. *But I do have to let them go.* A part of me will always love them. That's okay, to love them.

I have some sober friends. I have to admit they're kind of boring. But not all of them. And hey, I'm new at this.

I'm still working on my stuff. Doing the work never stops. I guess not. Today, I'm having a very good day.

Some days are hard. Some days, I really want to get my hands on a bottle of bourbon. I mean, it's like the thought of drinking bourbon takes over my feet and just wants to take me to a liquor store and hang out there until I find some guy to buy me a bottle. I talk to my sponsor. I talk to Rafael. Rafael says God helps keep him sober. Maybe God wrote *sober* on Rafael's heart. Maybe he wrote *sober* on mine.

But today! Today is *not* a hard day. To begin with I had this great dream last night. The snow was falling softly and I was walking the labyrinth. I was completely naked and I wasn't even cold. I was perfect. That's how I felt. I felt like I was a perfect human being. I had never carried that word around inside me. It was as if I was living in summer even though it was winter. My heart didn't have all those pieces of paper anymore—it had leaves. A thousand summer leaves. And as I kept walking toward the center of the labyrinth, it started snowing green leaves—just like in Rafael's journal. The sky was brilliant blue and it was so amazing.

When I reached the center of the labyrinth, everyone was there: Mark and Lizzie and Annie and Sheila and Jodie and Maggie and Rafael and Sharkey and Amit and Adam.

Even my mom and dad and my brother. They were there. And they were all perfect and whole. They weren't broken anymore. They all looked like angels.

When I woke up, I was crying.

This time the tears didn't mean *sad.* They meant *happy*.

After writing down my dream, I studied the painting I'm working on. It's a painting of me walking down a road. I have my heart in my hand and the road is leading to the sky. I remembered Adam had told me that anyone could have come along and erased the sketch I'd done in pencil. But this time, no one's going to be able to erase me. No one.

After lunch, I'm going to leave school early. Rafael is going to pick me up and we're going to the courthouse. Rafael, he's going to adopt me. I guess the subject came up because I asked him if I could call him dad. I don't know, but I have this thing inside me that needs to have a father. And

Rafael has this thing inside him that needs to have a son. Yeah, I know I just turned nineteen, yeah, I know that. But I guess a part of me is still a boy. I used to wig out about that because I thought that I shouldn't feel that way. But I *do* feel that way. So, I'm going with what I feel.

I remember the day when I asked Rafael if I could call him dad. He didn't say anything. He didn't have any words in him. Tears in his eyes meant *Yes, you can call me dad.* You know, my dad, he's dead. And I loved him and I'll always love him. He did the best he could.

But I have Rafael now, *and he really is my dad.*

I've decided that this is the good thing about God. He gives you second chances.

So this afternoon, I'm going to get a new name. I'm not going to be Zachariah Johnson Gonzalez anymore. I'm going to be Zachariah de la Tierra.

I am in love with my new name.

I'm remembering the old Zach. I'm looking in the mirror at the new Zach. My eyes are hazel. Today they look green.

I pick up my cell phone and decide to call Adam. I haven't spoken to him for months. I press in his number and wait. His voice mail answers and I smile at the sound of his voice. I am leaving him a message. "Hey, Adam. It's me, Zach. Remember the happiness scale? Today, I've reached a 10 on that scale. Wow! A 10! I woke up this morning and discovered God had written *happy* on my heart. Adam, I'm having a great day."